A LOVER IN LUXOR

THE GRAND TOURS OF THE ARISTOCRACY
BOOK 3

LINDA RAE SANDE

Twisted Teacup
PUBLISHING

ALSO BY LINDA RAE SANDE

The Daughters of the Aristocracy

The Kiss of a Viscount

The Grace of a Duke

The Seduction of an Earl

The Sons of the Aristocracy

Tuesday Nights

The Widowed Countess

My Fair Groom

The Sisters of the Aristocracy

The Story of a Baron

The Passion of a Marquess

The Desire of a Lady

The Brothers of the Aristocracy

The Love of a Rake

The Caress of a Commander

The Epiphany of an Explorer

The Widows of the Aristocracy

The Gossip of an Earl

The Enigma of a Widow

The Secrets of a Viscount

The Widowers of the Aristocracy

The Dream of a Duchess

The Vision of a Viscountess

The Conundrum of a Clerk

The Charity of a Viscount

The Cousins of the Aristocracy

The Promise of a Gentleman

The Pride of a Gentleman

The Holidays of the Aristocracy

The Christmas of a Countess

The Knot of a Knight

The Holiday of a Marquess

The Snow Angel of a Duke

The Ivy of an Earl

The Heirs of the Aristocracy

The Angel of an Astronomer

The Puzzle of a Bastard

The Choice of a Cavalier

The Bargain of a Baroness

The Jewel of an Earl's Heir

The Vixen of a Viscount

The Honor of an Heir

The Rose of a Sultan's Son

The Ladies of the Aristocracy

The Lady of a Grump

The Lady of a Sultan

The Pursuit of a Duchess

The Lords of the Aristocracy

The Abduction of an Earl

Beyond the Aristocracy

The Pleasure of a Pirate

The Making of a Mistress

The Bride of a Baronet

The Caton of a Captain

Puss and Pots

The Betrothal of a Baron

Masquerade Meow

The Grand Tours of the Aristocracy

A Courtship in Catania

An Affaire in Athens

A Lover in Luxor

Revenge of the Wallflowers

The Wager of a Wallflower

Stella of Akrotiri

Origins

Deminon

Diana

The Lyon's Den (Dragonblade Publishing)

The Courage of a Lyon

The Lady of a Lyon

The Loyalty of a Lyon

Note: Translations of select titles are available in German, Italian, Spanish and Portuguese.

CHARACTER LIST AND FAMILY TREES

Will Slater, Earl of Bellingham (1792), heir to the Devonville marquessate

Barbara Higgins Slater, Countess of Bellingham

Donald Slater (1811), illegitimate son of Will and Barbara, father of Antony, Marchese Montblanc

Nicoletta D'Avalos (1815), Marchesa Montblanc and wife to Donald

David Slater, Viscount Penton (1819), heir to the Devonville marquessate

Randolph Forster (1817), heir to the Gisborn earldom, nephew to Will

Diana Henley Forster (1820), wife to Randy and second cousin to Randy, Tom, and David

Thomas Forster (1819), nephew to Will

Harold Tennison, Earl of Everly (1791)

Estelle Jones Tennison, Countess of Everly (1795)

Helen Tennison (1821)

Bradley Tennison (1840)

Character List and Family Trees

PROLOGUE

September 1839, Mayfair

From the moment Thomas Forster, spare heir to the Gisborn earldom, entered the mansion belonging to Lord and Lady Morganfield, he knew he had to be on his very best behavior.

Everyone who was anyone in the *ton* had probably been invited, as was the rest of his extended family. Even though they only had a few days in London before they were to set sail for the Mediterranean, his grandmother, Cherise DuBois Slater, Marchioness of Devonville, had seen to it they had invitations to every event scheduled during the Little Season.

Even if they were to be in London for less than a week.

Having outgrown his last pair of satin pantaloons and matching top coat, he'd been forced to find new ones at a men's shop in Bond Street. While there, he had picked out a number of embroidered waistcoats, several shirts, longer pantaloons, and some cravats, sure there would be enough room in his trunk for the new clothing.

"You certainly appear rather dapper this evening," his older brother, Randolph, commented.

"As do you," he replied, not bothering to look. The two had ridden in the same town coach along with their cousin, David Slater, Viscount Penton, who was at that moment engaged in a rather flirtatious exchange with at least three young ladies about to enter the receiving line behind them.

They hadn't even made it into the ballroom, and already, David was charming the young ladies.

Tom couldn't help but stare when they did make it to the top of the stairs leading down to the what already appeared to be a crush.

He had always thought the ballroom in Devonville House rather grand, but this one seemed far larger—probably due to the mirrored panels mounted on the walls at both ends and the number of chandeliers that hung from the high ceiling. He tried to mentally calculate how many candles might be lit to provide the glittering spectacle he saw at the bottom of the stairs—all manner of silks and satins, turbans and feathers, gold and silver worn by aristocrats both young and old. He gave up when David joined them.

"Why did you stop here?" his cousin asked.

"I think we're to be announced," Randy said, nodding to the butler who hurried to take their names and titles. "Which means you get to go first."

Not the least bit shy, David immediately moved to the top of the stairs, and when his name and title were spoken in the loud baritone of the servant, he nodded and skipped down the steps as if he didn't have a care in the world.

Before he had reached the marble tiled-floor, a bevy of young ladies surrounded him, curtsying and holding out their dance cards.

"He's barely one-and-twenty and has absolutely no intention of marrying before he's seven-and-twenty, and yet they *love* him," Tom complained when Randy finished giving the butler their names.

"Don't despair, brother. I expect you'll have your name on a number of dance cards before you've had a chance to take your first glass of champagne from a footman," Randy remarked.

"From your lips to—"

"Lord Randolph Forster and The Honorable Thomas Forster," the butler announced.

Forced to begin his descent, Tom stared straight ahead and remembered halfway down to display a more pleasant expression than what he was sure appeared to be fright. Even without looking, he knew his older brother was smiling. Surely the glare from his white teeth made the ballroom seem more brightly lit than it had been when they were at the top of the stairs.

Randy had always been more self-assured, more confident in situations such as this. He had two years on Tom and knew most of the young men their age from their time at Oxford. Some of those very classmates were already in the ballroom, ready to greet them with good-natured jibing and reminders they weren't usually part of the Little Season.

"Card room, refreshments, or..." Randy waved to indicate the young ladies standing in the company of their mothers or chaperones. "Dancing?"

Tom glanced around, his attention immediately going to a young lady who was not glued to an older matron but was holding a glass of champagne as she watched the growing crowd at the bottom of the stairs. "I think I shall see to filling in some of these dance cards," he replied, leaving his brother's side without another word.

Before he had made it halfway to the young lady with the champagne, Tom knew his brother was besieged with requests from mothers wanting to introduce their daughters. Securing a betrothal to an heir to an earldom would be a feather in any doting mother's mobcap.

Tom decided there was definitely one benefit to being a spare heir—the matrons barely noticed him.

"Good evening," he said as he approached the young lady.

Her eyes rounded and she glanced both left and right, as if she couldn't believe he was addressing her. "Good evening, sir," she replied, nodding.

"I couldn't help but notice you are not accompanied by a chaperone. Does that mean...?"

"My mother is somewhere nearby," she replied. "But I don't believe we've met?"

Tom shook his head. "We have not. I am rarely in the capital. Uh..." He glanced around, searching for someone who could perform the introduction. When he didn't see anyone he knew, he said, "My name is Thomas Forster." He bowed as he reached for her white-gloved hand.

A quizzical expression appeared before she dipped a curtsy. "I am Helen. Lady Helen," she amended, a brief grimace crossing her face when he brushed his lips over the back of her hand. "Forster... as in Gisborn?" she guessed.

"Indeed. I'm the spare," he admitted, glad he had found a top coat that allowed him to shrug his shoulders. Had he not acquired the larger one earlier that day, he feared the sleeves would have torn out of their seams if he attempted to dance.

"What brings you to London, Mr. Forster?"

Tom managed to snag a glass of champagne from a passing footman. He shifted his feet so he was no longer facing her but standing at a right angle, sure he would be scolded by her mother at any moment. "My cousins and I are about to embark on our Grand Tour."

Her eyes once again rounded. "Oh, I am so jealous."

Giving a start—he hadn't expected such a response from a young lady—Tom chuckled softly. "You like to travel?"

"I'm sure I would if I ever had the chance," she replied. "Oh, I've been all over England of course, but I should love to tour the Continent, see Africa," she gushed. "Go to my grandmother's home country."

"Home country?" he repeated, sure she was about to mention Germany.

"Greece," she stated. "One of the islands of Greece."

Tom guffawed. "I... I would not have guessed," he said. "We're planning to go to Greece. To Athens, of course. Mayhap some of the islands." He glanced around again. "Might you allow me a dance this evening, my lady?"

"Of course."

She held up her wrist, and he wrote "Forster" on the line for one of the waltzes. He couldn't help but notice there were no other names on the card, but then, the ball had barely begun. "You're allowed, I hope?" he asked. "A waltz?"

Helen grinned. "I am. I rather doubt there is anyone here who is not allowed," she added.

"Oh?" he replied. "My mother once mentioned she could not waltz during her first year in Society. Apparently she could perform it at some place called Almack's, although she had to have some sort of special dispensation to do so."

Tittering, Helen said, "My mother wasn't allowed, either, but the first time she waltzed with my father at a ball, he stepped on her foot."

Tom nearly choked on the sip of champagne he had drunk and regarded her with disbelief. "You... you're not joking?"

Helen's light laughter lit up her features, its musical sound bringing a brilliant smile to his lips. "I am not. And although they were not betrothed until a year or so later, I rather doubt she held that unfortunate dance against him."

"Well, I should endeavor to avoid stepping on your slippers during our dance, my lady," he said, hoping his wince went unnoticed. He hadn't actually practiced the waltz in over a year. It wasn't as if he had much of a chance where he lived near Bampton-on-the-Bush.

"She was far more annoyed when he didn't seem to recognize her the next time they met," Helen commented.

"How could he not?" Tom asked in confusion.

"Well, she was in the water. The Aegean Sea, to be exact. So her hair would have been wet."

Tom swallowed at the thought of meeting a young woman in the Aegean Sea. "He must have thought her a mermaid," he guessed in awe.

"Aphrodite, actually," she said in a hoarse whisper, one of her blonde brows arched in a tease.

Sure his face was red with embarrassment—was she suggesting her mother had been unclothed at the time?—Tom dipped his head and took a long draught of the champagne, nearly draining the glass of its bubbles.

"Oh, dear. Now I've said too much—or embarrassed you—and you're wondering how you can remove your name from my dance card," she said in mock dismay.

He shook his head. "No. No," he replied, waving a hand to emphasize his response. "I was actually thinking of how fortuitous it was for him to have met the love of his life so far from England. As if..." He paused. "As if he was granted a second chance."

From the expression on Helen's face, he knew he had redeemed himself. "Perhaps when it becomes too much of a crush in here, we can take a turn in the gardens? I understand Lady Morganfield is quite proud of her roses."

Helen nodded. "I'd like that, Mr. Forster."

"*There* you are, darling."

Tom stiffened at hearing the sound of Cherise, Marchioness of Devonville. "Grandmama," he said, turning to bow to the beautiful matron who had married his grandfather about the same time his mother had married his father. "Lady Devonville, have you met Lady Helen?"

Cherise dipped her head as Helen performed a deep curtsy.

"Of course, darling. It's good to see you this evening, Lady Helen. I am in need of Thomas, though. There are those who do not believe he exists since he's so rarely here in London," she claimed.

"Of course, my lady," Helen said, dipping another curtsy.

Tom gave her a beseeching look before he was led away through the crowd.

"He seems rather amiable," Stella Jones Tennison, Countess of Everly, remarked as she joined her daughter at the edge of the ballroom.

"Indeed," Helen replied, finally draining her champagne. "Nearly as much as Penton."

Stella arched an elegant brow. "They are cousins, are they not?" When Helen responded with an uncertain glance, she added, "I am led to believe the entire family is amiable."

Knowing to what her mother's hints were leading— possible marital matches—Helen decided it best she change the subject. "Did you enjoy your dance with Father?"

"I did, and I still have all my toes," Stella replied, grinning in delight.

About to mention it would be hard for her father to step on them given her mother's expanding belly—the countess was due to give birth the following January—Helen decided against teasing her mother. The poor woman's emotions seemed to change on a moment's notice these days. At least her father knew what to do, although it frequently required the two of them to be behind closed doors. He was far more free with his kisses of late, too, but his displays of affection were at least limited to the confines of their townhouse in Mayfair.

At least, as far as she knew.

"Will he be dancing with you?"

Helen lifted her wrist so her mother could see the entry on

her dance card. "The waltz," she said, arching a brow as she grinned. She quickly sobered. "But don't get your hopes up, Mother. He's about to depart for his Grand Tour," she warned.

Stella allowed a long sigh. "Did you have *your* hopes up?" she asked in a quiet voice.

Shrugging, Helen said, "I know better these days." Her eyes widened when she realized two young men were standing behind her mother, apparently waiting for her. "Good evening," she said, her simple words enough to have her mother happily stepping aside.

Within minutes, she had several more lines filled in on her dance card, a situation which pleased her mother and gave her hope for the immediate future.

Apparently Thomas Forster's attentions had convinced other young bucks that they should seek her company.

*L*ater, when he appeared at the appointed time for their waltz, Helen was still catching her breath from the last dance—a Scotch reel with Lord Penton. "Hello again," she said, managing a curtsy.

Tom bowed and seemed uncertain for a moment. "I do hope my cousin didn't step on your slippers," he said, his gaze darting to David.

Although she hadn't known for certain the two were related, Helen was happy for the confirmation. "Even if he had, I would have forgiven him. He's a very amiable young man," she said, watching as the topic of their conversation smiled and greeted every other young buck as if they were long-lost friends. His behavior with young ladies was the same, and she wondered how many knuckles he had already kissed that evening. "If he's not careful, he's going to find himself betrothed before the evening is over."

Tom's guffaw and subsequent smile resulted in a dimple

appearing at the base of one cheek. "It would serve him right," he commented jovially. He sobered somewhat and glanced about the ballroom before he leaned closer and asked, "Would you prefer to walk in the gardens over dancing, perhaps?"

Torn between heartily agreeing to the suggestion—the ballroom had grown quite warm—and suspicion as to the young man's motives, Helen was about to reply that she would prefer to dance when he stepped even closer and added, "I fear I might step on your toes since I've never waltzed with anyone but my... my *brother*." This last was said in a whisper, and it was almost impossible not to giggle at hearing his admission.

"A walk in the gardens will be most welcome," she replied, placing a hand on his arm. "Tell me, Mr. Forster—"

"Thomas. Or you can call me Tom," he interrupted.

"Thomas," she said, rather surprised he would give her permission to use his Christian name when they had only just met. "Have you enjoyed your evening?"

"Oh, very much, although it has mostly been in the company of my grandmother's friends," he replied. They made their way to the back of the ballroom, darting around pockets of people in conversation. He held open a French door for her, and they both inhaled deeply upon leaving the ballroom.

"I didn't realize Lady Devonville was your grandmother," Helen said as they made their way along the pavers. A series of Japanese lanterns bobbed in the slight breeze, casting their shadows on the clipped lawn of the garden.

"Step-grandmother, actually," he replied. "On my mother's side."

Helen struggled to remember what she had read in *Debrett's*. "So... David, Viscount Penton, is your—"

"Cousin," he stated. "He's going with us on our Grand Tour."

"Us?" she prompted.

"My oldest cousin, Donald Slater, will be our guide. My

older brother, Randolph—he's the heir to the Gisborn earldom —and then…" Here he paused and cleared his throat. "My aunt and uncle are traveling with us as well."

Helen had to place a hand over her mouth lest she laugh at hearing his last comment. "So you will be on your very best behavior," she replied.

"I try to be all the time," he countered defensively.

She aimed a look of disbelief in his direction. "'Tis a pity," she replied. "I might have been compelled to allow you a kiss," she teased. She heard his inhalation of breath and immediately wished she could take back her last words. "I am teasing," she stated.

"Oh," he said, the sound of disappointment evident in his voice.

They walked along in silence until they reached the row of rose bushes that lined one side of the property. Backed against a hedgerow and edged on the front with tiny white flowers, only the lighter colored blooms showed in the light from a quarter moon.

"Do you have a favorite?" he asked.

Helen glanced down the row and pointed to some light pink roses, their darker centers almost black in the darkness. "Those are especially lovely," she remarked.

He led them to stand before the pink blooms, reaching out to pull one of the largest closer. "The color of a blush on a maiden's cheeks," he whispered, remembering how his mother described the roses she had planted in her garden outside the orangery behind Gisborn Hall.

"An embarrassed maiden," Helen said.

"Something tells me you are not easily embarrassed."

She inhaled sharply, the sound almost a scoff. "Perhaps I am merely cynical."

He turned to face her. "You are not old enough to be cynical," he argued.

Helen didn't meet his gaze, her attention still on the roses. That is, until two of his fingers touched her cheek to gently turn her face to his.

His lips were on hers before she quite knew what was happening. Firm pillows pressed to her lips, her mouth open from the momentary shock at his bold move.

For a moment, she didn't quite know what to do. She had imagined at least a hundred times what a kiss was supposed to be like—imagined what she would do in return—but the reality added texture and warmth she had not considered, a suckling sensation that was both pleasant and erotic, and a wash of warm breath over her cheek that held hints of champagne and amber and something spicy.

Despite wishing the kiss would continue, his lips left hers. His forehead touched her forehead, though, and remained there as he seemed to contemplate what to do next.

"I should apologize—"

"Oh, please don't," she whispered.

"I've wanted to kiss you since the moment I met you," he murmured.

She pulled away enough to stare at him in surprise. "You have?"

He nodded. "All I could think was that I would most assuredly step on your toes if we danced, and so I tried to think of what I might do that would save your slippers and keep me from displaying embarrassment undoubtedly redder than those roses." He motioned to the pink roses. "Even so, I fear my face is quite red. Did I do it right?"

"Do it right?" she repeated.

"The kiss?"

Helen blinked. "How would I know?" she asked in a hoarse whisper. "It's not as if I've ever..." Here she clamped her mouth shut and took a half-step back. The momentary spell that had been cast over them seemed to dissipate as quickly as it had formed.

"It was so pleasant," he stated. "I didn't really know what I was..." It was his turn to stop speaking.

"You're claiming *you've* never kissed before?" she asked in disbelief.

He shrugged, his broad shoulders emphasizing the simple response. For a moment, she imagined him capable of lifting her over one of them and carrying her to who-knew-where so he could do who-knew-what with her.

Mayhap behind the hedgerow.

The thought had her heart rate increasing so she could practically hear her pulse in her ears.

"I haven't," he affirmed. "Although, I would like to do it again with you. That is... if you're of a mind to be kissed again."

Torn between running back to the ballroom or holding her ground and engaging in a second kiss with the spare heir, Helen closed the distance between them, gripped a lapel in one gloved hand, and pressed her lips to his.

She wasn't expecting one of his arms to encircle her waist, but she was glad for the support. Glad for the warmth the front of his body provided for the front of hers. Glad that their second kiss was at least as pleasant and pleasing as their first.

Better, even, since neither paused with uncertainty at the beginning as they had with their initial kiss.

The ending, though, could have been so much better. Especially if Lady Devonville hadn't called out Tom's name from somewhere near the French doors.

"Apologies," he said, annoyance apparent in his voice.

Helen blinked several times, stunned by how he jerked away from her. She nearly allowed a curse but immediately understood why he had ended it so abruptly when she heard his name called out by his grandmother a second time. "You're forgiven," she whispered. "Go. I'll return to the ballroom in a moment."

"Are you sure?" he asked, his brows furrowed in confusion.

"Of course," she said, giving him a gentle shove to send him on his way.

"I look forward to seeing you again," he said. He bowed and hurried off.

Holding her breath until she was forced to let it go, Helen dipped her face into the nearest rose and inhaled, allowing the heady floral aroma to replace the intoxicating scent of Thomas Forster.

She would not soon forget it, nor the kiss they had shared.

CHAPTER 1

A CREATURE FROM THE RIVER

A year-and-a-half later, February 1841, the Nile Delta, Egypt
Of all the creatures Lady Helen Tennison expected to see on the banks of a river leading to the Nile, a crocodile was not one of them.

Nor was her baby brother, who at the moment seemed intent on becoming said crocodile's breakfast. How had he managed to escape their guide's tent and toddle all the way to the water's edge was a mystery she wasn't prepared to solve just then.

"Bradley!" she cried out, racing to scoop up the boy from the bank of the river. If she'd had the breath, she would have cursed the bell skirt of her gown, for when she was attempting to escape with her brother under her arm, she nearly lost its hem in the jaws of the dark green creature.

"Oh!" her mother cried out in shock, joining her to assist with the babe. Right behind her was Harold Tennison, Earl of Everly, holding a pistol in one hand. He stopped short and was in the process of aiming it at the crocodile when the beast determined it was outnumbered. It turned with great haste and slipped back into the dark water before Harry could get off a shot.

He lowered the weapon and let out his breath in a *whoosh*. He turned to see his wife and daughter still racing away from the bank of the river, his spare heir's arms gripped between them so the poor boy was dangling nearly a foot above the ground. His own shoulders spasmed at the thought of what Bradley's were experiencing at that moment.

He allowed a sigh of frustration.

Nothing about this trip to Egypt was going quite as he had expected.

A quarter of a century ago, before he was married and the father of three, he had been able to go on expeditions all over Europe and in the Mediterranean to search for unusual fish and plants, or to research trees and birds, his only concern his own well-being.

With his heir, Alexander, now married and safely back in London with his new wife, Margaret, Harry had thought he might resume his worldly treks—even if his half-Greek countess had recently bestowed him with another son. The boisterous boy didn't seem to understand the concept of his status as the "spare heir"—this wasn't the first time he seemed determined to commit suicide—but then he was barely a year old.

"That was entirely too close," Helen huffed, when she managed to reach the area where their dragoman was cooking their breakfast on an open fire. While Nabil had slept in the tent, they had spent the night in a nearby house, the surrounding area shaded by the leaves of banana trees. Their breakfast was to include several of the sweet yellow fruits.

"What *was* that?" Stella asked, taking her son into her arms. He settled onto her hip, his grin making it apparent he had no idea how close he had come to death-by-reptile.

"A crocodile," Harry replied. "They are..."

"Quite a nuisance," Nabil remarked. He was perched on a boulder that might have at one time been part of a nearby temple, a map spread out before him. "It's best you stay away from the riverbank whilst you are dining."

Helen glanced at the blanket her mother had spread out on the ground, half-eaten foodstuffs strewn about, some in the shade of a parasol she had planted into the ground. Not far away was the edge of the desert, its slightly reddish cast due to the morning light.

About to say, "Do tell," Helen couldn't when her mother pulled her into an embrace.

"Thank you, darling. I never would have reached him in time," Stella murmured. "Last I saw, he was asleep."

Bradley joined in the hug, his happy babbling at odds with his mother's terror.

"You're welcome," Helen replied, grinning down at her brother. "It was not as if I was going to let that awful thing take him," she added. Turning her attention to her father, she asked, "Were you thinking to add one of those to the aquarium in your study?"

Harry barked a laugh. "No, even though the young ones are quite small," he replied. "I do not think they would suit."

"Small?" she repeated in disbelief.

He pointed to Bradley. "Smaller than him," he said.

"Our son is far larger than most babes his age," Stella remarked. Her breathing had finally returned to normal, but the way her blonde brows puckered, Helen knew she was wishing she had remained at their townhouse in London.

Helen wasn't, though. Despite the momentary fright, she had been enjoying the trip up the Nile Delta from the Mediterranean. Every day she awoke to new sights. Water buffalo, strange birds, and the ruins of ancient temples lined the banks of the river that provided Egyptians with the means to live.

When her father had announced his intentions to take

them to Egypt, she had imagined desert sands for as far as the eye could see. Dunes dotted with giant pyramids and camels, Arabian horses and caravans. The greenery along this part of the Nile—and indeed the entire Delta—had been unexpected. Now that they were finally camped along the bank of the Nile —the source of the various waterways that had helped create the delta—Helen was beginning to understand why the river had been so important to the ancient Egyptians. Why it was apparently still so important.

Everything happened close to the river. Everyone lived near the river.

Contrary to what she had believed, Egyptians weren't desert dwellers. They grew crops and tended their animals and homes all within a mile of the water.

She had also imagined heat so intense, she would feel wilted before their daily luncheon. Instead, the weather had been particularly kind to their small party. She had even been forced to wear a shawl during dinner, for when the sun dipped below the horizon, the night air grew cool.

The following day, they were to arrive in Cairo to see the pyramids and the head of a sphinx at Giza.

"Nabil says we will reach Cairo later today," Harry said, stowing the pistol in a trunk. "We can expect to find accommodations there."

"A real bed?" Helen asked, her eyes betraying her dislike of the cots in which they had been sleeping for the past few nights, tents of mosquito netting protecting them from the biting insects.

Nabil chuckled. "Real beds," he affirmed. "Good food. Ancient pyramids."

Helen grinned. "I can hardly wait," she said. "I look forward to whatever we discover."

Glad to hear his daughter was amenable to what was to

come, Harry took his son into his arms and hoisted him over his head.

Bradley giggled in delight. "You and your sister are the very best travelers," he said, aiming an apologetic glance at his wife.

Stella merely shrugged. "I knew what to expect," she said.

Helen studied her mother for a moment, realizing she spoke the truth. Even though Estelle Jones Tennison, Countess of Everly, was the daughter of a duke, she had spent most of her youth on an island in the Aegean Sea, far from the luxury of Mayfair.

Although Helen didn't expect to miss the creature comforts of the Everly townhouse, she was looking forward to spending some nights in a building with real walls and a real bed.

She didn't want her sleep interrupted by a hungry creature.

CHAPTER 2
NEWLYWEDS AWAKEN

eanwhile, on a dhahabîyeh out in the river

The sound of footsteps overhead had Randy Forster, heir to the Gisborn earldom, emerging from a deep sleep. He reached out to ensure his new wife, Diana, was still next to him, grinning when she rolled to face him.

"Good morning, sleepyhead," she whispered, her lips upturned at their corners.

"Good morning, gorgeous." He leaned toward her and kissed her forehead. "What are you doing awake so early?"

She tittered, a sound he found as welcoming as he did amusing. As a woman determined to remain a spinster when he had met her atop the Acropolis in Athens, Diana rarely smiled, nor was she easily humored. For some reason he hadn't yet sorted, Randy had been immediately attracted to the young woman.

"Trying to determine if it's your brother or David walking about up on the top deck," she replied. "I believe it's Tom, but as to why he's up there, I have to admit I am rather curious."

"It's Tom," he affirmed, recognizing his younger brother's

cadence. He lifted his pocket watch from the nightstand, his eyes widening. "I *am* a sleepyhead," he added. "It's nearly nine o'clock." He lifted himself onto an elbow and listened for a moment. "And it feels like we're moving rather fast."

"The wind is in our favor," Diana remarked. "Our captain said this is the best time of the year to sail up the Nile."

He scoffed softly. "Are we in a hurry?"

Diana once again tittered and stepped off the small bed. Given the size of their compact cabin, she had to shimmy sideways to reach her trunk.

Randy suppressed the urge to groan when she bent over to open it and retrieve some clothes. His very first view of her had been of her bum, the perfect upside-down heart-shaped derriere encased in a pair of men's breeches.

She wasn't wearing anything at the moment, due to the fact that he had stripped her of her nightrail the night before, prior to them ever climbing onto the small bed. She also seemed oblivious to the discomfort she was causing him and his manhood.

"Are you staring at my bum?" she asked, her attention still on the clothes in the trunk.

So... not oblivious.

"I am and you know it, you minx," he accused, managing to inflect some humor into his otherwise serious response. Despite what he wanted to be doing with his new wife— engage in the sort of bed sport in which they had enjoyed once he had her completely naked—he pulled on a pair of pantaloons. "But if my brother is up on the roof..." He paused to listen and grunted when the sound resumed. "He must have seen something."

"Agreed," she replied. She held up a day gown next to a pair of breeches. "I can't decide," she added.

The daughter of Viscount Jasper Henley, Diana regularly

engaged in her father's avocation of archaeology. She was clever, too, and gifted—or cursed—with the ability to remember everything she had ever heard, read, or seen.

She also possessed a body Randy found irresistible. Given all her traits, he supposed he'd had no choice when it came to convincing her to marry him. Although he had offered to be her lover for life if she remained a spinster, he knew he would always regret it if she couldn't one day be his countess.

As for if she was regretting marrying him, he reveled in the reminder of the words she said to him every night before they slept.

"I love you, Randolph Forster."

For the first week after their civil wedding ceremony in Athens, she had added, "Please don't make me regret it."

Ever since, he had done his very best to improve upon his lovemaking skills—in seeing to her pleasure before taking his own. Other than having studied illustrations or read about lovemaking in books, neither one of them had any experience prior to their wedding night.

They had certainly learned much from one another since that night late in September.

"Mayhap neither," he whispered, referring to the clothes she held out. He swallowed, his eyes darkening with desire.

Diana dropped the folded items onto the bed and turned around as if she intended to look for something else. Bending over, she glanced back at him. "Perhaps you should come help me choose," she whispered. Instead of rummaging through the trunk, she braced her hands against the cabin wall.

The sight of her upturned quim had Randy gulping. He quickly divested himself of his pantaloons before moving to stand behind her. Gripping her hips with his hands, he gasped when one of her hands reached between her thighs to cradle his ball sac before guiding the tip of his manhood to her entrance.

"You're already wet," he whispered in surprise, inhaling sharply when he realized he was already half-buried inside her.

"I've been awake longer than you," she whispered.

"We've not done it like this before," he murmured, sliding his hands up along the sides of her torso until his fingertips brushed the tips of her nipples.

She gasped when he pressed further into her, and when she arched her back, he was suddenly buried to the hilt. She gave up her hold on his balls to press her palm against the wall, requiring both hands for leverage.

"I fear I'm going to come too soon," he warned, pulling halfway out before he thrust into her.

He felt one of her hands cover his right hand to guide it to where their bodies met, and he understood what to do. Pressing his thumb against her swollen womanhood as he pulled out of her, he felt her body respond even before he heard her soft cry. Rubbing harder as he thrust into her over and over, he knew he couldn't hold off his release.

At the same moment his seed spilled into her, her channel contracted around his manhood, pulling him deeper into her while her breath caught. To stifle her cry of pleasure, she turned her head to place her open mouth against her upper arm.

For a moment, Randy saw only stars as a maelstrom of pleasure gripped him and didn't seem to let go. Dizzy and delirious, he lowered his face to the space between her shoulder blades, one hand cupping a breast as the other took purchase on the wall for support.

"Well, this is certainly a novel way to start the morning," Diana whispered after a moment, her breathing finally returning to normal.

"If I died this very moment, I would miss you the most," he whispered hoarsely.

Diana gasped and straightened, sending him falling backwards onto the bed. "Don't you dare die on me," she countered, turning to follow him down onto the bed. She ended up atop him, grinning in delight.

He chuckled, although he quickly sobered when the thumping atop the roof began again. "I won't," he promised. "I think it's best I discover what's going on out there, though."

"Agreed," Diana replied. She rolled off of him and returned to the trunk.

"The gown," he said. When she gave him a look of confusion, he added, "Wear the gown. Save the breeches for when we reach some ruins," he suggested.

She nodded, watching as he pulled on his smalls and pantaloons. "I'll hurry, but I to need clean myself before I dress," she said.

Pulling on a shirt, he nodded. "There's water in the pitcher," he said. "Will you need help with your gown?"

"I can manage," she assured him. "But I'm only going to wear one petticoat. There isn't enough room on this ship for these huge skirts," she complained.

"I won't mind," he replied, grinning as he buttoned his waistcoat. "I'm going to forego a top coat." Pulling on a pair of boots, he stood. "Do I look like you've just had your way with me?"

Giggling, Diana moved to stand in front of him, reaching up with a hand to spear his hair with her fingers, smoothing it into some semblance of order. "There," she said proudly.

"Thank you." He kissed her first on the lips and then on the forehead.

"You're welcome. Now, be off with you. I need some privacy. If anyone asks, I—"

"I'll tell them you're reading," he said, gesturing to a small pile of books on the cabin's only nightstand.

She lifted a shoulder. "Thank you."

He winked at her and took his leave of the small cabin to discover whatever it was that had his brother up on the top deck.

CHAPTER 3
BREAKFAST ON A BOAT

*M*eanwhile

Holding his cousin's binoculars to his face, Thomas Forster studied the shore—and the young woman and babe he caught running away from the water. He let out a low whistle.

"What is it?" his cousin, David Slater, asked. He moved to take the pair of telescopes from Tom, surprised when his cousin gave them up so easily.

"*Who*, is more the question," Tom murmured, making his way to the back of the sailing vessel. Given the number of cabins and the fact that it had space for a kitchen and a dining table and chairs up top, the *dhahabîyeh*, named *The Cleopatra*, was practically a houseboat. The large sail, located at the front on a mast that leaned in the direction of travel, was completely unfurled and filled with the morning's wind as was the small one that extended well past the back of the ship.

When they had boarded the day before, Will Slater, Earl of Bellingham and former commander of *HMS Greenwich*, had studied the design for a long time, curious how the equivalent of a main mast would work at such an angle. Once they were on their way, he marveled at how easy it was for one man—their captain, George—and a young boy to crew such a craft. When George learned Will had captained a naval vessel, he invited him to take the wheel once they were well into the Nile.

"We must be careful of the sand bars," George had explained. "And other hazards on the river bottom."

Happy to wait his turn at the wheel, Will enjoyed watching the shoreline along with the rest of the family as they departed the port at Alexandria and made their way to a tributary in the Delta that provided direct access to the Nile. Now that they were on a waterway that was much wider and proved to have a slower current, Tom expected his uncle would be at the wheel for most of the day—once he finally emerged from his cabin.

Tom climbed the ladder leading to the top deck—the roof of the cabins—careful to maintain his balance as he stared at the distant shore.

David aimed the binoculars in the direction of where he had seen his cousin looking and scanned for signs of life. He spotted a man near the bank of the river, holding what he was sure was a gun, and behind him, a young woman hurrying away with a babe in tow.

No. Make that two women, although one was considerably older than the other. The babe appeared as if its arms were strung between them, and he rolled a shoulder in sympathy.

He lost sight of the two women when the man headed in their direction, blocking them from David's view. From seeing only his back, David was sure he was garbed in a white shirt, waistcoat, pantaloons, and boots.

Familiar clothes.

They appeared much like those he and his cousins had been wearing every day of late. Their group of six had made their way from Athens, Greece aboard a steamship to Crete, and after a fortnight on the largest of the Cyclades Islands, they had departed for Egypt on a sailing vessel.

Upon reaching the port in Alexandria, David's father, William Slater, Earl of Bellingham, had contracted with a ship's owner to take them to Cairo. Although he had hoped to extend the trip as far south as Luxor—the site of ancient Thebes—Will was told he would need to find a different vessel in which to continue the trip up the Nile. Despite his generous offer, the owner had reluctantly declined but assured Will there would be sailing vessels available for hire for such a trek.

"Did you recognize anyone on shore?" Tom called down to his cousin.

Torn from his brief reverie, David once again lifted the binoculars to his face. This time, he briefly caught the profile of the man, scoffing when he realized the gentleman seemed familiar. He attempted to refocus the lenses, but by the time he redirected them, the ship had moved too far up river for him to make out any details. "I take it you did?" he countered as he glanced up at his cousin, shading his eyes from the morning sun with a hand held to his forehead.

Tom walked the length of the top deck before he turned around and retraced his steps. From this distance, he couldn't be positive as to the identity of the young woman with the babe, but she certainly looked familiar.

Too familiar.

The memory of a kiss he had shared with her came to mind —as it frequently had done during their Grand Tour—and he had to tamp down the excitement he felt.

Tamp down his ardor, too, for his manhood had begun twitching at the same time he remembered the kiss he had shared with Lady Helen next to the roses in Lady Morganfield's garden.

He would have thought that after nearly a year-and-a-half, he could have forgotten about those stolen kisses, but they only seemed more vivid in his brain.

She seemed more vivid.

Although he had kept her from being discovered in his company by returning to the ballroom without her, her entire identity had been difficult to learn. He hadn't wished to raise suspicions with his grandmother by asking about Lady Helen, though. He had instead waited until their party had departed London before asking his Aunt Barbara if she was familiar with Lady Helen.

She was not.

His uncle, however, knew exactly who he meant. "She's Everly's daughter," he had said during one of their dinners with the ship's captain.

For any more information, Tom didn't dare ask anyone, preferring instead to help himself to the captain's copy of *Debrett's Peerage and Baronetage*. Although it had been a decade out of date, Lady Helen was listed along with her older brother, Alexander, as the only offspring of Harold Tennison, Earl of Everly, and his countess, Estelle Jones, daughter of the Duke of Westhaven and a woman named Astria Zabat from an island called Mykonos.

So what Helen had told him about her mother that night at the ball was true. She was half-Greek, but she was also a duke's daughter. He couldn't remember her mentioning anything about that when any other young lady might have led with such information.

Lady Helen was a duke's granddaughter!

Given the British had helped the Greeks with their war for independence, it shouldn't matter if a young lady was of Greek descent. He found the thought rather enticing, especially now that they had visited Athens and spent time in several archaeological sites, including the Temple of Poseidon at Cape Sounion and the ruins at Delphi. Should he ever see Lady Helen again, he would be able to regale her with stories of his time in Greece.

Tom scrambled down the ladder to discover his cousin

waiting for an answer to his query about what—or rather who —he had seen onshore. "I was probably only seeing things," he said dismissively.

David frowned. "Who did you *think* you saw?"

His hands moving to his hips, Tom shook his head. "Someone we met in London. At that ball we attended before we left for Sicily," he replied. "It's nothing, really," he added dismissively.

Chuckling, David considered the possibility. "Well, I suppose there are others who have ventured this way from England for their Grand Tours," he said. "But... that man seemed a bit long in the tooth to be on his."

"Watch who you're calling too old to be on his grand Tour," his father, Will, said as he joined the young men from inside one of the ship's four cabins. At eight-and-forty, most might have thought the heir to the Devonville marquessate too old to be traipsing about the Mediterranean on a Grand Tour. His years in the British Navy acting as a commander followed by over two decades as foreman for his brother-in-law's farms had served him well when it came to his physique, and it didn't hurt that his male ancestors had all seemed to live well past seventy.

"Apologies, Father, but that man back there..." David paused to wave in the direction of the shore.

"What man?"

"It was more than just a man," Tom said, when he joined his uncle and cousin. "Looked more like... like a family," he added. "An older man and woman, then a younger woman and her babe. I think she was rescuing him from something. Something on the ground that was large and dark."

"Whatever the man was going to shoot," David said, his eyes rounding.

"That would have been a crocodile," George announced. Three pairs of eyes turned to regard the captain of the ship and their dragoman for the trip to Cairo with curiosity. "Very dangerous, especially the large ones."

Will's eyes rounded. "I had quite forgotten about them," he said under his breath.

"You've seen them before?" Tom asked in alarm.

"You all have. There were a couple of them at that menagerie we attended whilst we were in London," Will replied. "The dark green reptiles with the long jaws and sharp teeth." He pantomimed the shape of a crocodile's head, extending his hands out in front his face.

"Oh, I remember now," Tom murmured, his gaze going to the south. The family on the shore had long ago disappeared and been replaced with marshlands featuring water buffalo.

"Sir, will we be having breakfast anytime soon?" David asked George.

Their dark-skinned guide chuckled. "I have been cooking all night just for you," he teased. "Please, help yourself at my table."

David glanced at his father, as if seeking permission.

"Go on," Will said. "I'll be right behind you."

"As will I," Barbara, his wife and mother to David said as she emerged from their cabin. Dressed in a light yellow day gown made from sprigged cotton, she appeared well-rested. Despite her attempts to remain under cover from the sun, her complexion wasn't nearly as pale as it had been when they left Oxfordshire the year-and-a-half before. "I don't know why, but I'm *famished*," she claimed.

Will did everything he could do to hide the smirk that threatened. He might have been eight-and-forty, but he certainly wasn't on death's door when it came to pleasing his wife in bed. The cooler temperatures at night had helped, sending her into his arms as soon as he was under the cotton bed linens. From there, he was eager to warm her even further, delighting in her pleas for more and her attempts to keep the sounds of her pleasure from penetrating the walls.

"As am I," Will agreed. He turned to George. "I wanted to thank you again for agreeing to take us to Cairo. I know packing enough food to feed these boys has to have overflowed your cargo space."

George waved a dismissive hand. "I have four myself, so I know how they eat," he claimed. "Besides, you paid well. You eat well."

When Will took a seat at the trestle, an assemblage of heavy wooden planks secured to the deck above the cabins, he turned his attention back to his nephew.

Tom, lost in thought, was oblivious to his uncle's gaze. He didn't even help himself to any of the bowls of stewed fava beans, coddled eggs, fruit, or hunks of cheese. The loaf of bread, purchased from a vendor the day before, had been broken in half. A pitcher of beer completed the offerings.

When Will poured him a glass of beer, Tom finally emerged from his reverie.

"A penny for your thoughts?" Will said, helping himself to a few pieces of fruit and one of the eggs.

Tom shook his head. "I would only be cheating you," he murmured. He took a drink of the beer, aware his uncle was watching him. A quick glance in his aunt's direction proved she thought something was wrong as well. He was relieved when David settled next to him, commenting on the fine weather as he filled his plate and announced he had begun studying a book he had purchased in Alexandria.

"Book?" his mother repeated. "Don't you mean a new library?"

David shrugged. "I thought it important I have the entire collection, even if it is all in French."

"What book?" Tom asked, confused by their conversation.

"*La Description de l'Egypte*," David replied, his French nearly perfect. "It was written by the savants Napoleon brought with him when he invaded Egypt. Four-and-twenty volumes filled with maps, drawings, and very detailed descriptions of what they discovered."

At the mention of Napoleon, Will stiffened. "Are these the same men who saw to removing statues and other artifacts to Paris?"

"Probably," David hedged. "But they're all in a museum now. For safe-keeping," he replied. "Much like what Belzoni took for the British Museum," he added, referring to an Italian who had been responsible for the early exploration of Abu Simbel, some tombs in the Valley of the Kings, and of the temples of Karnak in Luxor.

Will seemed to relax, although Tom knew he was bothered by the pillaging that had taken place at some of the other historical sites they had visited on this trip. "Are these books anything like Pausanias' *Descriptions of Greece*?" he asked, referring to the books they had used for reference whilst they were in Greece.

"They are, although these are far more exact in terms of their drawings," David replied. "They include measurements."

"And the illustrations are very well done," Randy announced, joining them at the trestle.

"You've seen them?" Barbara asked, angling a cheek when he leaned over to kiss it.

"From over Diana's shoulder," he replied. "She was reading quite late last night and was back at it again this morning. She'll be along shortly." He helped himself to some of the foods. "Apologies for my tardiness. I was sound asleep until I heard footfalls on the roof."

"That was your brother," David said, adding more eggs to his plate.

"Save some for Diana," his mother scolded him, at the same

moment George appeared with more food and a bunch of small bananas.

"So what, pray tell, had you up on the roof?" Randy asked, turning his attention to Tom.

His brother stiffened. "I saw some people on the shore. They were..." He shrugged.

"Dressed like us," David finished for him. "I'm fairly sure I recognized the man with the gun."

"Gun?" Barbara repeated in shock.

"He was aiming it at the..." He hesitated to mention more, as if he feared frightening his mother.

"A crocodile," George stated, placing another plate of cut fruits on the table. "The beasties are everywhere in this river."

Barbara exchanged a quick glance with her son and husband. "Those atrocious animals we saw in the menagerie?" she asked, her face screwing into disgust. "With the long jaws and large teeth?"

"That would be them," Will affirmed.

"They stay close to the water's edge. As long as we are moving, we needn't worry they will come aboard the ship," George assured her.

For a moment, she didn't appear convinced. "Did he shoot it?"

David shook his head. "I didn't hear a gun shot," he replied.

"Who did you think it was?"

At that moment, Diana appeared, her hair swept up in a bun atop her head. She was dressed in a pale blue gown and wore a shawl around her shoulders. "Good morning. Please accept my apologies," she said, her color still high from that morning's lovemaking. "I've been reading and didn't realize breakfast was already served."

"You're forgiven, Diana, and, oh, you look so pretty this morning," Barbara commented.

"Thank you," Diana said, taking the remaining seat at the

table next to David. "Did I hear correctly that there's been a crocodile sighting?"

"Not close enough to see directly," David replied. "I was using the binoculars."

"What made you think to even look?" she asked, nodding to George when he set a cup of licorice tea before her.

"Oh, well, I saw people on the shore. I'm fairly sure the man was Everly."

Will gave a start. "Everly... as in the Earl of Everly?"

David nodded. "Isn't he a naturalist, I think they call them these days?"

"Indeed," Will replied, his brows furrowed in thought. "I saw him at the Morganfield ball we attended before we left London."

"Did he mention he was planning a trip to Egypt?" Barbara asked.

Will shook his head. "No, but I did tell him where we were off to. I don't think I've ever seen a grown man appear so jealous. He even remarked that he missed his days of traveling," he commented. "In addition to the fish, he used to bring back exotic plants and birds from his excursions."

"I hear he has a most impressive conservatory as a result," Barbara remarked. "All *glass*." This last was said with a good deal of awe, for at the time when it was built, glass had been taxed at rather high rates.

"Speaking of glass, isn't he the one who has that large aquarium in his study?" David asked. "With a contraption that creates bubbles and another that keeps the water warm?"

"He is the one," Will acknowledged. "Quite an accomplishment, but then he is as inventive as Henry," he added, referring to Randy and Tom's father, the Earl of Gisborn. "I wonder what he's searching for here in Egypt?"

"Perhaps we'll see him again on this trip," Diana remarked. She held up a banana. "Although I would recommend he take a banana tree back to England, I can't imagine how he would do so. They're rather large."

Will guffawed. "Considering the size of some of the the statues that are in the British Museum, I rather imagine a banana tree would be manageable."

The others at the table snickered before they returned their attentions to their breakfasts and plans for what they would do when they reached Cairo.

All except for Tom. He was lost in thought, an image of a young lady with a baby in his mind's eye.

CHAPTER 4
ACCOMMODATIONS AND EXPECTATIONS

*T**he following day*

As Nabil piloted his felucca between the hazards of the slow moving Nile, Harry, Earl of Everly, struggled to read a letter he had been carrying with him since their departure from London.

"It appears I am no longer able to read French," he grumbled, his gaze going to his wife.

Ensconced on her lap, their year-old son blabbered with excitement while Stella watched the scenery. "Would you like me to try?" she asked, reaching out to capture the brittle paper when he offered it to her. She had to hold it out beyond the reach of Bradley, who immediately took interest and wanted it for himself.

"Come here, you little troublemaker," Helen said, moving from the other side of the felucca to take her brother into her arms, careful to duck her head under the bottom edge of the single sail that propelled the sailing vessel up the Nile.

Happy to join his older sister, Bradley continued to babble incoherently before ending his sentence with "dada".

Harry chuckled softly. "I do wonder if we'll ever know what he's trying to say," he murmured.

"Well, I can tell you what Monsieur Jacques LaSalle is trying to say in his letter," Stella said, holding up the missive that included seven creases and looked as if it had taken a trip around the world, been dunked in a cup of tea, and been stomped on by a pair of riding boots before its delivery to their townhouse in Mayfair.

"Oh, good. Do enlighten me," Harry replied in a pleading voice.

"It's not your French, darling, but rather his poor penmanship," Stella remarked. She held up the letter and recited, "Upon your arrival in Cairo on or around the fifteenth of February, your guide, Monsieur Nabil Al-Maghrabi, whom you shall meet in Alexandria on or around the third of February (given the current schedule of the ship you wish to take from London), knows to send word to me via courier upon your arrival so that I may meet you at the dock in Cairo and arrange transport to my..." Here she paused and shook her head. "I don't recognize this word '*riad*'."

"Oh, I know what that is," Helen piped up before her brows furrowed. "It's the Moroccan word for *house*." Her face displayed confusion. "But I don't know why he would call it that for a house in Cairo."

"LaSalle's house is no doubt of better construction than what we'll usually be seeing on this journey," her father commented. "He probably had the wood shipped in from Anatolia or Venice and the tile from Rome. He is a man of considerable wealth."

"How did you even learn of him?" Stella asked.

"He was recommended by someone at White's. They said he frequently hosts the bureaucrats that travel back and forth between India and England." He waved to the missive. "Does he mention anything else in his letter?"

She nodded and resumed reading aloud. "Your request for accommodations comes at a rather popular time for tourists it would seem, for I have already made arrangements for another family from England to stay at the *riad*."

Here, Stella paused when Helen gasped with excitement. Her face reddening when she realized both parents were staring at her, she said, "Oh, please, do go on."

Stella hesitated reading aloud, though, and instead read in silence before she made a strange sound in her throat. "It seems we are to *share* the accommodations in Cairo but that the *riad* is quite large with more than enough bedchambers and servants to see to our comfort."

"Hmpf," Harry replied, his manner suggesting he wasn't pleased with the arrangements. "Does he say anything else?"

"He wishes us safe travels and looks forward to meeting us in Cairo," Stella replied. "Where he will introduce us to the *dragoman*..." She glanced up, her expression conveying confusion. "What does that word mean?"

"The guide he mentioned earlier in the letter. A dragoman is an interpreter as well as a guide. He'll know English and Arabic and the routes we should take," Harry explained.

"Oh," she breathed. She continued where she left off in the letter. "The dragoman will take us to the pyramids at Giza and arrange for another to take to us to Memphis, should we wish to go to the necropolis located there." Here she screwed up her face in a grimace. "Necropolis?"

"Memphis was the site of many tombs and pyramids," Harry explained. "All of which were burial sites for the early pharaohs—the kings of Egypt."

"And the queens," Helen chimed in.

Her father chuckled. "Yes, the queens, too."

"What of the weather? Shouldn't it be raining this time of the year?" Stella asked, her gaze going to the cloudless sky.

From where he was manning the rudder at the back of the

felucca, Nabil said, "This is our rainy season, my lady." He waved. "Tonight I will be sure your tent is well away from the river as I expect it is raining upstream." He pointed south. "In Nubia. We may have rain this evening."

Stella glanced south and then turned to face the north. "This makes no sense," she said, her attention going to the river.

"That's because the Nile flows in the wrong direction," Helen replied. "It starts somewhere south of Egypt and flows north until it reaches the delta and the Mediterranean Sea."

"Lady Helen has the right of it," Nabil said. "And you will be very welcome at Monsieur LaSalle's *riad*. Very large. Very elegant. Even if it doesn't have a roof."

"What's this?" Stella asked in alarm. "No roof?"

"No roof over the courtyard, Mother," Helen explained. "But the courtyard probably has a tile floor, where the water is captured in a drain for use in the garden."

Stella glanced at her husband, who shrugged. "She has the right of it," Harry said. "I am most excited about the prospect of finding a new hibiscus plant."

"Oh, Monsieur LaSalle wrote about it at the end of the letter," she said, returning her attention to the missive she still held. "I didn't recognize the word at first." She used a forefinger to follow the written words before reciting, "The flower you seek is in the garden of the *riad*. There are many plants, mostly with red blooms. Should you require to uproot one for your needs, please do plant a piece of it in its place. Or you may decide there is a more desirable specimen on your travels. They are quite common. Do enjoy the tea. Regards, Jacques LaSalle."

"Enjoy the tea?" Helen repeated. "That seems like an odd way of ending a letter."

Nabil cleared his throat. "I do not mean to eavesdrop," he said from the back of the felucca. "Monsieur LaSalle is referring to hibiscus tea. A favorite among the Egyptian people. It was the tea of the pharaohs."

Stella gasped. "I do believe I've had hibiscus tea in London," she said. "Red, is it not?"

"Indeed," Nabil replied. "Good for digestion. I have some in our stores on board. I will serve it after dinner if you would like."

"That would be most welcome," Stella said. She turned her gaze on her husband. "I do wonder with whom we will be sharing the *riad*," she murmured.

"Well, if they're English, at least we'll be able to converse should they be of a mind to do so," Harry commented.

"Oh, I'm quite sure they will," Helen said, her gaze on her younger brother. She bussed him on the forehead, which sent him into a fit of giggles. The two resumed the clapping game she had been attempting to teach him ever since they left Alexandria.

Her father furrowed a brow before he turned to Stella. "Is there something you need to tell me?" he asked in a hoarse whisper.

Stella shook her head. "I'm quite sure I don't know who she is talking about," she whispered. "I was hoping *you* might know."

He shrugged before his face displayed a curious expression. "What is it?"

Hesitating, as if he couldn't trust his conclusion, Harry chuckled softly. "Do you recall meeting the Earl and Countess of Bellingham at the Morganfield ball? He is Devonville's heir?" he clarified. When she didn't appear to remember, he added, "A few months before you gave birth to my spare heir?"

Stella considered the query for a moment before her eyes widened. "Barbara," she whispered. "She was the Earl of Greenley's daughter... *sister* now, of course," she corrected. "She was about to leave for the Mediterranean with her sons and nephews. For their Grand Tour," she added with excitement.

Harry chuckled softly, his attention going back to his daughter and young son. "Remind me to tell you the rest of what I know tonight," he whispered, his manner suddenly secretive.

Scoffing softly, Stella seemed about to put voice to a complaint, but Nabil spoke before she had a chance.

"If you would be so good as to direct your attention to the south, you will see something of interest in the distance."

Even Bradley turned his head to see what their guide indicated when the felucca suddenly veered toward the southeastern bank of the Nile.

"The pyramids at Giza!" Helen exclaimed, standing and hoisting her brother onto her hip so she could move closer to the starboard side of the sailing vessel.

"You know of them?" Nabil asked in surprise.

"Of course. Ever since we decided to take this trip, I have read everything I could about Egypt," she replied, never taking her eyes from the three triangles barely visible on the horizon.

Harry and Stella exchanged curious glances before they turned their attention to the pyramids. "How far away are those?" he asked.

"Twenty miles as a bird flies," Nabil replied. "By the Nile..." He shrugged. "Five-and-twenty?"

"So... we only have one more day on the river?" Helen asked with excitement.

"Indeed. We will camp near here," Nabil announced, apparently a cue for his young assistant to see to taking down the sail. "And tomorrow, we shall arrive in Cairo." The felucca coasted toward the shore, where an ancient dock bobbed in the water. Within a few minutes, the Tennisons were on the shore and making their way to higher ground for a longer look at the pyramids.

Helen's attention wasn't on the ancient monuments, though, but rather back on the river.

If everything worked the way she hoped, two months of careful planning was about to be rewarded. Knowing her father would wish to camp along the river rather than make the trek to Cairo directly, she had suggested a modified schedule for their family to follow in the hopes their arrival in Cairo would coincide with the arrival of the Bellinghams.

Although she didn't know the exact schedule of when the Bellinghams and their son and nephews would arrive in Egypt, she had an approximate itinerary thanks to Cherise, Marchioness of Devonville.

The grandmother of Tom Forster was more than happy to share what she knew when she hosted them for tea a few days before their departure from England.

Including where they were to stay.

She gave her brother a kiss on his forehead, grinning as she contemplated seeing Tom again.

CHAPTER 5
AN INTRODUCTION TO CAIRO

The following day at the port at Cairo

Although the dock where George had tied up the *dhahabîyeh* was busy, it wasn't as chaotic as the other ports the Bellinghams had experienced on their trip. There were porters, of course, and all manner of donkeys, camels, and horses to see to cargo, but the number of people was considerably less.

Awake earlier than usual, Barbara watched the activity from where she was seated on the upper deck. Although some of the cargo was familiar, much of it was not. Especially a line of dark, linen wrapped packages, each about five feet long, laid out on the planks of the dock. As she watched, two men loaded them into a wooden crate, and it wasn't until they were handling the last one that she realized just what it was she was seeing.

Mummies.

"Ew," she murmured, deciding she best return to her cabin and finish packing.

. . .

hen the last of the trunks had been off-loaded from *The Cleopatra* and were stacked on a dray cart with a single donkey, George finished his discussion with a well-dressed man and turned to introduce him to Will. "Monsieur DeSalle is the gentleman who has a *riad* available for your stay. Many rooms, a cook, and servants. He frequently hosts Englishmen on their way to India, so he is familiar with your ways," he explained. "He says you should be very comfortable during your stay, but I am to tell you there will be three more English people coming, probably later today. Maybe you know them?"

Will chuckled. "I rather doubt it. I'm rarely in London and unfamiliar with those who see to the offices in India," he replied,

"You are an earl, no?" DeSalle asked in English, holding out his right hand.

"I am," Will acknowledged.

"My other guest is as well. Harold Tennison—

"The Earl of Everly," Will finished, scoffing softly. "We thought we saw him on the banks of the river yesterday."

"He is a savant? Come to research plants?" DeSalle asked, obviously curious about the aristocrat's avocation.

"He is a... *naturalist*, I believe is the term he uses to describe himself. A member of the Royal Society. Well-traveled, too. I look forward to seeing him again."

"I expect his arrival at any time," DeSalle said, nodding to a robe-garbed man who approached him and bowed. "Ah, our *hantours* have arrived. There are three for your party," he said, waving to a line of horse-drawn carriages that had pulled up just beyond the dock. "They will see you to my *riad*."

"I look forward to meeting the Countess of Everly again," Barbara murmured, her words meant for Diana. "I think I will recognize her from the Morganfield ball we attended prior to our departure."

The younger woman grinned. "I recall meeting her when I was young. My father and her husband are both members of the Royal Society," she explained before realization dawned on her features. "You must be at your wit's end with all these men," she added.

"Really, it's no different when we are at home," Barbara replied on a sigh. "But there I have a lady's maid and Hannah—your new mother-in-law—and there are women in the village of Bampton with whom I can speak when I am there," she explained. "Here I feel as if I am a fish out of water."

Diana gave her a sympathetic glance. "I fear I have been of no help in that regard. I have spent so much time in the company of my father and brothers, I am not much of a conversationalist, nor am I in possession of any gossip to share."

"Oh, you are doing fine, darling," Barbara assured her. "I do think the boys already think of you as one of them as opposed to a sister."

Resisting the urge to wince, Diana nodded. "Perhaps it is merely due to Randy, but I do find I like my new brother and your son far more than I do my own brothers," she whispered.

Barbara tittered as she opened her fan and waved it in front of her face. "I will keep your secret," she promised. "No reason to let these ruffians know they are appreciated," she added in a tease. She was prevented from saying more when they were ushered to the hantours.

Topped with fabric coverings from which tassels dangled from the edges, the black carriages were manned by robe-garbed drivers, their heads wrapped in turbans. Each man held the reins of the single horse hitched to their hantour.

· · ·

ill helped Barbara up the high step into one of the hantours while Randy did the same for Diana in another. Tom and David ended up in the last carriage, but before they climbed aboard, they stopped to admire the small horse in front. "This is an Arabian," David announced in awe, finally tearing his attention from his binoculars to give the dark brown beast a look.

"It's so small," Tom remarked, his gloved hand smoothing along the horse's withers to its flank. He winced at feeling the ribs so close beneath its hide.

"We're so used to draft horses and bays, any other horses appear small to us," David reasoned, climbing into the carriage. Given the harsh afternoon sun, he appreciated the carriage's flat roof, although the sides remained open to provide unimpeded views of the city.

They watched in fascination as the carriages cleared the dock, and for the first time since they had docked, David had the opportunity to view the pyramids at Giza through his binoculars. "They're so close," he said in awe. "They're just across the river."

Tom took the instrument from him, and despite the rough road, he was able to make out three of the pyramids before buildings interrupted his view. "We'll see them up close on the morrow," he commented, giving the binoculars back to David.

"From atop a camel?" David asked, his expression suggesting he was looking forward to the experience. He lifted the binoculars to his face and continued to study the horizon when he could.

"No doubt," Tom replied, not sharing his cousin's enthusiasm.

David grinned in delight, aiming his binoculars at a pair of young ladies carrying baskets from a nearby market. When one of them caught him staring, he waved and smiled.

They did not return his greeting, and he lowered the binoculars to discover Tom grinning at him.

"We should take advantage of our time here to do some shopping," David remarked. "George said we should buy gold items."

"You mean... like jewelry?"

"Rings, necklaces, anything made of gold. They'll be small. Easy to transport and give as gifts when we return to England," David explained.

"Good idea," Tom said. "Especially since it would seem there is a jewelry shop right next to where we are to stay," he murmured, watching as their *riad* came into view.

He decided he was going to like Cairo.

CHAPTER 6

TALK OF TIGHT SPACES AND
HISTORIC PLACES

he following morning
When Randy awoke with a start, he immediately lifted himself onto an elbow and blinked at the candle lamp on the nightstand. From the lack of light bleeding around the edges of the room's only window, he knew it was still dark outside.

"Apologies. I didn't mean to wake you," Diana said. She was sitting up in bed, an open book resting in the crook of her arm. Reaching out, she smoothed her free hand over his sleep tousled hair.

Randy furrowed a brow. "Have you been reading all night?" The last he could remember, she had fallen asleep with her head in the small of his shoulder, her legs tangled with his and one of her hands pressed to his chest. The thought of what she had been doing a few minutes before made his morning tumescence even more apparent, his member tenting the bed linens.

"No, darling," she whispered. "But it's nearly dawn. I wished to finish the entry in this book about the Great Pyramid of Khufu before we go there."

"That's today," he said, sitting up straighter. He glanced over, noticing the page she was studying included a drawing. "What's that?" he asked, pointing to a double line that appeared as if it was inside the structure.

"The passage into the pyramid," she replied, tracing a finger from the entrance to where the corridor intersected with another that led up to an open chamber. The initial passage continued downward until it was completely under the ground and beyond the footprint of the pyramid. "I'm going in there," she stated, pointing to the Grand Gallery.

"What?"

She glanced over at him, her expression blank. "Would you like to join me? The passage is a bit tight, I think. Only a little over three feet by three feet, and it's at a fairly steep angle, but many have done it," she went on, not aware of how his face had paled at hearing her description of the tunnel into the pyramid.

"Just a few years ago, some additional chambers were discovered," she added. "They are apparently covered in red-painted hieroglyphs, and there is graffiti left from the builders. Can you imagine?" she asked rhetorically. "They wrote their names as well as the various names of Khufu, and did it over forty-four hundred years ago." This last was said with a good deal of excitement.

Although he tried to show enthusiasm, Randy remained reserved in his reaction. "It sounds very interesting," he replied.

Diana set the book aside and stared at him. "What's wrong?"

"Nothing. Nothing at all," Randy replied, pulling the bed linens from his body as if he intended to get out of bed.

Despite his nakedness, Diana's attention remained on his face. She reached out and captured his arm. "Randy, what is it?"

For a moment, he looked as if he wouldn't respond, but he finally settled back onto the bed and allowed a long sigh. "I... I don't think I can go in there." He waved a hand in the direction of the book.

She displayed a look of disappointment followed by worry. "You needn't be frightened. There isn't anything in there," she said. "Everything of value was looted long ago and—"

"It's not that," he said.

She dipped her head. "Will you tell me what has you hesitating so?"

He clamped his mouth shut so hard, she could see a muscle jumping along his jaw line. She leaned over and placed a kiss there.

"I don't wish for you to... to think me a coward," he whispered hoarsely.

She scoffed. "I would never think that," she countered. "Randy, darling, please tell me what's troubling you."

Wrapping an arm around the back of her shoulders so he could pull her closer, he said, "I cannot abide small places. Being inside them. It drives me mad."

"Oh," she said, her mouth dropping open as understanding dawned. She turned in his arms and lifted a finger to stroke his cheek. "Were you trapped in a cupboard when you were very young?"

He blinked. "How... how did you know?"

She shrugged in his arms. "I did it to Michael once," she said, referring to her oldest brother. "Locked him in a wardrobe when we were playing hide and seek—"

"Tom did it to me. I think I was four at the time."

"He was so angry when I opened the door, he chased me out of the house," she went on, her attention on her mind's eye. "I had to run all the way down to my father's dig site in the Greco-Roman quarter, over a half-mile away," she continued. "Of course I was in trouble once Father learned the truth of the matter."

Randy didn't try hiding his smirk. "Serves you right," he murmured.

"So I suppose I shouldn't suggest we try anything in a small alcove or a box-bed," she said, one blonde brow arching suggestively.

He blinked as he stared at her. "You mean… sexual congress?" he asked in a whisper. "In an alcove?"

She lifted a shoulder. "You just never know. But should I feel so inclined whilst in the vicinity of an alcove or one of those bed cupboards, I'll be sure to control myself."

Randy's mouth dropped open. "You minx," he accused. "If it's large enough in which to engage in sexual congress, then I shan't have any trouble. But that…" He pointed to the drawing of the internal passage of the pyramid. "That is too small."

Diana sighed. "All right. But please don't tell me I can't go," she said softly.

He shook his head. "I wouldn't dare," he said. "But I would feel better if someone went in with you. Just in case something *is* in there… or something happens." He considered who would be in their party that day. "I don't know if Tom would want to—"

"David will," she interrupted. "He talked about it last night at dinner."

Randy nodded. "All right. Will you do a drawing whilst you're inside that chamber?"

"I rather doubt I'll be in there long enough," she replied. "Besides, I'll have to take a lantern. I expect it will be pitch black inside."

Not having thought about the lack of light, Randy visibly shuddered. "Perhaps our guide will know more."

"I expect so," she agreed. She leaned over and kissed him on the lips. "Thank you," she whispered.

He returned the kiss, wrapping his arms around her waist to pull her closer. "What sort of husband would I be if I didn't let my archaeologist of a wife go inside the largest of the Seven Wonders of the Ancient World?" he countered.

"The very worst," she replied, grinning. "Speaking of wonders," she added, readjusting herself so she was straddling his hips. Reaching down, she grasped his member, her long fingers sliding down the length of him as she touched the wet tip with her thumb. She smoothed the pearlescent bead to the edge of his ridge with the pad of her thumb while she used the finger of her other hand to lift his ball sac.

Randy inhaled sharply and groaned as she continued stroking him. When he begged to be inside her, she lifted her hips and guided his turgid manhood to her entrance. Slowly settling onto him, she took him in inch by inch until he completely filled her.

Although he would have liked her to ride him slowly, to take her time and shift her hips and tease him until he couldn't take it anymore, Randy knew from the light showing around the drapes that they were running out of time. He placed his thumb where their bodies met and rubbed her womanhood, delighting in her cry of surprise and pleasure. Twisting their bodies so she was beneath him, her knees pressed to his thighs, he thrust into her over and over and allowed his release much sooner than usual.

Diana blinked several times as he collapsed atop her, the last of her orgasm leaving her boneless. "A wonder, indeed," she whispered.

Randy chuckled as he rolled off her and announced they had to get dressed. "If we're not at breakfast, they'll wonder what's become of us."

Diana tittered. " I rather doubt that."

CHAPTER 7
RIDING A SHIP OF THE DESERT

*T*wo hours later, across the river in Giza

Despite having awakened early that morning so he could spend time in the nearby gold shop he had spotted on their way to the *riad*, Tom's perusal of the jewelry had to be cut short when their party was ready to leave for their excursion to the pyramids.

Having pared his choices down to a gold ring with a lapis lazuli stone or a silver pendant with a ruby, he opted for the ring and paid the shopkeeper. He didn't bother trying to haggle, which seemed to bother the shopkeeper.

It bothered David even more, but they had run out of time. "You have someone in mind for that?" he asked, motioning to the ring.

Tom shrugged. "Maybe," he replied, knowing his lack of a definitive answer would drive his cousin to distraction.

In reality, the sight of someone he hadn't seen since the Morganfield ball had him remembering what it had been like to kiss her. What it had been like to hold her in his arms. Of what it felt like every time he saw her in his mind's eye.

Lady Helen Tennison was in Cairo. Staying at the same *riad* as they were. And when he had spotted her the night before, she looked as glorious as he remembered her. With any luck, they might find a private garden in which they could reenact their kiss.

He tucked the ring into his waistcoat pocket and joined his aunt and uncle for the trip to the edge of the desert.

From his precarious perch atop a camel, Tom now watched his younger cousin as David seemed to be engaged in a staring match with the beast to which the cameleer had assigned him.

His knees tucked beneath his bulky body in the reddish sand, the camel gazed at David, its long-lashed eyes wide and —dare Tom hope?—full of mischief.

When David leaned to the left, the camel's neck waved to his right, mirroring David's movement. When he leaned to the right, the camel followed suit.

"If you're trying to hypnotize him, it's not going to work," Tom called down to his cousin. "Besides, you don't want him half-asleep or he'll dump you on your bum."

David gave him a quelling glance. Only the day before, their dragoman had explained the concept of hypnotism, saying the unfamiliar word as a means to explain the concept of 'temple sleep' employed by the ancient Egyptians. The practice involved traveling to a temple to sleep in a darkened chamber and then await a dream that would reveal a cure for whatever ailed them.

"I'm merely introducing myself," David replied, moving to the side of the camel. Gripping the T-shaped handle, he threw one leg over the strange saddle, and when the cameleer motioned for him to lie back, he did so.

He had already paid witness to the others having the done the same as a means to stay on their camels, for when the beast's back legs unfolded, its back end rose while the front remained on the ground. Then there was that moment of sudden adjustment before the front legs unfolded and the camel was finally on all fours—and not always happy about having a rider.

At least Aunt Barbara had been able to mount hers without incident, the sidesaddle an odd contraption that provided two seats instead of only one. Once her beast was on fours, she was able to arrange her skirts over the other seat.

Although Diana had opted to wear breeches and boots, she was happy to accept a camel with a sidesaddle. She grinned in delight as she watched her husband fuss over her mount. "Don't delay the inevitable, darling," she warned, nodding to where the cameleer held the reins of his mount.

Randy sighed. "You're sure you're all right?"

"I am fine," she replied, tightening the straps of her straw hat beneath her chin lest the slight breeze send it flying.

"I'm a bit jealous you're riding him."

She inhaled softly, her grin replaced with an expression of surprise. "If it's any consolation, I'm not taking him to bed," she whispered. "Besides, there's only one stud I have any intention of riding, and I as I recall, he bucked me off this morning." Her eyebrow arched in a tease, and Randy knew his face reddened with embarrassment.

"If it's any consolation, I rather enjoyed the ride," he countered. "But then I always do."

She lifted a hand to her lips, pretended to kiss her palm, and blew it in his direction.

He pretended the kiss had been real but said, "When you go into the pyramid, could you let David go ahead of you?"

She furrowed her brows. "Why?"

"Because if he's behind you, I fear he'll grow to appreciate a particularly shapely bum."

Diana tittered. "Oh, all right. He can lead," she agreed. "But I'm giving him the directions."

Randy nodded his appreciation.

Only the hour before, he had spoken with David about

joining Diana for her expedition into the largest pyramid. They had returned from a gold shop where he had found a chain on which she could wear her wedding ring when she was on expeditions. His cousin's initial enthusiasm had soon turned to suspicion, though.

"Wait. Why aren't *you* going in?" he had asked.

Randy flexed his broad shoulders. "I rather doubt I could fit. Diana claims the passageway is rather small. I shouldn't wish to get stuck," he explained.

Although David responded with a guffaw, the answer seemed to satisfy him, for he readily agreed. "It will be good to see something with a real archaeologist."

If the comment had been made in jest, it didn't seem that way as Diana's eyes had widened in surprise—and appreciation. "You do realize you're now my favorite cousin?" she had asked, a grin lighting her face.

Preening in a manner better suited to a dandy, David had bowed deeply and thanked her for her regard as the others in their party chuckled.

*R*eluctantly, Randy moved to mount his camel. Having watched the others, he merely mimicked their moves, his expression blank as the camel rose to all fours in a much smoother manner than David's had done.

Apparently his cousin's attempt to hypnotize his camel had not worked in his favor.

A trio of riders from another nearby herd approached, Lord Everly leading the way. From his relaxed stance atop his mount, it was apparent he had experience riding a camel. A lead rope was connected from the back of his saddle and attached to a ring strung through the nose of Lady Everly's camel. Lady Helen's mount was behind hers and attached in the same manner.

"You've done this before," Will accused as the earl approached followed by his countess and Lady Helen. The babe, Bradley, was not with them.

"It's been ages ago, but yes," Harry replied. He glanced back to ensure Stella was all right. "They have the oddest gait. You simply have to roll with it," he suggested. "Think of it like riding a ship, but instead of being on the water, you are in the desert."

"Indeed," Stella and Will replied in unison.

From where he sat atop his own mount, Tom couldn't help but stare at Helen. Although he realized now he should have expected to see her with her parents, he hadn't been entirely sure she was the one he had seen with the babe on the shore of the Nile.

Dressed in a bright yellow day gown and a straw hat adorned with daisies, Helen was the epitome of a fresh-faced young lady out for a morning ride.

For a moment, he imagined her riding him. Her long limbs straddling his hips, her kid-gloved hands pressed to his shoulders as he rolled his hips beneath hers.

He wondered if her blonde hair was long or merely shoulder-length. If it was long, it would brush over his bare chest, tickling his skin as she rode him.

From the fitted bodice of her gown, he knew she was blessed with breasts befitting her Greek namesake. Although the daughter of Zeus was a mortal, she had been worshipped as the tree goddess.

Leave it to Lord Everly to come up with the perfect name for his only daughter.

As for worshipping her, Tom imagined undoing the fastenings of her gown until he could remove the bodice and hold the soft white orbs in his hands. The thought of those breasts had him wondering what they would look like. How they would react to his touch.

Would her nipples harden if he simply rubbed his thumbs over the rosy tips? Or would he need to pull her down so he could use his tongue and mouth to coax them to readiness? The thought of suckling her nipples had the oddest sound coming from his throat, and he had to stifle further thoughts of Helen and her nipples when the front of his riding breeches suddenly tightened.

He glanced down to discover his camel had turned its head to the side, one eye pinning him as if in rebuke.

That's when he realized the others had already set off in the direction of the pyramids. He nudged the T-bar, and the camel lazily moved forward. Immediately understanding Lord Everly's comment about camels being the ships of the desert, he soon learned how to simply roll with the odd gait.

"They are closer than I thought," Diana called out to Randy, her grin apparent in the morning sun. Only a few wispy white clouds interrupted the bright blue sky above. On the eastern horizon, a hazy band of red rested above the line where desert met the sky.

"There are more of them than I thought," Randy replied, noticing smaller, stepped-style pyramids beyond the three larger buildings.

"For the queens and daughters," she said.

His gaze went back to her, his pride in her swelling when he noticed how well she was riding. If she could handle a camel while holding on with only one hand, he could only imagine how well she would do on a horse once they returned to England.

"Even the surfaces of the larger pyramids look as if they are stepped. Like they have stairs," he commented, his gaze on the closest pyramid.

"Now they do," she agreed. "But they didn't used to. Such a shame."

"What do you mean?" he asked. Given how his uncle and cousin rode on the other side of Diana with Barbara's camel attached to the back of Will's, he knew they were listening intently to their conversation. He hadn't expected to learn more until they reached the base of the largest pyramid, the Great Pyramid of Khufu, where Lord Everly said a dragoman was to meet them.

"The pyramids were never meant to be climbed," Diana explained. "When they were built, they were sealed with an outer casing of polished stone held with mortar, and the edges were fitted so perfectly together, it was difficult to see the joints. When the sun shined on them, they gleamed like gold, especially at the very top."

"What happened to the outer casing?" David asked, his gaze going from the base to the top of the largest pyramid.

"Time. Erosion from wind and water," she replied with a shrug. "And theft. I'm quite sure those outer stones have been used in other building projects in the area."

"What a shame," Barbara commented. "Still, they are rather majestic as they are now."

"Indeed they are," someone said from their right. Garbed in a long robe and a *keffiyeh*, the bronze-skinned man rode an Arabian with ease.

The camels suddenly seemed to take their cue from him, increasing their gait to match that of the horse he rode. It was then Randy noticed the Tennisons were directly behind him.

"This is Salman," Harry called out. "He is our guide today."

The Bedouin lifted a hand in a wave. "Apologies I was not there when you arrived to meet your camels," he said. "I am not used to Englishmen awaking so early."

"You are forgiven, of course," Will said. "May I ask how is it you speak such good English?"

The guide chuckled, his white teeth in sharp contrast to his darker skin. "Necessity," he replied. "I make my living sharing the secrets of my ancestors with travelers. I do so with those from many lands, hence I must speak English, French, and German in addition to my own Arabic."

"How impressive, Mr. Salman," Helen said. "And might you tell us about your mount? He is a warm blood, is he not? An Arabian?"

Straightening in his saddle, Salman acknowledged her query with a nod. "He is indeed, my lady. Perhaps I shall allow you to ride him for the trip back."

Helen dipped her head, as if hiding the blush that suffused her face. "He would no doubt be a more comfortable ride," she replied, unaware of who was listening to her every word.

CHAPTER 8
AN AWKWARD REUNION

From where he rode his camel near the back of his family group, Tom turned and stared at the young lady who brought up the rear of the Everly procession.

He had been aware of Helen for their entire ride from the hotel. Hearing the sound of appreciation in her voice directed at their ruggedly handsome dragoman had him experiencing profound jealousy. Their talk of horses seemed to convey double entendres, but he couldn't sort exactly how.

From the way Salman seemed to puff out his chest and ride even straighter on the small horse, Tom knew the guide was enjoying the young lady's attention.

How could he not?

She looked like a bright desert bloom given her gown, gloves, and hat, a matching shawl threaded through her elbows to keep the sun from her arms.

"He is the perfect horse for the desert, my lady," Salman said in response to Helen's query about his Arabian. "Small, fast, nimble. Do *you* ride, my lady?"

At suddenly becoming the center of attention, Helen blushed. "I do, sir, but not often," she replied.

"Because you live in a city and not in the country?" Salman guessed.

"Yes, I suppose," she replied.

Tom fumed when the dragoman slowed his mount so he was riding between them. Despite the fact that he could still see over the top of Salman given how much taller the camels were than the guide's small mount, Tom was now positive the guide was flirting with Lady Helen.

"What is it you ride? A cold blood?" Salman asked.

"An Irish walker," Helen replied. "He is easy to ride but quite proud."

"I do not know of these 'Irish walkers'," Salman said, his expression conveying doubt.

"It's an Irish Sport Horse," Tom stated. "They are known for their athletic abilities and gentle temperament."

"Ah," Salman replied, turning his attention to Tom. "And what do you ride, sir?"

"A Cleveland bay," he said. "They are—"

"Originated in Yorkshire, did they not?"

Tom gave a start, not expecting the guide to be familiar with the breed. "Yes," he replied.

"Their coloring is exceptional," Salman stated, waving to his own Arabian as if to show his horse was the same color of reddish brown as the bay horses in England.

"Uh, I suppose."

"Ah, we are here," Salman announced, spurring his horse so it moved up to join the camels at the front. They had paused when they reached the shade from the largest pyramid, the lead cameleer already dismounting and joining a young boy who had several camels kneeling at the edge of the pyramid's shadow.

The two quickly saw to Will's camel, the beast first kneeling and finally settling so his back legs were tucked beneath him. Once Will had stepped off, he hurried over to stand next to

Barbara's mount.

"I'll catch you," he said, holding his arms up.

She only hesitated a moment before she leaned toward him and fell into his arms, tittering until her booted feet were safely on the sandy ground.

Meanwhile, Diana's camel had already kneeled, and she was stepping off when Randy said, "How did you do that?"

Grinning, she moved to the side of his camel and had the beast kneeling with a couple of clicks of her tongue. "They want you off just as badly as you wish to be off of them," she said, before moving to assist Tom with his camel.

Meanwhile, the cameleer had moved onto Harry's mount.

"I appreciate your help," Tom said, his gaze on Helen. He was in the middle of dismounting when their dragoman rushed to Stella's camel. Since it was attached to the back of Harry's camel, it had begun kneeling before Harry had a chance to help her down from the sidesaddle.

Seeing his opportunity, Tom hurried to stand next to Helen's camel. "Might I assist you, my lady?" he asked. He frowned when he noticed she was watching their guide help with her mother, and jealousy once again had him fuming. "Or not?"

Helen turned to regard him with furrowed brows. "I'm still terribly high up," she said, her eyes wide with indecision.

"Hold on," he instructed, waiting until her camel knelt before he reached for her waist.

Helen gasped, her gloved hands moving to grip his shoulders as he lowered her from the sidesaddle.

For that brief moment before her feet touched the ground, when Tom was lowering her, he inhaled deeply and held his breath as her body brushed down the front of his.

They stared at one another a moment before she blinked. "Thank you, Mr. Forster," she said.

"You're welcome, my lady," he replied, wincing slightly at hearing her formality.

She patted the side of the camel's neck. "I do wonder what Bradley would have thought of riding a camel. I don't know if he would have been frightened or delighted. He's just over a year old, you see."

Reminded of the babe, Tom did his best to hide his disappointment. He lifted her hand to his lips, and brushed them over the back of her knuckles. "I did notice you left him behind."

"I found a nurse to see to him for the day," she explained. "She has a babe about the same age, so he shan't miss me."

Although he wanted to ask her about the boy's father, they were interrupted when Salman called out, "Let us begin here." He was waving them to a spot at the base of the largest pyramid.

"Such an interesting man," she said, so only he could hear.

Tom bristled at hearing Helen's enthusiasm, and he reluctantly held out his arm for her. Helen placed hers on it, and from the way her brows knitted, he knew she was confused by his manner. Not about to mention the reason for his dislike of the guide, he pretended interest as they joined the others who stood and stared up the rough face of the Great Pyramid of Khufu.

"She looks so familiar. Who is she?" Helen asked.

Tom furrowed a brow, following her line of sight to discover she was staring at Diana. "My new sister, Diana," he whispered. "She and Randy have been married about six months."

"Henley?" she asked in surprise.

"Indeed. You know her?"

Helen nodded. "From school. Although... well, she wasn't there much. Always off to Sicily. Is that where Lord Forster met her?"

He shook his head. "Athens, actually. Henley has a new dig

site on the Acropolis, but I think Randy had made up his mind about taking her to wife long before her father even arrived in Athens to begin his position."

Helen sighed. "I suppose the breeches helped draw his attentions?" she teased.

Tom's eyes widened. "Uh... I... I couldn't say," he stammered. "I think he likes her because she's... well, she's clever. Knows a lot. Remembers everything."

"Huh," Helen replied softly. "Imagine having to travel two-thousand miles to meet the woman who is to be your wife," she murmured. "When you're both from England."

Tom held his breath a moment. Was she talking about Randy and Diana? Or someone else?

And where was the father of her babe?

"It is a bit odd, I suppose," he replied.

With that, the two turned their attentions to the dragoman and listened intently.

CHAPTER 9
PYRAMIDS PROVE TO BE A PUZZLE

"Pyramids were the burial places of the great pharaohs," Salman stated, spreading his arms wide as they faced the structure. "This, the largest of all the pyramids, was built for Khufu and his queen Henutsen. Khufu ruled for twenty-six years, and this pyramid took his entire life to be constructed."

"When was this, sir?" Helen asked.

"Ah. In your calendar, two-thousand, five-hundred, eighty-nine BC."

"But the kings of Egypt did not expect to remain in their tombs for long. When they died, their bodies were mummified—prepared for the afterlife—which they believed would allow them to live on as gods," he explained.

"Mummified?" Barbara repeated, her eyes widening.

"Ah. You wonder how this was done?" Salman asked.

For a moment, she looked uncertain. Will cleared his throat. "If you do not elaborate, she will pester me for the details long after you're gone," he teased.

"Will," Barbara scolded.

Salman grinned. "Our ancestors were the first to develop the process of embalming a body, first by removing their organs, then drying the body with salt, followed by wrapping it in strips of linen secured with perfumed oils and resins," he explained. "The entire process took seventy days." He paused a moment. "You will no doubt see some mummies whilst you are shopping,"

Murmurs of surprise sounded from the group before he continued. "Then the processional would occur, when the mummy was placed in a sarcophagus—like a coffin, but highly decorated—and taken into the burial chamber, deep within the pyramid." He waved to indicate the dark area on the face of the pyramid.

"Through that particular opening?" Tom asked, his gaze having taken in the entire side of the pyramid to determine there was only one small breach, about a third of the way up from the ground.

"Possibly," Salman hedged. "That is where Giovanni Belzoni broke in about fifteen years ago," he replied. "And your Colonel Vyse continued the exploration six years ago."

"Did he find anything?" Randy asked, his eyes widening when he realized Diana was no longer by his side but had made her way to the end of the wall they faced.

"Nothing," Salman stated. "The tomb had long ago been looted, even before the Ottoman Caliph al-Mamun forced his way inside from somewhere near the top, we are told," he explained. "Like others, he sought treasure."

"When did he break in?" Randy asked, his attention still on Diana. She had begun climbing the pyramid, carefully picking her way up the blocks. She carried the same satchel she had used in Athens when she was on her archaeological expeditions, the leather strap secured across her back and over one shoulder.

Occasionally she paused and seemed to study something

before she moved laterally for a few feet. Once she found a negotiable path up, where the blocks were not so large, she would resume climbing but always stop as if she was examining the stone.

"It has been a thousand years and another score ago," Salman said, his gaze following Randy's.

"Eight-hundred twenty AD," Tom said quietly. He knew Helen turned to stare at him, but he kept his attention on the guide.

"He was not the first, though, since we know the tomb was looted long ago."

"What would they have found?" Helen asked.

Salman beamed at her, which had Tom bristling. "There are accounts written by Arabs describing three mummies, a ruby the size of an egg, a sarcophagus filled with gold, and a corpse in golden armor holding a sword," he explained, using his hands to help in his descriptions. "They, of course, are lost to time, for we have not seen the likes of such since."

His audience displayed expressions of disappointment, but Will leaned his head in Barbara's direction and whispered, "Queen Victoria probably has it."

"Will," she scolded. "Her ruby isn't *that* large," she said.

"And what of the other pyramids here?" Harry asked, his expression suddenly awestruck when he realized how far up the side of the pyramid Diana had climbed.

Apparently noting the earl's concern, Salman's attention went to where Diana was hurrying along a row of blocks towards the opening. He smiled. "It seems she will soon reach the entrance," he said. "But she will need a lantern if she is to see anything inside."

"She has one," Randy said. He had watched her pack her satchel that morning, not surprised she included a *fanoos* and the means to light it. The small lantern was probably meant to be more decorative than utilitarian, but it lit their hotel room in a pleasing light. "Is there anything she should know? Before she goes in?"

Salman lifted a shoulder. "There is a rope inside. She may need it to climb up to the chamber, for the passage is steep," he explained. "It will be hot in there, and the passage is not large." He angled his head and arched a brow. "But then, she is not large." His attention was suddenly diverted, and he left Randy's company to return to his horse.

"I'm going in," David said to the dragoman, handing his binoculars over to Tom.

"Then you will take this with you," Salman replied, handing him a lantern from his saddlebag. "And this."

David glanced at the rolled document the guide had pulled out with the lantern, the crude drawing a map of the inside of the pyramid. "You are going in the Robber's Tunnel," he stated. "Which means you will turn sharply to the left to get to the ascending shaft. Do not continue down when you see this corridor," Salman instructed, pointing to the intersection where a passage continued downward. "Only go up."

"What if I miss the corridor?"

"You will not, but if you did, you would go down under the ground, into an unfinished chamber," he explained, motioning to indicate the area beyond the footprint of the pyramid. "Nothing to see there. A wasted trip," Salman said.

"Not even paintings or carvings?" David asked.

The dragoman shook his head. "This was built before they did such things in the tombs," he replied. "You will see inscriptions—hieroglyphics—when you go to the newer tombs."

"Understood." With a canteen hanging from around his neck, David scrambled up the side of the pyramid, his route not nearly as intentional as Diana's had been. A moment later, he joined her at the chevron-topped entrance into the pyramid, the stones expertly joined to handle the stress and weight of the blocks atop them.

Randy moved closer to the base, directly below the opening. "Please don't be long," he called up.

Diana struck a Lucifer match on the rock and lit her *fanoos*. "Does Mr. Salman have any recommendations for me?" she countered, shaking the match until the flame blew out.

A grimace crossed his face. "Salman says it is hot and that the passage into the King's Chamber is small," he responded, obviously not sharing her enthusiasm for exploring. "There is a rope for when you need it," he added. "You will go straight and then to the left, and then when you can, you must go up."

"I have studied the drawings," she reminded him. She pointed to a spot further up the north face. "I am glad I am not going in that way."

"As am I," he called up. The entrance above where she stood was for the descending passage and would have required her to travel downward at a fairly steep angle to reach the ascending passage. Although Randy was fairly sure she could have negotiated the passage, she would also have had to climb up to get out.

Randy knew she had not only studied the drawings, but that she remembered every bit of their detail. He thought of changing his mind and telling her she was forbidden from going into the pyramid, but he knew she would never forgive him if he did. The opportunity to explore an ancient wonder wasn't something that happened very often. And this, the Great Pyramid, was the only remaining Ancient Wonder of the World.

"I love you, my sweet, so you had better come back to me," he shouted. "But if you're not back in an hour, I am coming for you." He paused a moment, his attention on his cousin, who had joined Diana at the entrance. A lantern dangled from one hand, but David set it down to remove his top coat and hat. He left them draped on one of the blocks near the entrance before retrieving the lantern.

Diana blew Randy a kiss, her hands encased in leather gloves, one gripping her lantern. A moment later, she followed David and disappeared into the darkness.

He grinned. "Where did David get a lantern?" he asked in surprise, his query directed to their guide.

Salman allowed a guffaw, waving to the saddlebags on the back of his Arabian. "I always carry a lantern with me," he claimed. "For those who insist they must go inside."

"I'm not so sure this is such a good idea," Barbara said, finally putting voice to a protest upon seeing her son disappear into the pyramid. "He's the sole heir to the Devonville marquessate," she added in a worried whisper.

"He will be fine," Salman stated. "As will the girl. There is nothing to fear. Well, except for an occasional snake."

Will gave the guide a quelling glance before he offered Barbara an arm.

Meanwhile, Harry made his way to stand next to Randy. "You let her go in there?" he asked in alarm.

Randy regarded the earl with an expression that suggested his query was mad. "Since I wish to remain her husband, then I must, my lord," he said. "Besides, she knows I am not comfortable in tight spaces, and Penton has agreed to accompany her."

"Are you just going to stand here and wait for her?"

Randy nodded in the direction of their guide. "I'm going to continue following him, my lord," he replied. "If they have not come out in an hour, then I will go in."

With one last glance to where Diana had disappeared into the pyramid, Harry shook his head and returned to his countess. "She's as bad as you," he said under his breath.

Stella beamed in delight before allowing a titter.

Salman cleared his throat, anxious to continue their tour. "This, the largest of all the pyramids in Egypt, was built for the pharaoh Khufu. The corners are aligned almost perfectly to the north, the south, the east and the west," he said waving his hands to indicate the directions. "The base is seven-hundred and fifty feet on each side, and at its tallest, it was about four-hundred and eighty feet."

"Was?" Harry questioned.

"It lost its *pyramidion*—its capstone—" He paused and held his hands in the shape of a small pyramid. "So it is not as tall these days," he said with a shrug. "About thirty feet of its height is gone."

"When?" Will asked, his brows furrowed.

"Probably before the Romans invaded," Salman replied. "Pliny the Elder and others from his time wrote of a platform located at the top, although it is no longer there."

"What are the blocks made of?" Barbara asked, her gloved hand pressed to one of the large stones making up the base.

"Local limestone. The outer casing, which was made very smooth, was white limestone from Tura and granite from Aswan."

"But how could they get these huge stones here to even build this?" Barbara asked, noting the size of the blocks that made up the base of the pyramid.

"Ah, by way of a barge on the Nile. The river used to come right here," he said, pointing to the end of the pyramid. "The river has changed course over the centuries, so it is no longer so close."

"When you mentioned snakes, were you referring to poisonous snakes?" Helen asked, a look of worry crossing her face.

"Indeed. There are the cobras and the horned vipers and many other vipers which can turn an excellent day into your last if they bite you," he claimed. "They live here in the desert," he added, waving to the sands beyond the pyramids.

"I have a pistol with me," Harry said, loud enough so Will could hear him.

"Are you a good shot?"

Harry shrugged. "I'm good if the target is up close," he claimed.

Barbara and Stella exchanged looks of shock.

"Follow me, and we will see the other pyramids," Salman said, waving for them to join him as he made his way along the base of the pyramid and onto the golden-red sandy ground beyond.

"Do those you guide often go inside the pyramid?" Will asked. He was quickly joined by Harry, who walked on the other side of the guide.

"If at least one did not, I would wonder why they came all the way here," he replied. "You are an explorer, Lord Everly. Surely you understand curiosity?"

"I do, but in my older age, I've grown to appreciate self-preservation. Besides, I don't think I can crouch that low for such a long distance to get through the passageways. My back would protest for at least a week after such an excursion."

Will nodded in agreement and paused a moment before asking, "What if they don't come out in an hour?"

"I will send Ari in to get them."

"Ari?" Will repeated.

Salman indicated the young boy who was holding onto the reins of several camels. "He is small, and he knows all the passageways."

"How much will it cost me if he must go in after my son and niece?" Will asked, hoping he had enough blunt on him to pay for a rescue.

Once again laughing, Salman said, "Enough for a decent meal."

Will and Harry exchanged glances of disbelief. "That's all?"

"These people are poor," Salman stated. "As it was for those who built these pyramids, they will work for food. A hunk of meat and a beer every day is all they required to build these pyramids."

"A bargain," Harry murmured.

"Agreed," Will said.

"It was an honor to be chosen to help build them," Salman said. "But it was hard labor. They could not do it for more than a few months before being replaced by others," he explained. He rounded the corner of the pyramid. "We now go to the back of this one to see the others," he called out.

Another five minutes passed as they walked and stared out on the desert. When they reached the back of the pyramid, other large, smooth-sided pyramids were suddenly visible along with several smaller step pyramids. In the other direction, a group of robed men were clearing sand away from another structure.

"Here is the pyramid of Khafre, the pyramid of Menkaure, and the pyramid of Khentkaus the First. She was a Queen Mother, and her tomb is merely a two-stepped tomb," he explained. "Never finished, probably because the original structure was not sound enough to support more blocks." He waved a hand to indicate part of the desert. "Imagine boats sailing past these structures."

"How old are these?" Tom asked.

"Khufu's pyramid was finished around the year you know as two-thousand-five-hundred and fifty BC," Salman replied.

"That old?" Barbara asked in surprise.

"These are not the oldest, my lady. The very oldest pyramids are in Memphis, and they are not smooth-walled as these were."

"The Step Pyramid?" Tom asked suddenly.

"Exactly. And the Bent Pyramid," Salman confirmed. "They are from twenty-six-hundred BC."

"Will we see those?" Barbara asked of Will.

He shrugged. "Possibly," he hedged.

"They are well worth the trip into the desert, but I would recommend you hire several carriages to take you there. For your comfort," Salman said. "In the meantime, do take the opportunity to walk around the other pyramids."

As their group broke into pairs, Tom once again offered Helen his arm, which left Randy the odd man out. With one last glance at the south face of the Great Pyramid, he followed the rest as they made their way to the next pyramid.

CHAPTER 10
INSIDE A DARK TOMB

*M*eanwhile

"You should probably remove your cravat," Diana suggested, watching as her second cousin took off his top coat and hat and left them on the stones just outside the Robber's Tunnel entrance. "Salman said it's very hot inside."

David glanced into the passageway. "I thought it would be much smaller," he said, undoing his knot and unwinding the long cloth from around his neck.

"It appears we won't have to bend down for this part," she said, lighting his lantern. "But there is a passage further on where we will."

With one last look in the direction of Cairo and their group below, the two set off into the pyramid.

"Why do you suppose this passage is so accessible while the other entrance is not?" David asked, glancing about as they made their way.

"This is tall enough for something large to be brought in," she replied. "Tall but not too wide," she added, pausing so she could lift her *fanoos* higher.

"Didn't pharaohs require a means to make the trip to the

afterlife?" he asked, following suit with his own lantern. Given how small the other passageways were that they had seen on the schematic of the pyramid, it hardly made sense that there be one near the exterior that allowed one to walk upright.

Diana inhaled softly. "A ship, yes," she said. "But would they have brought it inside the pyramid?"

He shrugged. "If so, it was probably brought in this way."

Although the going was easy at first, the limestone walls far enough apart that they could practically walk side by side and the ceiling high enough so they didn't have to crouch down, circumstances changed when they reached the sharp bend to the left.

A number of blocks seemed to have been moved around, and it was apparent why.

"That's the way down," David said, noting how the entrance to the descending passage had been blocked.

"And this is the way up," Diana said, finding the square opening to her right. She crouched down and held out the lantern in front of her, the light illuminating the smooth-walled gray stone passage for several feet.

"Allow me," David said. When she seemed about to argue, he added, "I promised Randy I would go first."

She stepped aside and let him enter first, and once she was inside the upward-sloping tunnel, she understood why her husband hadn't wanted David behind her.

Her view was of his bum.

"Is there a rope?" she asked.

"Not sure we'll need it," he said, his booted feet gripping the stone well enough that he didn't slip backwards. "But here it is."

The thick coarse hemp was tucked into the corner. Diana gave it an experimental tug to be sure it was attached to something.

"If you don't mind, I'm going to pick up the pace," he said.

"Good idea," she said, anxious to get through this part of the pyramid.

David scrambled up the passageway, his breathing becoming more labored until he reached the end. He turned and took her lantern as she stepped out and straightened. "Oh," she said in surprise, her gaze immediately going to the high ceiling.

"I think this is the gallery," David said, holding the lanterns up to the walls. No paintings or carvings adorned them, though, and he scoffed. "It appears it's all gone," he said with disappointment. "There should be paintings, at the very least," he added.

"According to those books you bought, everything was taken a long time ago," she replied, reaching for her *fanoos*. "We have some more climbing to do."

David turned around and understood what she meant. At least the sloping passageway was wider and its ceiling rather high, but it was also longer than the others they had been through and the temperature was noticeably warmer. "Do you suppose the air in here is over four-thousand years old?" he asked.

"Some of it, no doubt," she replied. "But without the casing on the outside, the structure isn't completely sealed. The blocks are fitted together rather well, though."

"Is that what you were examining outside? While you were climbing?" he asked as they made their way up.

"Indeed. I was curious as to how precise the blocks were cut. They are exceptionally well fitted," she claimed. "But inside—"

"They are not," he finished for her, his lantern illuminating some blocks to prove her point. "I suppose they didn't need to be."

They remained silent for the rest of the climb, conserving

their breath until the floor beneath their feet suddenly flattened and the walls of the passage disappeared.

"We're in a chamber," he said in a quiet voice, his words echoing. Even the sound of his breaths seemed to resonate off the smooth stone walls.

"The burial chamber," she agreed, rushing forward. Her boot steps echoed loudly on the stone floor, and she didn't stop until her lantern lit a rectangular stone box.

"Is ... is that a sarcophagus?" David asked, his excitement evident.

"Such as it is," she replied, lowering the lantern into the hollowed out block of granite. There was no lid, and one corner at the top had been damaged at some point—probably when the lid had been pried off. Knowing the lid would have been slid into place along a series of grooves and held in place with pegs pounded into holes, she swept her light around the upper edge, pausing it upon finding the pegs broken off. "Damn tomb robbers," she whispered.

David chuckled at hearing her curse, watching as her *fanoos* showed the inside bottom corners to be straight and square.

"There's no decoration on this at all," David said, using his lantern to illuminate the exterior of the coffin. "And the marks from chisels and drills are definitely evident." His disappointment sounded in the tone of his voice.

"It was probably quite beautiful at one time," she guessed, sighing as she held out the *fanoos* and walked the perimeter of the chamber. Although the sound of her sigh was amplified inside the empty chamber, only gray stone walls showed in the light.

Gray stone walls and a human face.

Her gasp of surprise and David's mighty yowl of fright echoed off the walls.

CHAPTER 11
A MOURNFUL SOUND
INCITES CONCERN

*M*eanwhile, *outside at the southwest corner of the pyramid*

Rather enjoying the opportunity to be escorted not just by one young man, but two—even if the older Forster was married—Helen stared up at the Pyramid of Khafre and sighed. "Can you imagine what it must have been like for a man to spend his entire life watching as people were building his final resting place?"

"If they did, they must have been in disguise," Randy replied. "From what Diana told me, only the high priests were allowed to see the king."

Helen scoffed. "How could they have any power if they weren't even seen by their people?" she asked in surprise.

"Probably because the priests were the ones with the true power," Tom murmured. A strange howling sounded from nearby, as if his words had upset the Egyptian gods.

"Did you hear that?" Helen asked, pausing mid-step.

"You've done it now, brother," Randy whispered. He, too, had stopped, cocking his head as if to determine the source of the faint but haunting sound.

He wasn't the only one. Up ahead, Salman's attention was suddenly directed on Khufu's pyramid. Randy followed his line of sight, frowning when he considered who might have made it. "Was that—?

"David?" Tom finished for him.

"Diana," Randy breathed, his concern evident.

The two exchanged quick glances and both set off at a run along the west wall of the Great Pyramid toward the north.

About to follow, Helen realized there was no way she could have kept pace with the two men. Instead, she joined the others to discover Salman displaying a look of amusement while everyone else appeared confused.

"Sir, why is it are you smiling?" she asked, tempted to hit him on his head with her parasol. "Do you take pleasure in the misfortune of others?"

Salman chuckled. "I should not, I know. But I am fairly sure there is a reason for the shout we heard."

"A snake?" she guessed, her eyes wide with fright.

"No. A pest to be sure, but not a snake," he said, shaking his head.

Helen's attention went to where the cousins had been running alongside the western base of the Great Pyramid, but they had already disappeared around the corner.

CHAPTER 12
A FRIGHTFUL FACE

*M*eanwhile, inside the burial chamber

Although a wide-eyed face lit by her *fanoos* was enough to have Diana's heart rate racing in surprise, it was David's reaction that truly scared her.

Never in her life had she heard such a frightening sound as what had come out of his throat. On top of that, the yowling scream's echo continued to reverberate through the burial chamber long after it had first sounded.

"David!" she admonished. "You'll wake the dead."

Behind her, the eventual heir to the Devonville marquessate stood wide-eyed with fright. "Isn't he already?"

She gave him a quelling glance. "It's just a boy," she said, lowering the lantern so the youngster didn't appear as a disembodied head. Bronze-skinned and thin, he was familiar and displaying an expression of amusement. "You were tending to the camels," she said, not making it a question.

The boy nodded. "Ari," he said, pointing to his chest.

"Diana," she said, placing a hand on her chest. She moved it to David's shoulder. "Lord Penton." She noticed how at the mention of "Lord", the young boy's eyes widened, as if he recognized the English title to be one of importance. He immediately sobered and bowed low.

Diana gave a start when she realized the boy didn't have a source of light. "Where is your lantern? Uh... *fanoos*?" she clarified, lifting hers slightly.

Ari shrugged. "No light, but I carry for you," he offered. "Escort you out."

Diana exchanged a quick glance with David, realizing the boy had negotiated the passages in the pitch black. He had probably done so since he could walk. "Don't we go out the same way we came in?"

He nodded. "Salman sent me. In case you are lost."

Bristling at the comment, Diana was about to put voice to a protest but instead said, "I wish to see the relieving chambers," she said, pointing up. "The ones that were discovered a few years ago. With the red-painted walls?" she added, hoping the boy understood.

Ari shook his head.

"What are the relieving chambers?" David asked, keeping his query low given how every sound echoed so loudly in the chamber. He had unrolled the map Salman had given him and was holding it in the light of his lantern.

"Above the burial chamber," she said, pointing to the crude rectangles in the drawing. "Apparently meant to safeguard the king's chamber should the roof collapse."

"That could happen?" David asked in surprise.

"The fact that they planned for the possibility is rather telling," she replied. "But then this was one of the early straight-sided pyramids, so they were probably still learning how to build them."

"What do you know of the relieving chambers?"

"Nathaniel Davison discovered the lowest one eighty years ago, and Howard Vyse found the others when he was last here in thirty-seven," she replied. "He, uh, used gunpowder to open up some passageways that lead up to the other four chambers," she added, grimacing at the thought of the interior masonry being disturbed. "He wrote that the walls of the upper chambers are covered in graffiti painted with red ochre," she explained. "Possibly with the names of the workers who built the pyramid, because they were painted prior to being put into place."

"How would he know that?" David asked, his gaze darting to see that Ari was listening intently to her words.

"Some of the inscriptions are upside down or sideways, and some are partially obstructed by other blocks," she explained.

David turned to the boy. "How do we get up there?" he asked, lifting his lantern in an attempt to illuminate any openings.

"The tunnel is high," Ari replied, pointing back toward the grand gallery. "No ladder. Not allowed."

"Can you show me where it is?" Diana asked. "The tunnel?"

"Diana," David said in a whisper. "We don't have the means to climb," he argued.

"I just wish to see *how* Davison got in," she replied.

"Lead the way, Ari," David said.

The boy turned and scampered through the short horizontal antechamber and into the gallery, turning and pointing up to the top of the east wall.

Bending down, David and Diana followed him. When they emerged into the high-ceiled gallery, David lifted his lantern as high as he could. He strained his eyes in an attempt to see evidence of a tunnel opening. Once Diana had added the light from her *fanoos*, the opening near the roof became evident.

"There it is," she breathed.

"Did you really wish to go through that?" David asked, studying her expression of awe.

"Not particularly," she replied, wiping perspiration from

her brow. "But I do wish someone had published a drawing or—"

"Like this?" David asked, turning over the map Salman had given him. On the back side were a series of marks made in four rows.

"I make those," Ari stated, one hand on his chest as he pointed to the papyrus.

"You did?" Diana asked. "You were in there? In the upper chambers?" She pointed up to the tunnel. "When?"

He shrugged. "With that man Vyse. I carried his *fanoos* and tools," he added proudly.

"And he had you document... write what you saw on the walls?"

His face screwing into confusion, Ari shook his head. "Salman did."

"Salman was his guide," David guessed. "He was there in the chambers? With you?"

Ari nodded. "He gave me charcoal and the map and told me to draw while we waited for the Englishman."

Diana and David exchanged knowing looks. A young boy—Ari would have been four or five at the time—would have grown bored waiting for the explorer to complete his work. Giving him a task to transcribe what he saw on the walls would keep him busy for a time.

"So.... which chamber is this?" Diana asked, pointing to the top series of hieroglyphics.

Ari held up two fingers. "Wellington's chamber," he said, obviously struggling to remember the pronunciation of the name. "Many cracks in the stones."

The comment didn't surprise Diana. The relieving chambers were meant to protect the king's chamber, but it also meant they would have to withstand pressure from the weight of stones directly above. "And this one?" She pointed to the next set of hieroglyphics down on the page.

He held up three fingers.

"Nelson's chamber," she said in a whisper. She pointed to the next set.

He held up four fingers.

"Lady Arbuthnot's chamber, which means this one is Campbell's chamber," she said, pointing to the last as Ari held up five fingers.

"The top one."

David took a long draught from his canteen before wiping the back of his hand across his brow. "It's terribly warm in here, and I think we best be going." He glanced over at Diana, wincing as if he thought she might argue.

"I'm ready to go, too," she said, rolling up the map before stuffing it into her satchel. She gave her *fanoos* to the boy. "Lead the way, Ari."

David nudged her elbow and asked in a whisper, "Are you sure?" Despite his quiet query, his voice still echoed.

She nodded. "He may show us things we missed," she said hopefully. "And it's downhill most of the way."

With Ari holding the *fanoos* ahead of her and David's lantern behind, her hands would be free. Placing a palm against the smooth polished limestone of the grand gallery walls, she carefully followed the boy by staying on a sort of curb that hugged the wall. A matching curb ran alongside the opposite wall, and in the middle, the sloping path was a few inches lower.

"This is how they would have transported the blocks," David said in awe. "I don't know how I didn't notice it before," he commented.

"We were climbing up that ramp," she reminded him, realizing now it was a way to keep traction as the side curbs were a smoother stone.

When they had almost reached the part of the tunnel that connected the grand gallery to the ascending passage, Diana remembered her husband's comment about following David. She turned her head, glancing over her shoulder to see where her cousin's attentions were directed.

David was staring at the walls and ceiling, his downward steps careful lest his boots slide on the limestone rock floor. "Do you suppose there are any openings?" he asked. "For air?"

"I'm certain there were. During the construction," she said. "They would have blocked them off when the final casing was installed, though."

"But that casing is mostly gone now," he reminded her.

"So air can get in," she agreed. "Perhaps light as well." She paused to allow him to go into the tunnel first.

"Are you sure?" he asked.

"Please. I shouldn't want Randy to chide you for staring at my bum all the way through this tunnel," she said with a smirk.

Even in the odd lighting, she could see David's face redden with embarrassment. "Won't he chide you about watching *my* bum?" he countered.

She tittered but quickly sobered when the light from the *fanoos* had nearly vanished down the tunnel. "Go," she ordered.

Crouching down to one side, David scrambled into the tunnel, Diana following close behind. They continued the trek down to the Robber's Tunnel, although they never quite caught up to Ari.

That is, until David nearly ran into him where the tunnel exited and turned sharply to the left. His shout of alarm had Diana stopping in mid-step before she cleared the tight passage.

The shout was followed by a curse and what sounded like laughter.

"What's happened?" she asked, finally emerging to stand upright. Before she quite knew what was happening, she was suddenly in her husband's embrace while David was pummeling Tom with one fist, the lantern precariously swinging about.

Ari stood off to one side, obviously confused.

"You scared me nearly to death," David accused.

"Fair's fair," Tom countered.

"What is he talking about?" Diana asked of Randy, when he finally let go of his hold on her.

"What happened in there?" he asked. "We heard a horrible yowling sound."

Diana lifted a hand to cover her mouth, but a titter escaped. "Ari appeared out of the dark, so we had a bit of a fright is all," she replied. "He's been most helpful, though," she added, ruffling the boy's hair. "He's a clever boy. If you have any coins on you, he deserves payment for his services."

Randy fished some money from his waistcoat pocket and handed it to the boy. "Thank you for escorting her," he said.

"She didn't need any help," Ari replied. "She is clever."

"Yes, she is," Randy agreed, offering his arm.

Diana lifted herself on tiptoes and kissed him on the cheek. "Come. Let's get out of here. I'm hot, and I'm thirsty."

The four hurried toward the faint light that indicated the entrance to the pyramid, all of them inhaling deeply of the fresh air when they made it outside.

The rest of their party, having completed their walk to the other pyramids, had returned and were about to mount their camels for the ride back.

Diana couldn't help but notice how Tom watched as Salman assisted Helen onto her camel. She was fairly sure she even heard him growl. Turning her attention to Randy, she lifted a brow.

"I'm not exactly sure what's going on with him," he whispered.

"It would appear he's been possessed by the Green Monster," she said. Mounting her camel, she held on to the handles as the camel unfolded his back legs, forcing her to lie back, until his front legs straightened and she was suddenly higher than Randy.

"You do that entirely too easily," he accused.

Tittering, she watched as the cameleer assisted her husband, and when their entire party was ready, she directed her camel to line up with the others for the trip back to the *riad*.

CHAPTER 13
TWO COUNTESSES CONVERSE

ater that day

Upon their return to the *riad*, the travelers enjoyed a late luncheon while Diana and David described their tour of the inside of the pyramid. Helen told of her encounter with an especially insistent street vendor who was peddling miniature carvings of sphinxes and pyramids. An anecdote of his experience with his camel was shared by Harry, which resulted in peels of laughter by everyone.

When the dishes had been cleared, several headed off to their rooms to take naps while three of the women moved to the parlor.

Reunited with Bradley, Helen immediately moved to join him on the carpeted floor.

"I always wanted a daughter," Barbara said, her gaze on Helen as the young woman played a clapping game with her younger brother.

"Well, you cannot have mine," Stella countered, her wan grin fading when she saw Barbara's serious expression. "Besides, you might yet find yourself with child."

"Oh, no," Barbara said, her head shaking to emphasize her answer. "I'm afraid David was my last."

"I thought Helen would be *my* last," Stella said softly. "So imagine my surprise when I discovered I was with child a couple of years ago. My oldest had just met and married Margaret. I thought to surprise Everly with my news after their wedding, but he already knew."

Barbara tittered. "We think they could not know such things, but Will was much the same when I was expecting David." Tears filled her eyes as she remembered the babe being placed into her arms after she had given birth, the relief she had felt at learning it was a boy.

That Will had a legitimate heir.

Now that babe was over twenty years old. He had already been secretly betrothed for a time. He was no longer—Diana's brother, Marcus, had already taken Jane Fitzsimmons to wife—but then, Barbara wouldn't expect David to be in the market for a wife until he was several years older.

Stella angled her head to one side. "There are babes without mothers," she whispered. "Mayhap you could take an orphan as your own and raise her," she suggested.

"I've put out the word in Bampton of my intent to do so," Barbara explained. "I suppose it's fortunate we've not had any motherless babes in the past decade or so."

Her attention once again darting to where Helen was playing with Bradley—her daughter was attempting to teach him how to throw a small rubber ball—Stella said, "Well, I rather doubt Everly would let you have Bradley, but there have been times on this trip when I would have gladly handed him over."

Barbara once again tittered. "Boys," she said in agreement. Her brows puckered. "You don't have a nurse for him?" she asked, her gaze scanning the area in search of a servant.

"We left London with one," Stella replied. "But we lost her in Malta."

Her eyes widened in shock. "Oh, I am so sorry."

Stella blinked. "Oh, she didn't die. She... she met a young man, fell in love, and stayed on Gozo. Our itinerary didn't allow for us to look for another nurse before we had to depart the island, so Helen has been a dear to help with him. I see to some of his feedings, of course. I have nursed him since he was born, but I could use the help."

Barbara held a hand to her mouth to cover her surprise at hearing Stella was nursing the boy. "Well, I suppose that's not so bad, and Lady Helen does appear to enjoy his company."

"She wants desperately to be a mother someday," Stella said.

"Did she leave behind any suitors in London?"

Stella shook her head. "She did not. A pity, really. She had two during her second Season, but nothing serious. I think she's is paying the price for me being half-Greek."

"Stella," Barbara gently scolded. The countess was a duke's daughter, and she had inherited her Greek mother's beauty and blonde hair.

Stella displayed an expression of worry as she watched her daughter. "I think she's a rather handsome young lady—"

"She is. Amiable as well."

"—but she has yet to host a serious suitor," Stella went on. "Her dance card is usually full, but there are never any flowers delivered to the house the following day. Everly assures me he has a dowry set aside for her, so I do not know what else it can be."

The giggles of the babe reached Barbara's ears, and she turned to see Helen racing the boy for the ball. His white gown, stained with the red sand of the desert, barely hid his knees from view. "Now there is a sound I miss," she said, grinning.

"Everly delights in it. Lifts him over his head and sends my heart into palpitations, I worry so that he will accidentally drop him."

"He won't," Barbara assured her. "He is his spare heir, after all."

Stella nodded. "I so appreciate you spending time with me, but I can see that at any moment, Bradley will be seeking sustenance."

"Will I see you again on this trip?" Barbara asked, sounding almost desperate with her query. "I have so missed the company of other women," she added. "English women."

Stella inhaled softly. "Well, I suppose that depends on where you're off to next," she remarked. "And when?"

"The boys wish to go to Luxor. Something about some half-buried temples in the sand," Barbara replied with a wave of her hand.

Stella displayed a brilliant grin. "I do believe the men in our lives have the same destination in mind," she said. "Which means we really must see to it that we travel together."

"That would be capital," Barbara replied with excitement.

"Everly says it's four-hundred miles south of here."

Barbara's mouth dropped open in shock. "That will take *weeks*," she whispered.

"We'll go on a boat," Stella stated. "A sailing barge of some sort. It's about a fortnight heading south on the river. It's not necessarily faster coming back even though the river flows north—something to do with the winds—when we'll be going with the current."

"Oh," Barbara said with relief. "That's not so bad, I suppose."

"The heat shouldn't be as bad this time of the year, but there may be some insects, so we'll need to sleep with mosquito netting," Stella explained.

"We've been doing so on the ship we were on coming from Alexandria," Barbara said.

"We really must have our men discuss this. Will you join us for dinner this evening?" Stella asked. "The cook here at the riad is excellent, and there is plenty of room at the table."

"For all *six* of us?" Barbara asked.

"Indeed. Come by at six o'clock. We can convene in the parlor and learn about everything you've done over the past year," Stella said with excitement. "I haven't seen your new daughter-in-law since she and Helen attended finishing school together."

The comment had Barbara blinking in surprise. "I... I wasn't aware Diana was in London long enough to attend Warwick's," she commented, referring to Warwick's Grammar and Finishing School.

"She wasn't, not really. But she did attend for a time," Stella said, "In between trips to Sicily." At seeing Barbara's thoughtful expression, she added, "If you're worried she won't make a suitable countess for Lord Forster when he inherits—"

"I am not," Barbara quickly interrupted. She dipped her head. "I cannot say the same for Randy's mother, however."

Stella sighed. "She's probably fluent in at least a few languages."

"Ancient Greek, Latin, Sicilian..." Barbara lifted a shoulder. "Actually, despite spending several weeks traveling with her, I don't really know all that much about her. I do know she wishes to continue her archaeology avocation, and she can paint beautifully. Oh, and she remembers everything she has ever heard or seen or read."

Tittering, Stella said, "Well, I'll see what I can discover during dinner this evening. She's probably a fascinating young woman. It's no wonder your nephew thought to take her as his wife. She'll never bore him."

Barbara nodded, her attention once again on Lady Helen and the babe. Helen had the boy hoisted onto her hip and was making her way in their direction.

"Apologies, Lady Bellingham," Helen said, managing to dip a curtsy despite the way she held Bradley. "I fear my brother is about to make his hunger known to all."

"It's fine, Lady Helen," Barbara said, coming to her feet. She chucked the boy under the chin and made a cooing sound, which had him displaying three pairs of teeth when he grinned. "I will see all three of you later this evening," she added, curtsying to Stella before she took her leave.

Although she hadn't had much say in the itinerary of their travels, Barbara was about to make her wishes known to Will. Having Lady Everly as a like-minded traveling companion would certainly improve the trip.

CHAPTER 14
PLOTTING THE NEXT ADVENTURE

Later that night

The last of the Egyptian dessert *omm ali*, a sort of bread pudding, had been consumed and the dishes removed when the ladies excused themselves to head to the parlor. The men remained at the dining table with glasses of *sobia* sitting in front of them. The creamy coconut-based drink was good, but it wasn't port.

As soon as the server disappeared, Harry reached under his chair and pulled out a bottle of port. Will chuckled. "You had better be prepared to share that," he warned.

"Fear not. I stocked up when our ship put into port at Sines," he replied, grinning as he poured five glasses of the liquor.

"It's very generous of you to share," Randy commented, holding up his glass in a salute.

The others held their glasses out and took a sip before Will asked, "Where are you off to next?"

Harry arched a brow. "I hear there are several varieties of hibiscus in Aswan."

"That's five-hundred miles away," Tom commented.

"Indeed. But easy enough to get there when traveling on the Nile. Where are you off to?"

David and Tom looked to Will, but it was Randy who said, "Diana is desperate to see the temples in Luxor. The city is on the river, about four-hundred miles south from here, so we'll have to arrange passage on a ship."

"You do know there are a number of temples along the Nile between here and there?" Harry asked. "And the Necropolis of Saqqara includes the pyramids at Dashur. They're only about twenty miles from here," he added.

"We'll go to as many as can be arranged," Will said. "Won't you?"

Harry allowed a shrug. "Truth be told, I hadn't considered our itinerary beyond Memphis, but we've come all this way. We really should see the ancient sites. My countess has not put voice to a complaint of our extended absence from London, nor do I expect her to..."

"So you'll go with us to Luxor?" Randy urged. "You might find other hibiscus there."

Chuckling softly, Harry nodded. "I hear there are a number of interesting birds along the Nile," he murmured. "Pigeons are apparently a delicacy here, so I can be on the lookout for them when I don't spot any flowers. So, I suppose we will."

"Luxor it is," Will replied with a grin, lifting his glass in a salute. "I'll see to finding us a *dhahabîyeh* that will accommodate both our families in the morning."

Harry suddenly stiffened. "Has anyone warned you about those boats?"

Will furrowed a brow. "If you're asking if I know what will be involved in hiring one, then yes," he admitted.

"I'll split the costs with you. We'll have to do the provisioning and prepare the ship for passengers," Harry warned.

"And paint it, I hear. But I think that can all be arranged."

"Then I say let's do this."

The others held up their glasses, obviously pleased with the plan.

om was the first to sober, his thoughts on a certain young woman and her babe. He had been doing the math in his head regarding Bradley's age, and he wasn't happy with what he had determined.

Had Helen done something to coerce him into the gardens that night before they left London? Something he had been unaware of? Because given the babe's age, it meant Helen would have been halfway through a pregnancy at the time of their meeting.

At the time they had kissed in the gardens.

Surely she would have known she was with child. He was sure she wasn't married, so had she intended to kiss him in the hopes he might propose marriage? Trap him knowing she would be giving birth to another man's child only a few months later?

He had thought her an innocent. Well, except for how she had returned his kiss, her manner betraying her eagerness at continuing the act of intimacy.

Perhaps she had been married and had lost her mate to an untimely death, he considered. Missed having a man in her life and was eager to exchange a passionate kiss in the gardens in the hopes of finding a new husband.

If she had been married, surely she would have used her husband's name or title when they were introduced, though. Why keep that information from a potential suitor?

He couldn't recall their exact words that night at the Morganfield ball. He couldn't even recall the words they had said to one another when they were in the gardens.

What he could remember was the intensity of the kiss they had shared. The profound sense of wonder he had felt. The look on her face when they had finally ended their elicit kiss and stared at one another as if their entire worlds had been turned upside down and inside out.

He could swear she was as surprised as he was by what had happened. Either that, or she was a very good actress, able to pretend she felt far more than she did whilst in his arms.

Earlier that day, she had gladly accepted the offer of his arm as they toured the area around the pyramids. He knew she had frequently directed her gaze on him, as if she wanted some sort of assurance he still held her in high regard. He had done everything in his power to act in a cordial manner, never giving away his suspicions nor encouraging her to speak her mind.

Coward, he thought. Had he simply asked as to her regard for him, Tom was sure Helen would have told him. He didn't know if he was ready to learn more about Bradley, though.

Not sure what to believe, Tom downed his drink in almost a single gulp and sat back to listen to the conversation of the others around him. At some point, he would have to confront Helen with his suspicions. Ask her outright about her intentions.

But he knew he wouldn't do so until he was sure about what he wanted.

CHAPTER 15
PREPARING FOR TRAVEL
WITH A TUMBLE

Two days later

Arrangements for travel to Memphis and beyond having been made—Will had found a captain with a luxury *dhahabîyeh* large enough to accommodate their party of nine plus the captain's daughter who would act as a nurse for Bradley—Stella completed packing her trunk and regarded her husband with a quirked brow. "I cannot decide if you are happy at the idea of traveling with Lord Bellingham and his family, or if you merely agreed to it out of some sort of sense of obligation," she said.

Harry paused in his own packing and aimed a look of surprise in her direction. "*Relieved* is more like it," he replied. "There is strength in numbers, and I will admit I am happy I won't be draining the Everly coffers from last year's harvest on this excursion alone," he remarked.

Not only had Will paid the captain and crew up front, but he had located one of his quartermasters from his days in the navy. The expat had settled in Cairo soon after the wars with Napoleon had ended, using his skills to help provision ships for British diplomats and soldiers making their way to India.

"I'm only having to pay for foodstuffs," he explained, "which I have reason to believe were a bargain given Bellingham's former quartermaster is seeing to it. I admit it is still more than I would have had to pay for only the four of us given they have three boys—"

"Really, darling, they are young men. You must remember how Alexander eats nearly everything that's put on the table."

Harry chuckled. "I do, and I am glad for the company."

Stella grinned. "Because it is mostly male company?" she countered.

He shrugged. "Can you blame me? After all the years of having Alexander to even out our numbers, I find I miss him." About to place several folded cravats atop some waistcoats, he added, "Bradley is not yet old enough to side with me during family arguments."

Tittering, Stella closed her trunk's lid. "I must admit I enjoy Barbara's company. She's not at all like so many of the aristocratic wives I've come to avoid in London."

Harry tossed a sheaf of papers onto the top of his trunk. "What about Lady Forster?"

Stella inhaled softly. "I cannot yet say," she admitted. At seeing his look of concern, she quickly added, "She's a lovely girl, but I cannot help but feel a bit intimidated. She's so... *knowledgable*. So clever," she claimed.

"More so than me?" he countered with a chuckle.

Unable to hide her grimace—she rarely had need to lie to her husband—Stella instead merely lifted a shoulder. "Barbara says she is possessed of the ability to remember everything she has ever read or seen in her life. Can you imagine?"

Raising his brows in fascination, Harry said, "I could have used that ability whilst in university," he murmured.

"Sometimes I wish you had it," she said softly.

Harry gave a start. "Why do you say it like that?" he asked, immediately on the defensive.

Stella tilted her had to one side. "There are times when I think you don't remember *our* past," she murmured.

"Oh, but I do," he insisted. "But I hardly think you would wish to remember it all." When she lifted a brow as if to encourage him to share, he added, "For example, I stepped on your toes during our first dance."

"That you did," she acknowledged.

"And then the next time we met, you were..." Here he swallowed. "Aphrodite. Rising out of the Aegean, wearing little more than a scrap of fabric." He made a growling sound in his throat. "I'll never forget that day as long as I live."

A blush colored her face, but Stella arched an elegant brow. "I shall never forget the look on your face that day," she whispered.

About to respond, Harry clamped his mouth shut and swallowed. He glanced at the door and then at the bed. Even before he had a chance to ask if she might join him there, Stella was up and in his arms, her fingers quickly undoing the fastening of his pantaloons. A second later, and she grasped his hardening member, brushing her thumb over the bulbous tip in a move she had done over a hundred times.

"Should I remove your gown?" he asked, breathless with excitement.

"Only the skirt," she replied, rather enjoying his expression of lust. She used her free hand to push his pantaloons from his waist, grinning when they fell on their own as he attempted to kick off his shoes.

Meanwhile, Harry fumbled with the fastening at her waist, and before the skirt had loosened its hold on her, he had the ties to her petticoats undone. The bell skirt and its support dropped to the floor in a *whoosh*. "I am so glad you haven't adopted wearing drawers," he whispered hoarsely, his hands lifting the hem of her chemise.

"I never will," she assured him.

He had her backed up to the bed, following her down as she lifted her knees to his thighs.

"As much as I want you right now, I think it best I pay some heed to a particular spot between your luscious thighs," he murmured.

Stella gave a start when he was no longer atop her but had slid down the side of the bed until his knees hit the carpeted floor. She expected him to put voice to a grunt or a curse, but not a sound of discomfort could be heard from him as he gripped her ankles in his hands and placed them over his shoulders. Then his head moved between her thighs and Stella knew he was as lost as she would soon be.

He wasted no time with teasing or tasting her, for his tongue entered her before retreating to allow his lips to suckle her engorged womanhood.

"Harry!" she whispered in surprise, unable to move given how he had her hips pinned with his hands. Forced to simply accept the delight his tongue and lips caused, the sharp darts combining with rolling waves of pleasure made her beg for more even as she feared she might faint from the intensity. A soft chuckle sounded in response from between her legs. "If you're feeling proud of yourself, you should be," she whispered on a giggle.

"You liked that, did you?" he countered, rising to his feet but grasping her ankles to keep them against the front of his shoulders. His manhood jutted out, the tip brushing against her quim before finding her entry.

"You know I did, but... *oh!*" she cried out, his cock filling her in a single thrust. His hands had once again moved to her hips, holding them in place lest his thrusts push her too far back on the bed.

"Damn, but you feel good, my lady," he whispered hoarsely, his thrusts settling into a rhythm as old as time.

"We've not done it like this since... *oh!*" she replied, well aware he was near to his release. He had moved a thumb to where their bodies met, the pad brushing against her quim in exactly the right spot to send her over the edge of yet another orgasm.

"Before Bradley was born," he finished for her, his eyes squeezed shut as his body spasmed. A growl sounded from his throat as he threw back his head.

Stella watched as all the life seemed to drain from him, the post-coital exhaustion soon forcing him to give up his hold on her ankles so she could roll to one side and allow him to fall onto the bed. Once he was settled next to her, she sighed. "I remember the first time we did it that way," she said, grinning. "I was pregnant with Alexander, and I was growing so round." She glanced over at him, her grin widening into a smile when it appeared he was already passed out.

"You thought I would take a mistress," he whispered, his eyes still closed. "That I would think you were no longer the most beautiful woman in the entire world."

Stella inhaled softly. "Harry," she whispered.

"I still do, my Aphrodite."

Leaning over to place a kiss on one of his eyelids, she allowed a long sigh.

"What is it?" he asked, his eyes opening to display his concern. He moved farther up onto the bed, pulling her along with him until their entire bodies were atop the bed. "Something has been troubling you ever since we left London. Out with it."

Stella shook her head in the small of his shoulder. "I fear Helen will end up a spinster," she said, angling her head to see his reaction. She had put voice to the same concern many times, but never like this, when she was in his arms and had his undivided attention.

"Why?"

Her eyes widening at hearing the simple query, she said, "Because I'm half Greek," she blurted.

His burst of laughter was most unexpected.

"Harry," she scolded.

Sobering, he inhaled and held his breath a moment. "I know your mother was not held in high regard despite being married to a duke," he admitted. "And it didn't help that Westhaven had an avocation that kept him away from London for years at a time," he added softly.

Alexander, Duke of Westhaven, had been an archaeologist, his search for Greek artifacts taking him to many of the islands in the Aegean. He had found his own Aphrodite on Mykonos and married her despite knowing he would face censure from the aristocracy back in London upon his return.

"But I rather doubt most even remember your mother these days."

"They don't have to," Stella whispered. "They need only look at me to—"

"Feel profound jealousy at seeing your beauty," he said, arching a brow as if daring her to counter his claim.

"You bounder," she said on a sigh.

"I know Helen isn't as gorgeous as you are, but I expect she'll exhibit an elegant beauty as she ages," he said in a soft voice. "But she'll be wed and have several children of her own long before that."

Stella gasped. "What makes you say that?"

Harry shrugged one shoulder. "Haven't you noticed how Thomas Forster looks at her?" he countered.

"With derision, you mean?"

Lifting himself onto an elbow, which sent her rolling onto her back, Harry stared down at his wife in disbelief for a moment. "Derision?" he repeated. "What makes you say that?"

She allowed a sound of disbelief. "I watched him while we were riding the camels. I saw how he looked at her during dinner. It's as if he cannot abide being in the same room with her."

Harry seemed to think about her examples for a moment before he shook his head. "First of all, it was quite obvious he was jealous of our guide's regard for Helen," he claimed. "And Salman knew it, I think. He was practically goading Thomas to do something."

"That's what you thought?" Stella asked in surprise.

Harry nodded. "He's also rather jealous of Bradley, although I haven't quite sorted why, other than he desires her attentions for himself."

Staring at her husband as if he had grown horns, Stella gave his words a good deal of thought before she settled her head back into the pillow. "She does spend a good deal of time with Bradley," she murmured. "She'll be a most excellent sister when he's older, I think. That is, if she's still living with us."

Harry grunted. "She's behaves as if she's his *mother*," he commented.

Inhaling sharply, Stella stared at him. "Are you saying she is a better mother to him than I?"

He shook his head. "Not at all," he quickly countered. "Only that if someone saw them together and didn't know any better, they might assume she was his mother."

Stella gave his words some thought before she suddenly gasped. "Do you suppose Thomas—?"

"Yes," he interrupted. "But you're not going to say anything to him," he added before she had a chance to finish her query.

She scoffed softly. "Why ever not?"

Harry chuckled. "I might be wrong," he replied. "But if I'm not, I think I will enjoy watching the young man decide whether or not he has true feelings for our daughter."

"Harry," she gently scolded.

"Let him squirm a bit," he said, ignoring her rebuke. "We'll be on the same boat together going up the Nile. There will be plenty of time for him to show himself."

Stella remained quiet for several seconds before she said, "What if he doesn't? Have any feelings for her, I mean?"

Harry lifted a shoulder in the pillow. "Someone else will, my sweet. She's a duke's granddaughter. An earl's daughter," he went on, as if lineage alone would be enough to secure a match.

Maybe lineage would have been enough back when he and Stella had met and married. He knew of many marriages of convenience. He also knew the partnerships didn't always lead to a loving relationship. He supposed that's why men hired mistresses and wives were allowed their own lovers once the heir and spare had been born.

Marriages of late seemed far different. As if this generation of young people had decided love matches were more important than politics or business or personal fortunes.

"*My* daughter," he whispered suddenly. "She's worthy of the very best match, dammit."

Rather relieved he seemed to have more confidence in the matter of Helen's desirability than she did, Stella settled her head back into the small of his shoulder and had just closed her eyes when she remembered they were supposed to be departing the *riad*.

"We have to dress, darling," she said, rising from the bed. "We'll be leaving at any moment." She turned to discover Harry snoring softly.

Sighing, she pulled on her skirts and was glad when Harry awoke on his own and resumed what they had been doing before carnal thoughts had interrupted their preparations.

Remembering his comments about the younger Forster boy, she couldn't help but grin.

Perhaps there was a young man who would fall in love with Helen.

Perhaps he already had.

CHAPTER 16
AN EXCURSION TO SAQQARA

The following day, a port close to Saqqara

Distant shouts, the neighs of a donkey, and the slight bump of the *dhahabîyeh* against a dock had Diana bounding out of bed and into a pair of breeches and a long-sleeved shirt. She was already pulling on a pair of stockings followed by her boots when Randy lifted himself onto an elbow and stared at her.

"What's happened?" he asked in alarm.

"We've docked, which means we're at Memphis," she said with excitement. "We're about to see some of the oldest man-made structures on this entire planet," she added happily.

"Oh," he replied, rising from the bed. "I quite forgot."

She gasped. "How could you?"

He chuckled softly. "Probably because I spent the night in the same bed with you," he teased. "Rather more comfortable than our most recent accommodations I might add."

Indeed, the *Dendera*, a rather new vessel, was far more luxurious than any other ship upon which they had sailed. The polished hardwood interior included a posh parlor and eight well-appointed cabins. The crew cabins and galley were below the main deck. A set of stairs led up to the top of the ship, where a covered dining area with seating for twelve and chairs for lounging were located. The crew were usually found in the open area at the very front of the ship. At the very back of the ship, where a last set of cabins were usually located on a typical *dhahabîyeh,* the deck was open but surrounded by a waist-high railing. A metal table and four chairs were the only furnishings, other than a rickety stool that was positioned next to the control for the rudder.

"You fell asleep on top of me again," Diana said. "But I'm happy to hear I'm more comfortable for you than the mattress at that *riad.*"

He chuckled. "I'm sorry about that."

"I'm not. It was rather chilly last night, so I appreciated your warmth." She rose from the bed and kissed him on the cheek. "I'm surprised your bum didn't grow cold though."

"If it was, I didn't notice," he murmured.

She grinned. "I'm going out to see if a dragoman has been hired yet."

Before Randy could respond, she took her leave of their small cabin and made her way through the thin corridor toward the front of the ship. Three of the four men who made up the crew were on the dock, seeing to securing the vessel with ropes. Noting the position of the sun, Diana realized they were on the west bank of the Nile.

She found the ship's captain, Mahmood, at the wheel. He widened his eyes at the sight of her but dipped his head. "Lady Forster," he said.

"*Sabah al-khair,*" she said by way of a morning greeting, glancing around to see a bustling port despite the early morning hour. A number of other ships were docked near theirs while several had cleared their moorings and were heading out to the middle of the river, no doubt for fishing. In the distance, a number of camels rested in the sand beyond the main thoroughfare, and a line of horse-drawn carriages were parked nearby. "Where might I find a dragoman to take us to the Saqqara Necropolis?"

The captain gave a start. "I expect he will find us, my lady," Mahmood replied, his grin displaying gaps where several teeth were missing. "You should allow your uncle to see to the arrangements, though."

Diana bristled. "Are you saying the guide won't speak with me because I am a woman?" she asked, annoyance evident in her voice.

The captain didn't have a chance to answer when Will appeared at her elbow. "He is," he said in a whisper. "But don't take it personally. This is a very patriarchal society," he added, using terminology she would understand given her background. In a louder voice, he said, "Mr. Salman suggested we hire a man called Omar. Said he had access to all manner of transportation and was quite knowledgable about the necropolis."

Before the captain had a chance to respond, an older man, his leathery face weathered by sun and wind and surrounded by a linen *shemagh*, stepped on board and reached for Diana's hand.

Startled, she watched as his lips brushed over the back of her knuckles before he straightened. "I am Omar, my lady," he claimed in barely accented English. "At your service."

Diana glanced at the captain, waiting for him to confirm the identity of the man.

"Your arrival is well-timed, Omar," Mahmood said dryly. "Almost as if you were expecting us."

"I was," Omar acknowledged. "Salman, your dragoman in Giza, sent word yesterday I was to expect you," he explained. "And he especially mentioned you," he added, turning his attention back to Diana. "Lady...?"

"Lady Forster," she said, wondering what Salman might

have included in his missive. She dipped a curtsy before turning to indicate Will. "This is my uncle, Lord Bellingham."

"Ah. An aristocrat," Omar acknowledged with a bow. "I understand there are others in your party, my lord?"

Will nodded. "There are nine of us," he said. He didn't include the nurse or Bradley in his number, thinking they would remain on board while the rest of them spent the day touring.

The number didn't seem to surprise the dragoman. "Five hantours will do then," he replied happily, referring to the horse-drawn buggies. "I have seen to it they are supplied with water and hay. Your ladies will bring their parasols, no doubt? A luncheon as well?"

"I'll see to it they do," Diana replied. "Will I be able to explore the inside of any of the pyramids?"

Omar displayed a moment of surprise. "You are not deterred despite your experience in Khufu's tomb?" he asked.

Diana blinked. "Not in the least."

"You were not... frightened?" he asked in surprise.

She shook her head before her eyes widened with understanding. "*I* was not the one who was frightened, sir. My cousin had a bit of a scare when a young boy appeared as if out of nowhere. Mere momentary fright is all," she explained.

"You are not deterred by claims of curses cast upon those who would enter a pharaoh's tomb?" he pressed.

She shook her head. "I am an educated woman, sir, and I am not superstitious."

Omar and Mahmood exchanged worrisome glances. "Perhaps you should be, my lady," Omar commented. "The heat inside the Red Pyramid is nearly intolerable, the air is very poor, and there is nothing to be found there but an empty chamber."

Will cleared his throat. "Exactly how many pyramids can

we see in one day?" he asked. "If we don't go inside?" He directed an apologetic glance at Diana.

"I will take you to Saqqara and Dashur where you will stand next to three pyramids… well, four if you count the small mound near one of them," he replied. "We shall see some off in the distance. And then there are many tombs and the remains of temples in Saqqara. What you call Memphis."

"I don't have to go inside a pyramid," Diana murmured.

Will furrowed a brow. "You're sure?"

She lifted a shoulder. "I've read the descriptions of these pyramids' inner tunnels and chambers. They are much like the one I was inside of at Giza."

"Very true," Omar said, waving a finger. "These were the first of many pyramids to be built, though, so they are not as… perfect," he added, wincing as if he knew he had chosen the wrong word.

"All the better," she said. She turned to Mahmood. "When might we be able to eat breakfast? And might you be able to make a luncheon we can take with us? We'll need water as well."

Will and Mahmood exchanged glances of amusement. "Here I thought *you* were the planner, my lord," Mahmood commented. He turned to Diana. "Your morning meal is ready, my lady." He waved to the table set up at the top of the ship. "I will have Ahmet prepare food for your travels and flasks of water."

"*Shukran*," she replied by way of thanks. About to say she would see to waking the rest of their party, she turned to discover most members of the two families were already making their way up the stairs to the dining table. "We shouldn't be long," she said, directing her comment to Omar.

"I shall have our transports ready when you are, my lady." He turned to Mahmood. "We shall meet you at the dock near Dashur late in the afternoon."

"I'll be there," Mahmood replied.

From their casual manner, Diana realized the two had taken other travelers on a similar trip in the past. Although the others would be grateful their dragoman was experienced, she knew Omar wouldn't allow her the freedom a younger guide might.

a n hour later
"I didn't realize the ground would be so hard out here," Tom said. Next to him, his brother was lounging in the buggy, his gaze directed at the horizon. Off in the distance, several triangular shapes interrupted the flat line of the desert.

"Me, neither," Randy replied. He had opted to ride with Tom so Diana and Helen could ride together. David would have been left alone in a carriage except he had talked Helen into allowing Bradley to ride with him.

Although they had expected the babe to be left on board with the nurse, Helen had put voice to a protest, claiming it was important he join them and that she would see to him.

The look on Helen's face had been almost comical when David lifted the boy into the buggy and then stepped up to sit next to the toddler.

Bradley beamed in delight, obviously not the least bit concerned he wouldn't be seeing his mother or sister for a half-hour or more.

"You're not funning me?" Helen had asked in alarm.

David shook his head. "I have two younger cousins I've taken on rides," he claimed. "At some point, I'll have one or two of my own babes I'll need to take in a curricle or a barouche."

"You'll have to hold onto him," she argued.

"I know," David replied, an arm reaching behind the boy so he could pull him closer. "Don't worry. I'm only going to teach him some new words." Before she could scold him, he winked and said, "Don't worry. I won't teach him how to curse."

The five hantours set off into the desert west of the river, the morning sun casting shadows directly in front of them. In the first vehicle, Omar sat on the bench with a young boy who handled the reins of the Arabian that trotted at an even pace. Seated behind them in the squabs were Diana and Helen—"ladies first," the guide had remarked before they set out—and following them were the other four vehicles.

"I was expecting more sand," Randy admitted. "But I much prefer this mode of transport over riding a camel." He fished a pair of eye-glasses from his waist coat pocket and put them on, grinning when the tinted lenses meant he didn't have to squint. "You should put yours on," he suggested, indicating the spectacles. Although they weren't particularly fashionable—most who wore them in England did so because they had syphilis—they did provide some eye protection from the harsh sun.

"What possessed our uncle to buy these things?" Tom asked as he examined the eye-glasses. There were two thin arms attached to the outer edge of a black frame in which two tinted glass plates were mounted.

"Probably the need to rid himself of the vendor who was peddling them," Randy replied. "I like them."

Tom snorted. "That's because Diana said you looked rather dashing in them."

Not about to argue, Randy smirked at his brother as his attention went to a pyramid of a most unusual shape—it featured a six-tier stepped profile.

The hantour halted next to the others while Omar and the drivers saw to helping everyone down from their seats.

Grimacing at seeing how Helen rushed to take Bradley from the carriage he was in—the boy had obviously enjoyed the ride given how he kept attempting to say the word 'horse' with David's encouragement—Tom made an odd growling sound.

Randy glanced between his brother and the toddler. "You don't seem to like him," he commented.

Shrugging, Tom said, "I can't believe she brought him. I thought she was going to leave him with the nurse."

His brows furrowing at hearing the contempt in his brother's voice, he scoffed. "I'm sure she will for shorter excursions. Maybe longer after Helen begins to trust the nurse," he said. "I rather doubt any woman is willing to leave her babe for such a long period when they've only just met."

Before Tom could reply, Diana rushed up to claim Randy's arm, and the two set off to join Omar.

The weathered dragoman took the scarf from in front of his face, lifted an arm in the direction of the pyramid, and announced, "*This* is the oldest stone and clay structure on the entire planet."

"How old?" Barbara asked, surprising the guide.

"Forty-four hundred years old, my lady," he replied. "The pharaoh Djoser, the first king of the third dynasty, had it built so the four corners mark the four directions of the compass," he said, waving his arms to indicate east and west. "What you see here is but a fraction of what once was a complex of temples and tombs surrounded by a wall. A vast city of the dead."

"He certainly knows how to keep our attention," Tom murmured, his comment meant for David.

"Shh," David replied. "I'm listening."

"Is it true there are four-hundred chambers under that pyramid?" Diana asked.

Omar gave a start. "Imhotep designed it to be so the pharaoh could live here after his death. So that he would have all that he needed in the afterlife."

"I don't suppose I could go down there?" she murmured.

Shaking his head, the dragoman said, "It is not safe, and I would suffer a scolding should someone learn I had allowed you inside."

Diana exchanged a look of disappointment with her husband.

"I didn't tell him that," Randy claimed in a hoarse whisper.

"Was the surface always so rough looking?" Barbara asked.

Omar brightened. "Ah, no my lady. At one time, it was covered in a layer of white limestone. When the sun shown, it gleamed like a giant, two-hundred-foot-tall diamond." He began walking toward some ruins off to the side of the pyramid. "Come, we will walk through what is left of the temples."

The group followed the dragoman through a crude opening in what had one time been the massive façade of a temple. Once beyond the entry, they made their way in between two rows of fluted columns, and the rubble beyond marked where walls had once stood.

"It is a ruin now, but one day, I think it shall be rebuilt," Omar remarked as he spread his arms to indicate the area.

When the group wandered back through the columns to regard the pyramid one last time, Randy found Diana seated on the ground, her sketchpad open and the shape of the pyramid already drawn. "You didn't waste any time," he remarked.

"I wish I could walk the perimeter," she replied, not looking up from her work. "See what's on the other side."

"The bottom tier is rubble," Omar said sadly. "Stones purloined to make other structures."

"The bane of every ancient temple," Randy commented.

"Indeed," Omar agreed. "I think you shall like the next one better than this, though."

"Oh?" Randy replied.

"The first successful attempt at a true pyramid."

Diana glanced up at Randy. "He's referring to the Red Pyramid," she said. "Will we see the Blunted Pyramid after that? The one they sometimes call the Bent Pyramid?"

The guide displayed a moment of disappointment. "You already know of it?" he asked.

"She's been reading books on Egypt since we left Alexandria," he explained. "And she remembers everything."

"Ah, but reading about it does nothing to blunt the awe of seeing it. No pun intended."

Diana suppressed a chuckle as Randy helped her to stand. "Will we stop at the Pyramid of Unas?" she asked.

Omar shook his head. "We can see it from here, so we will not stop there," he replied, pointing in the direction of a mound that might have been mistaken for a hill in the middle of the desert. "As you can see, there is not much to it. One can barely tell that it was at one time a pyramid."

"Then let's be off," Randy encouraged. He escorted her back to the hantour she shared with Helen, and a few minutes later, they were off across the flat desert.

CHAPTER 17
TWO YOUNG LADIES CONVERSE

An hour later

Helen was about to lift Bradley into the hantour she was sharing with Diana when her mother hurried over to take the boy into her arms. "He can ride with me, darling," she said. "With all this fresh air he's had today, I expect he'll sleep most of the way to Dashur."

Given the distance from the pyramids at Saqqara to those they would see near Dashur, Omar had said to expect the trip to take nearly an hour-and-a-half.

Helen watched as her father helped her mother into their hantour, the two disappearing from view behind the curtains that hung from the hood of the equipage. The lightweight fabric did little to lessen the heat of midday, but it did help to keep out the red desert dust kicked up by the other hantours.

"You're so good with him," Diana remarked. "Might I ask, did his father not wish to come along on the trip?"

Helen blinked. "Bradley's father?" she asked in confusion. "But... he did." She suddenly scoffed but displayed a grin. "His father is *my* father. What I mean to say is, Bradley is my brother."

It was Diana's turn to blink. "Oh. Given his age and how he's usually with you, I just assumed he was *your* son," she replied. "Forgive me."

"Oh, it's all right," Helen replied happily. "I rather like that I seem to be doing it correctly. Motherhood, I mean. I want children of my own so much, you see."

Not surprised to hear the admission, Diana said, "From what I recall of our time at finishing school, you're not much younger than I am."

"Only a year's difference," Helen acknowledged.

"But being here means you'll be missing the Season," she reasoned. "Or did you leave a beau back in London?"

Helen stiffened. "Uh, no."

When she looked as if she might say something more, Diana arched a brow. "But... you... have someone in mind?" she asked, arching a brow as if in a tease.

Her gaze darting about as if she was trying to decide how to respond, Helen finally nodded. "When I encouraged my father to arrange this trip to Egypt, it was because I hoped... well, it was because I knew when Lord and Lady Bellingham were expected to be here."

Diana gave a start. "You *wanted* to be in Egypt at the same time as we were?"

Helen nodded.

"But why?"

Dipping her head, Helen seemed reluctant to to respond. "Because I knew the Forsters would be here."

Diana blinked before her eyes rounded. "You came because..." She stopped, about to mention her husband's name before she scoffed and suddenly inhaled. "Because Thomas is with us," she whispered.

"Please, don't tell anyone," Helen begged.

Momentarily confused, Diana seemed to think for a

moment before she reached out and took Helen's gloved hand in hers. "Are you in love with him?"

A grimace passed over Helen's face before she finally nodded. "I think so. I was more sure before we left London. Absolutely positive before he left London."

Not having been in London in some time, Diana was momentarily confused. "You had reason to believe he might feel affection for you?"

Helen nodded. "He... he kissed me during a ball. In the gardens. The night before they departed London."

"The Morganfield's ball?" Diana asked.

"That's the one. How is it *you* know of it?" Helen asked.

Although Diana had been in Girgenti on Sicily at the time, she had heard tales of the fête from Randy and his aunt. Overheard David and Tom speak of it. It had been at that ball that David Slater had arranged a betrothal of convenience with Miss Jane Fitzsimmons as a means of providing her protection from unwanted suitors.

"In a round about manner, I acquired a sister because of that ball," Diana replied. When she noted Helen's look of confusion, she explained what had happened. "Penton's pretend betrothal with Miss Jane worked perfectly until my brother Marcus met her. He's friends with her brother, Antonio—from school, you see. When they arrived in Athens, my brother and I had only recently taken up residency in a house arranged for our family's use while my father was to work on the Acropolis."

"Oh, how interesting," Helen whispered.

"I was with Marcus when he met Jane. I could tell he felt affection for her. Or lust, at the very least. I often wonder if he wanted me there because he thought to introduce me to Antonio." She rolled her eyes. "The future Lord Reardon."

"I hear he is the most handsome heir in all of Bath," Helen said, her brows waggling.

"His features are rather easy on the eyes—and you will not share what I just said with my husband."

"Oh, I won't," Helen promised, tittering softly. "Do go on with how Jane became your sister., though"

Diana grinned. "Well, the day following their arrival in Athens, we were all up on the Acropolis when Lord Penton and the Forsters appeared. They were on the next leg of their Grand Tour... and when Marcus discovered Penton was supposedly betrothed to Jane—"

"He challenged him to a duel?" Helen guessed, her eyes wide.

"They never actually came to blows," Diana assured her. "But once David confirmed that Jane returned Marcus' affections, he graciously stepped aside so Marcus was able to marry Jane."

"Oh," Helen breathed. "How romantic."

It was Diana's turn to display a grimace. "Penton never was going to marry her. He's my age—far too young to be considering matrimony given he'll eventually be a marquess," she reasoned.

Helen angled her head to one side. "So is that when you and Lord Forster fell in love?" she asked, her voice nearly a whisper.

Diana dipped her head. "I suppose it was," she admitted. "He was most insistent we should be together..." She swallowed, remembering how he had already accepted her desire to be a spinster and had offered instead to be her lover. "Or married," she murmured before allowing a wan smile.

"You don't regret marrying him," Helen stated.

Diana giggled. "No, I do not," she admitted. "The way Randy speaks of matrimony with his brother, well, I suppose it should come as no surprise that Thomas would be amenable to marriage earlier than his age would indicate." She sighed. "I admit I have noticed Thomas watching you. When you haven't been looking."

Helen inhaled softly. "When I catch him staring at me, he turns away," she countered. "I was sure..." She stopped speaking and sighed. "I think I've made a mistake in talking my father into bringing us on this tour," she said quietly.

"You have not," Diana countered, reaching out with a hand to place it on Helen's arm. "Lord Everly seems quite engaged with it all. He and Lord Bellingham are getting on as if they are long lost friends," she added. "And he's certainly enthralled by those flowers he's been studying."

"Hibiscus," Helen stated. "They are used to make tea here, but he wants some for his conservatory back in Mayfair. He's quite the botanist. A naturalist."

"Ah," Diana replied thoughtfully. She regarded the younger girl for a moment before she said, "Do you still feel affection for Thomas?"

"I think so. I would like to know that he returns my affections, though. Before I would ever do anything like... kiss him again."

"I concur," Diana replied. "Which has me wondering if Randy knows what happened at that ball." She paused, her expression thoughtful. "Would you like me to ask him what he knows? Mayhap mention how I've noticed Tom's regard for you?"

"You won't tell him why?" Helen countered.

Diana furrowed a brow. "I won't," she assured her. She chuckled softly before her eyes rounded. "If you end up married to Tom, we'll be sisters."

Helen grinned. "I'd like that," she admitted.

"And the sooner you're wed, the sooner you can become a *real* mother."

Helen beamed in delight. "I once told Mother I might have to take Bradley off her hands."

"She wouldn't allow you to, though," Diana said, although there was a hint of a question in her voice.

"Oh, there are days when she simply hands him to me," Helen said without a hint of amusement. Her sudden grin betrayed her words. "My parents were not expecting to have another child after me, and although we had a nurse when we left London, we... lost her in Malta."

"Oh, dear," Diana replied. "How awful."

"Oh, not like that," Helen said, waving a gloved hand as if to erase her initial words. "She met a man there, you see. Love at first sight, I think, and they decided to marry, and she stayed behind on the island of Gozo."

Diana dipped her head. "Still, it must be a challenge to travel with a baby."

Helen lifted a shoulder. "It's not so difficult. Well, unless he runs off and almost gets eaten by a crocodile, or manages to escape from his bed in the middle of the night, takes off his nappy, and pees all over the floor."

"Oh, dear," Diana replied. Laughing, she settled back in the squabs. "I cannot imagine having a babe," she said. "But I'll have to, of course. At least two if I'm to do my duty as a future countess."

"You'll have a nurse to help," Helen reasoned. "And given Lord Forster's brothers and sister Grace, I expect he'll do fine with having children of his own."

"He has said as much," Diana admitted. "He seems to think I'll simply pack up a babe much like I do my satchel when I'm off to do some digging."

Helen lifted a shoulder. "That will work until the baby starts to crawl," she commented. "Once he starts walking, though..." She shook her head from side to side. "You'll be chasing him more than you will be digging. *That's* when you'll leave him with his nurse."

Diana didn't reply, her attention on the scene directly ahead of them. She inhaled softly.

"What is it?" Helen asked, her gaze following Diana's.

"The Red Pyramid," Diana said in awe. She glanced to the left, searching the horizon for signs of another pyramid. An odd shape protruded from the ground, darker in appearance than the red sandstone that made up the Red Pyramid. "That's the Black Pyramid," she murmured. "Or what's left of it," she added sadly. "It's in worse shape than I thought."

"Are we going to stop there?"

Diana shook her head. "We will at the Red Pyramid, and if you look off beyond it, you can just make out the last one we'll see today," she explained, referring to a distant bump on the otherwise flat horizon.

"I can't imagine how they built these out in the middle of... nowhere," Helen commented, leaning forward to gaze out beyond the side curtains.

"The Nile has changed course over the centuries," Diana commented, sniffing the air. "It's closer than you think, and I would bet money they cut a canal into the desert leading to the site so they could bring all the blocks by way of a river barge."

Helen's eyes rounded at hearing Diana's comment. "You would bet money?" she repeated in shock.

Diana grinned. "Don't tell anyone else I said that. My father used to say it when he was sure of some find he uncovered." The driver's sudden yelp had the Arabian slowing his quick trot to a walk until it was in the little bit of shade provided by the pyramid. The other hantours lined up next to them, their occupants slowly stepping down and stretching their stiff limbs after the hour-long ride.

"This, my friends, is the Red Pyramid," Omar announced, his arm held out as if he was introducing a friend. "It is named for its rusty red color and is the largest of all the pyramids here at Dashur. Come into the shade and I shall tell you all about it."

Although she stood with Randy for a few minutes, listening to the dragoman's recitation, Diana pulled her sketchpad from her satchel and soon slipped away to explore on her own.

CHAPTER 18
A TOUR OF DASHUR

*O*n the eastern side of the pyramid

"Well, this one seems rather well preserved," Barbara remarked as Will led her away from the hantours to where their dragoman stood. Meanwhile one of the drivers hurried over with two collapsible chairs and set them up on the hard ground while another spread out a large woven blanket. He held his hand out to indicate she should take a seat. "I'm not infirm, but I think I shall take him up on his offer," she said to Will.

"As will I," Will murmured, pulling out his pocket watch to discover it was already past two o'clock. Despite the breakfast they had been served on the ship, his stomach grumbled.

"If you are hungry, now would be a good time to eat your picnic luncheon," Omar said. Another driver appeared with their basket of food and yet another brought more chairs and another blanket. "We are protected from the breeze on this side of the pyramid, one the local people refer to as the Bat Pyramid."

"And that one?" Will asked, his gaze directed toward a dark

pyramid that looked as if its sides were angled in halfway up the structure.

"Ah, I will talk about the Bent Pyramid in a moment," Omar replied.

"It seems to be appropriately named," Stella commented, before she turned her attention to the one that rose in front of them. At the apex, the sun was barely hidden by its triangular top. Rays of light splayed out as if from the pyramid itself.

Within a few minutes, their luncheon was spread out on the blanket in the small bit of shade provided by the pyramid, the ladies and older gentlemen seated in the wooden chairs while the younger men lounged about on the blankets. Bradley climbed onto Helen's lap, his grin widening once she had him seated so he faced the dragoman.

"They call it the Bat Pyramid because...?" David prompted, his face screwed into a grimace.

"There are bats inside," Omar acknowledged, his white teeth gleaming when David made a sound of dismay.

"This looks as large as those we saw at Giza," Harry remarked, before he helped himself to a hunk of cheese and some flat bread.

"Almost," Omar agreed. "Khufu and Khafre are larger, though, and were only made possible because this one was successful."

"Successful?" Tom repeated.

"*This* is Egypt's first successful attempt at building a true smooth-sided pyramid," Omar stated proudly.

"Old Kingdom, is it not?" David guessed.

"Indeed. The Pharaoh Sneferu—he was the father of Khufu and Khafre—oversaw the construction of four pyramids during his reign. This was the third, built we believe starting in 2575 BC, and is estimated to have taken between ten and seventeen years to complete."

"What were his first two pyramids?" David asked, helping himself to a *kofta*, a sort of meatball flavored with seasonings.

"Ah. A complete failure and an almost failure."

A series of gasps of surprise sounded at the guide's words. "Failure?" Will repeated, helping himself to a *kofta* from the small basket containing a number of foods that could be eaten without utensils. The cook on their ship had obviously understood they would be eating in the desert.

"There was once a Pyramid at Meidum, but it collapsed sometime in our antiquity," Omar explained, pointing off in the distance to indicate where it might have been located.

"And the 'almost failure'?" David prompted, his gaze directed at what was left of the Black Pyramid, thinking the dragoman was referring to it.

"You will see that one next," he replied, pointing toward the south. Given where they were located on the eastern side of the Red Pyramid, they couldn't see it.

"This one looks rather squat," Randy remarked, holding his hands together so his middle fingers touched while his hands matched the angle of the sides of the pyramid.

"At a perfect forty-three degree angle," Omar stated. "You see, Sneferu discovered with the Bent Pyramid..." He once again pointed to the south. "The original fifty-four degree angle was far too sharp—too steep—which was probably the angle used to build the Pyramid at Meidum," he said, obviously pleased to have such an interested audience. "When it displayed signs of instability—it may have even partially collapsed while it was under construction—the angle was abruptly changed to forty-three degrees." He waved an arm to indicate the pyramid behind him. "So forty-three degrees was chosen for this one, and as you can see, it has survived almost forty-three hundred years because of it."

A murmur of appreciation passed through the group.

"Third time was the charm," Randy commented. He

glanced around, and when he didn't see Diana, he excused himself from the group and went off in search of her.

"Has it always been this reddish color?" Stella asked.

Omar held up a finger. "This is a good question."

Stella beamed in delight.

"No." When he didn't immediately say anything else, she scoffed. He chuckled, obviously amused with himself. "It once had a veneer of polished white limestone completely covering it," he finally replied. "Now, imagine how magnificent it must have appeared on a day such as this," he said, his hands spread wide. "There are reports that when the sun hit the top of it, it glowed as if it was made of silver and gold, which is actually a possibility for what is called the pyramidion—the very top of a pyramid. You see, the pyramid builders used to cap their creations with a material we call *electrum*, a sort of combination of gold and silver and other metals," he explained.

"The reflection must have been blinding on a sunny day," Will commented.

"The god Ra at his finest," Omar agreed, obviously pleased the earl had provided the perfect setup for his comment.

"Can we go inside this one?" David asked, as if he was anxious to do so. Apparently, he had forgotten about the bats.

Omar winced. "You can, but it is terribly hot, and the air inside is very poor," he replied.

"Worse than Khufu's pyramid at Giza?" David pressed.

Nodding, the guide said, "You ask as if you made the trek inside that one?"

David nodded. "I did."

Omar's eyes widened. "You are a brave man."

A round of chuckles greeted the comment, and David's face reddened with embarrassment. "I was merely startled when that boy appeared from out of the darkness," he murmured in his own defense.

"How does one get inside this pyramid, and was anything found in there?" Tom asked with excitement.

Rolling his eyes, Omar inhaled and sighed in resignation. "The entrance is accessible," he admitted, once again pointing toward the south. "But it requires you climb one-hundred-and-twenty-five steps to get to the entrance. *Steep* steps. Then you must go down through a two-hundred foot passage that leads to two antechambers."

"Have *you* been in inside?" Helen asked, her hands wrapped around her baby brother's middle. A bonnet covered his head, and he was seated so he faced outward. He seemed as interested in the giant wall of red limestone in front of them as he did the *kofta* he gripped in one hand.

"I have," Omar replied. "The antechambers feature nearly forty-foot high corbeled ceilings, and there is an even higher corbeled burial chamber. Very impressive once you climb up to it."

"Was anything *in* there?" she asked in awe.

He angled his head first to the left and then to the right. "When it was first entered, it is said there were some human remains found. Fragmentary, at best," he clarified. "But they were thought to be of Sneferu himself."

A collective awe sounded throughout his audience.

"I will allow you time to eat your luncheon, but should you have questions, I will do my very best to answer them," he said.

The group turned their attention to the various foods spread out on the blankets, the young men helping themselves to second and third helpings of the savory meatballs. When no one asked any questions of their guide, he sauntered off in the direction Randy had gone only moments earlier.

.   .   .

"Here you are," Randy said as he approached Diana, his wife sitting crossed-legged on the ground as she sketched the face of the pyramid which included the access to its entry. "I feared I would discover you had gone inside by yourself."

Diana glanced up from her sketchpad. "It has been tempting, but from what I read of this tomb, it's quite hot inside. Easier to navigate than the one at Giza, though."

"Omar said the air is of poor quality. I feared you might faint should you go in there," Randy said as he lowered himself to the ground. He held out a napkin filled with a variety of foods. "I wasn't sure what you might like, so I brought a bit of everything."

She gave him an appreciative grin before leaning over to buss him on the cheek. "You are a dear," she said, plucking a *kofta* from the napkin. "I'm starving." She bit off the end of it and made a humming noise.

Randy grinned before directing his attention to her drawing. "Will you paint it?" he asked.

"Maybe," she responded, her quick strokes having already outlined the pyramid and the curving line of stairs that led to the opening halfway up the south-facing surface. "The color will be quite a challenge to match."

"Is it what you expected?" he asked, his brows furrowed with worry. He hadn't read any of the books on Egypt she had been reading every night before they turned out the lights, and he was curious as to her expectations.

She stopped drawing and regarded him with an expression of surprise. "Better, I should think, although I do wish some of the veneer was still intact. That and the pyramidion," she commented. "I read that it was coated in—"

"Electrum," he interrupted, grinning when her blonde

brows rose in surprise. "Omar told us about it," he added sheepishly.

"Then he is a good dragoman," she stated.

"He seems quite proud of what his ancestors built."

"He should be," she said, using the edge of her charcoal to shade some of the steps she had added to her drawing. "This pyramid is a result of trial and error—"

"The first successful straight-walled pyramid," he finished for her. "Built at a forty-three-degree angle. White limestone veneer, now missing."

She closed her sketchpad and returned it to her satchel. "Someone was listening," she teased, helping herself to a piece of flatbread.

Randy pretended offense. "Don't expect any more information from me. I left before he finished." He offered her the last *kofta*, and when she declined, he finished it off in a few bites.

Easily coming to her feet, Diana placed her hands on her hips and regarded the stairs directly in front of her. "I am tempted." She reached out and offered a hand to Randy, who grunted as he struggled to stand.

"To go inside?" he asked in disbelief. He attempted to brush the red dust from the back of his top coat, wincing when he only managed to smear it on the superfine.

"At least go part way up," she replied. "For the view," she claimed, waving to the Bent Pyramid three miles off to their right.

He regarded the fairly shallow stairs followed by the steep stone steps. "I'll go with you. So we can help each other," he offered.

She fished a pair of kid-leather gloves from her satchel and pulled them on, and he followed suit with the pair he had stuffed into his top coat pocket when they had started the picnic.

Diana set off climbing the man-made stairs leading up to

the pyramid's exposed building blocks. Randy followed, admiring her bum as she scrambled up to almost the halfway point of where a dark rectangle indicated the entrance. When she turned around on a particularly large block, he was still a few steps down, and his gaze was directed at her midsection.

"Have you been staring at my bum?" she accused.

"Yes," he replied, struggling to catch his breath as he joined her on the same step. "It's all that's kept me climbing." He panted a couple more times before his breathing seemed to even out. "I thought you were going to stop when we reached the stones," he complained. "How is it you're not winded?"

Diana chuckled. "We're not that high up," she countered, tempted to ignore his comment about her breathing. "Mayhap fifty feet. As for not being particularly winded, I am younger than you," she added with a prim grin. She decided not to remind him that she had spent most of her life following her father around on his digs, climbing ancient marble and stone steps into a variety of temples and tombs.

Her gaze swept the horizon to the south. The larger of two dark silhouettes on the horizon appeared to be a pyramid with walls angled in about halfway up. "That is the Bent Pyramid," she commented.

"Was that one a pyramid?" Randy asked, his gaze directed on what was left of the Black Pyramid. The odd-shaped mound was even darker than the Bent Pyramid, and nothing of its current shape would suggest it had at one time had four walls.

"It was," she acknowledged.

"What happened to it? And who was buried there?" he asked.

"Amenemhat the Third and his queens," she replied. "He was supposedly the first pharaoh to have his wives buried with him. The pyramid was once called 'Amenemhat is Mighty' because it used to be rather large, but it suffered from structural problems and obviously fell apart."

"Wrong angle?" he guessed.

Diana lifted a shoulder. "It was built during the Middle Kingdom, so they knew what angle to build it," she reasoned. "But it likely collapsed because it was too close to the river, and because it was made of mud bricks rather than stone," she explained.

"The groundwater probably softened the bricks," Randy reasoned.

"Indeed. Once the limestone veneer was removed, that's the color that was revealed."

"Hence the name," he finished for her. "What a shame."

Diana nodded. "Well, I rather imagine the rest of our party is going to miss us if they don't already."

Randy glanced down the steps and winced. Even though they were only a quarter of the way up the side of the pyramid, it felt rather high. Too high. "How far up did you think we were?" he asked.

"Only about fifty feet, I think," she replied, her attention on the Bent Pyramid. "The entrance is at about a hundred feet," she added, her gaze going up the face of the pyramid where a makeshift platform marked the entry.

"Only?" he repeated.

Diana glanced over at him, her brows furrowed. "Is this the highest you've ever climbed anything?" she asked.

He swallowed. "Maybe."

She looked down the face of the pyramid, the steps they had navigated not nearly as evident from this angle. "Let's be on our way, shall we?"

He lifted his gaze to the horizon. "I, uh, never thought going down might be more difficult than climbing," he groused as Diana stepped in front of him and began making her way down, bending into almost a sitting position before reaching down with a booted foot to feel for the next step. Her kid-gloved hands gripped the stones as she went.

"Just follow my bum," she teased.

Attempting to copy her lead, he stopped on the next step down and took a steadying breath. "Diana," he called out. "This seems far steeper than forty-three degrees," he complained.

She turned and glanced up, alarm showing on her face. Immediately understanding his hesitance, she said, "It is rather steep, darling. I think it would be safer if we faced the rocks and went down backwards. Sort of crawl down."

When he saw her do just that, he followed suit, his moves far more careful than they had been when they were climbing. Once the steps were less steep, he finally turned around and bounded down the rest of the stairs to discover Omar watching them, which meant the dragoman must have come around the southeast corner when they were both facing the pyramid. They hadn't seen him when they were surveying the horizon.

He glanced back up to where they had been and frowned. From the ground, he spied the block upon which they had stopped. "It certainly doesn't look as if we were fifty feet up," he murmured.

Diana winced at seeing how the golden-red dust of the desert covered his boots and pantaloons. "Do not discount your achievement, darling." She turned and made her way to the guide, wondering how long he had been watching them. "I did not go inside. I didn't even make it all the way to the entrance," she said before Omar could ask. Randy finally joined them, his face red with exertion.

Or perhaps the sun. His top hat barely provided any shade for his face.

"I am glad you did not go inside. There are bats," Omar stated, as if he thought the mention of them would be a deterrent for her.

Diana tittered. "I thought you were going to say 'snakes'," she replied.

"There could be some of them as well," the dragoman

commented. He waved for them to join him as he headed back the way he had come. "The others should be done with their picnic," he explained. "I told your captain I would have you at the dock this afternoon to meet the *dhahabîyeh*. He is probably already there."

By the time they rejoined the others on the east side of the pyramid, the remains of the picnic had been removed and everyone was heading for their respective hantours.

"Ride with me?" Randy asked.

Diana directed a quick glance in Helen's direction, and the young lady nodded her understanding.

Especially when Tom helped Helen up and into a hantour.

CHAPTER 19
A MOST AWKWARD CONVERSATION

A moment later

Helen's heart raced as Tom offered his gloved hand. "That's very kind of you," she said, stepping up into the hantour and settling into the worn leather squabs. "Will you join me?"

Tom stepped back, his gaze darting to the one in which his brother was about to climb into. When he didn't see Diana, he bounded into the carriage. "Yes, I suppose I will. Seems Lady Forster is riding with my brother."

Pressing her bell skirts closer to her thighs to make room for him on the bench seat, Helen watched as he removed his top hat and sat back. "Did you enjoy the tour?" she asked.

He nodded. "Indeed," he replied. "And you?"

"Very much, as did Bradley. I think he was as enthralled as my father."

Tom stiffened at the mention of the babe. "He, uh, seems to a be a rather happy baby."

"Oh, very much. Unless he's hungry, and then he has no problem voicing his complaint," she replied. "He's riding with Mother now and will be asleep before we reach Dashur."

Tom nodded. "I admit to being rather surprised when we came upon your family in Cairo."

"The feeling was mutual," she said. "Of all the places to find others from England..." She allowed the sentence to trail off. "Was Egypt on your original Grand Tour itinerary?"

"It was," he acknowledged. "Randy insisted we go, but I think David... uh, Penton," he corrected himself, "He was equally interested."

Helen dipped her head. "But not you?"

He finally directed his gaze on her and lifted a shoulder. "I admit to ambivalence. I would go anywhere my cousins wish to go. I certainly don't regret coming here, although..." He used a glove in an attempt to brush some of the desert dust from the knee of his pantaloons. "The sand is certainly troublesome."

"Isn't it?" she agreed. "I'm beginning to think all my gowns will have reddish-gold hems by the time we return to England."

They sat in silence for a moment, and Helen considered whether or not she should bring up the matter of their kiss during the Morganfield's ball. She was saved from doing so when Tom spoke first.

"Will you go back to London directly from Egypt?" he asked. "When we're finished with our tour?"

She remembered her mother and Lady Bellingham mentioning their respective itineraries when they were in the *riad* parlor in Cairo. "My mother wants to go to Rome before we head back to England," she replied, deciding it wasn't really a lie since her mother had put voice to such a request.

"Not Greece?" he asked in surprise.

Helen inhaled softly. "Oh, I'm sure she'd like to go to her birthplace," she replied. "She was born on Mykonos. An island in the Cyclades."

"Have you been?"

She shook her head. "It hasn't been safe to travel in the

Aegean, what with the war between the Ottomans and Greeks," she replied. "But… I would like to go."

"We were in Athens before we came to Egypt," Tom said before he chuckled softly. "That's where Randy acquired his wife."

"Acquired?" Helen repeated, giggling softly. "You make it sound as if he bought her at a shop," she teased.

He scratched the side of his nose. "Found her in a temple on the Acropolis, is what he did. I don't know if it was love at first sight or if he merely thought it was his duty to provide protection for her, but they do seem to love one another."

"Indeed," Helen agreed.

"Although my younger sister—"

"You refer to Grace?" she asked.

"Yes," he said, his expression conveying discomfort. "Before we left on this tour, she had begun to adopt the practice of wearing my younger brother's breeches, much to my mother's dismay," he explained. "So when I first met Diana, and she was wearing them, and I was left wondering what was happening in the world of ladies' fashion."

"For her avocation, it makes perfect sense," Helen replied. "Perhaps your sister can claim a similar excuse?"

He started to open his mouth and closed it, remembering the night before the decision had been made that four cousins and an aunt and uncle would be departing England for a Grand Tour. The night they had brought in the last of the harvest before the heavens had opened up and rain poured down.

Grace had joined them in the fields, garbed in George's breeches and working just as hard as any of the rest of them and the tenant farmers who were employed for the Gisborn fields. "Well, I doubt she plans to be a farmer," he murmured, "but should she marry one, she certainly knows what's required for success." For a moment, he seemed awestruck.

"I rather doubt Lady Grace is going to marry a farmer," Helen commented.

Chuckling, Tom nodded. "Agreed." His expression suddenly sobered. "She'll be having her come-out next year." He scoffed. "It's hard to believe she'll be eighteen years old."

"Her name has already appeared on the list," Helen said.

"The list?" he repeated.

"The list of daughters of aristocrats available for marriage," she clarified.

Tom blinked. "Oh." He frowned. "Are you aware of any young bucks who might have mentioned her name?" he asked in alarm.

Helen hid her amusement behind a gloved hand. "I heard Farringdon has her under consideration," she said, referring to Raymond Roderick, the oldest legitimate son of the Marquess of Reading.

"Reading's whelp?" he asked in disbelief. "Farringdon is barely a year older than I am," he claimed. He scoffed again. "How did they even meet?"

"Who says they have?" she countered. When he turned and regarded her with a questioning stare, she added, "She is not the only one. There are dozens on that list." *Including me*, she almost added. Farringdon wouldn't really consider her, though. She was practically on the shelf.

"Are you still on that list?" he asked, his gloved hands rubbing the tops of his knees.

Helen blinked. "I am."

He glanced over as if he was surprised to hear it. "Oh."

She straightened in the squabs. "Why did you say it like that?"

Obviously uncomfortable, Tom dipped his head. "I've been away from England for some time. I realize I cannot expect... *situations...* to remain unchanged," he stammered.

Helen furrowed her brows. "Situations?" she repeated.

He nodded.

Suddenly understanding he was referring to her, she blinked several times. "Well, I certainly haven't been kissed by anyone since... since I last saw you in London," she stated.

Tom's eyes rounded. "You haven't?"

"I haven't," she insisted. "And since I am *here*, I am missing this Season, but..." She sighed. "I don't mind, really. Thomas, I wouldn't trade this opportunity to see the world..." She waved to the up-close scene of the Bent Pyramid to their right. "For all the entertainments London has to offer."

Before he had a chance to respond, the hantour suddenly came to a halt and Omar's voice sounded from somewhere to their right, his words describing the dark pyramid.

When the carriage resumed its trek to Dashur and their ship, the two sat in uncomfortable silence until they were nearly to the dock.

"I agree," Tom stated suddenly.

"Agree... with what?" she asked in confusion.

"I wouldn't trade this Grand Tour for a Season in London. For... *three* Seasons," he corrected himself, as if he just then realized he would have been away from England for that long by the time they returned to British shores. He chuckled as the hantour came to a halt. "But then, I've never attended one, so I'm not really sure what I'm missing."

Helen narrowed her eyes and allowed him to help her down. Before she had a chance to shake out her skirts, Bradley came running up, his arms outstretched.

"Oh, dear, you're awake," she said on a sigh. When she glanced over at Tom, she saw his expression change to what appeared to be one of disgust, and she blinked. "Thank you for riding with me," she said, wondering at the sudden change in his demeanor. She lifted Bradley and settled him on her hip, wincing when she saw how much of the reddish dust had been ground into his white gown.

"You're welcome," he said curtly, giving her a slight bow before turning toward the *dhahabîyeh*.

He didn't offer his arm before making his way on board.

Sighing in resignation, Helen waited until he had disappeared down the central corridor before boarding.

CHAPTER 20
A CONVERSATION ABOUT A BROTHER

*E*arlier, in another hantour

By the time she was seated, Diana couldn't see whether Tom had joined Helen in her hantour or not.

"What is it?" Randy asked, leaning forward in an attempt to discover the subject of her curiosity.

"*Who* is the more appropriate question," she replied.

He removed his top hat and raked a hand over his sweat-dampened head. "All right. I'll play along. Who?"

"Your brother."

Randy stiffened. "What about him?"

"Is he in love with Lady Helen?"

The carriage suddenly jerked into motion, the Arabian following the line of other hantours as they headed south for the short trip past the Bent Pyramid.

"Not that I'm aware," he answered carefully. "Whatever gave you that idea?"

Diana winced. "Has he ever made mention of Lady Helen?"

Randy shook his head. "Not directly."

"What's that supposed to mean?"

He sighed. "He doesn't seem particularly happy about her

being with a babe is all," he commented. "Now that you bring it up, I do wonder if he wishes some of her attentions were on him instead of Master Bradley." He paused before he asked, "Why did you ask?"

Moving closer on the bench so their thighs touched, Diana lowered her voice to a whisper, as if she feared the driver might overhear her. "Did you know Tom kissed Lady Helen at Morganfield's ball? The night before you left London?"

Randy blinked twice. He straightened on the bench and directed his gaze straight ahead. The town of Dashur and the Nile beyond was already visible on the horizon. "Damnation," he muttered. "He never said a *word*," he added, turning to regard her with surprise. "The cur. He used to tell me everything."

Diana gripped Randy's hand in hers. "Have you formed an opinion of Lady Helen?"

He shrugged. "She seems a fine young lady. Good breeding—"

"Even though she's part Greek?"

He once again frowned. "Her grandmother was a duchess," he commented, as if her ancestry didn't matter.

"Is. She's still alive," Diana corrected him.

"Rather gorgeous, too, from what I remember, although I was just a boy when I last saw her," he added, acknowledging her comment with a nod. "More than a decade ago. Westhaven was still alive, and they were at a garden party," he explained, referring to Alexander, Duke of Westhaven. "Did you ever meet him?"

Diana nodded. "Of course. He and my father share the same avocation," she reminded him.

The hantour halted suddenly, and Omar's voice sounded from somewhere up ahead. "To your right, we have the Bent Pyramid. Built in twenty-five-sixty BC, its interior consists of two chambers. The burial chamber includes a sarcophagus, and there is a smaller chamber with three niches where statues once resided." He appeared in their line of sight when he moved closer to the pyramid. "Much like what happened to other pyramids, the outer casing limestone was removed by treasure hunters. We go now to Dashur where your ship awaits," he said. After a moment, the hantour once again jerked into motion as the driver touched the Arabian's back with his crop.

"Well, as for Everly, he seems rather clever. He's a member of the Royal Society," Randy said, picking up their conversation where they had left off.

"And the son? Alexander?" she prompted.

"Have you ever *seen* him?" he countered.

She lifted a shoulder. "Once or twice."

"And you didn't swoon from paying witness to his excessive handsomeness?"

Diana blinked before she broke out into a fit of giggles. "Oh, dear, I did not," she claimed. "But it sounds as if you did?" she teased.

He made a sound of protest. "I met him at school. Trust me when I say that with his looks, he could have gotten away with behaving as an arse, but he never did." Dipping his head, he said, "I will admit I am relieved he is happily wed. I shouldn't want you considering a tumble with him."

Diana scoffed in disbelief. "Randall Forster," she scolded, although she was grinning in delight. She leaned over and kissed his cheek. "So... Lady Helen passes all the tests for consideration as a potential wife?" she asked.

It was Randy's turn to blink. "Of course." He suddenly stiffened. "You're thinking Lady Helen and Tom. Together?" There was a bit of disbelief in the query, although no indication he found fault with the idea.

"Married, yes," she acknowledged.

Randy settled back into the squabs and let out a chuckle. "He doesn't stand a chance, does he?" he asked rhetorically.

Diana's good mood sobered. "Actually, he hasn't shown Helen the slightest bit of interest this entire trip," she said on a sigh.

"Actually..." Here Randy stopped and chewed his bottom lip. "I think he has, but I've been misinterpreting his attentions." His gaze seemed set on something in his mind's eye.

"What do you mean?"

"I've seen him watching her," he admitted. "When she's been holding the baby. I know he wants children. Eventually. We've talked about how many we might have," he said, lifting a shoulder.

Diana's eyes widened, but she decided now was not the time to learn on how many he wanted. "And?" she prompted.

"Well, now I think he's merely jealous of Bradley, which has me wondering who the father is. Did he stay behind in London, or is she widowed? Or..." His face displayed a grimace. "Did someone ruin her?"

Diana covered her mouth with a hand, glad to learn she wasn't the only one who didn't know the truth about the babe. "Lord Everly is Bradley's father," she stated.

Randy sat up straight and stared at his wife for several seconds before she added, "Bradley is Helen's little brother. Everly's spare heir."

"That *dog*," Randy said in awe.

Wincing, Diana waited for him to clarify.

"He's old enough to be that boy's grandfather, which is part of why I thought he was Lady Helen's son."

"So you thought that, too?" Diana asked in a quiet voice. "Now I don't feel so foolish. She's such a good mother to him."

"Exactly. Which means she would make an excellent mother for her own babes," Randy murmured.

The hantour turned as they approached the river, and

Diana glanced out to see that theirs was one of the last to arrive at the dock. She wasn't surprised to see *The Dendera* already moored and Captain Mahmood stepping off the ship to greet his passengers.

"Don't tell him," Diana stated.

"What?"

"Don't tell Tom about the babe being Helen's brother."

Randy frowned. "Why ever not? He's probably as confused as we were."

"Yes, and let's leave it like that," she said at the same time the hantour came to a halt.

Randy didn't make a move to exit the equipage, his attention still on his wife. "What's going on in that gorgeous head of yours?" he asked.

Diana arched a brow. "If he does have feelings for her, then the babe shouldn't make a difference."

He considered the comment a moment. "True," he finally said. "Unless he believes the father is alive and back in London. Or... or that she was ruined and left with child," he said, his eyes filled with concern.

"Which would have had to have happened *before* Tom kissed her at the Morganfield's ball."

Randy gave the comment some thought before he said, "Huh." When he noticed the driver glancing back at them, he realized they needed to depart the hantour. He fished a coin from his pocket and handed it to the man.

"*Shukran*," Diana said, following Randy out of the carriage.

The driver waved.

When they were free of the hantour and on their way to the ship, Diana entwined her arm with Randy's. She glanced up at him. "So... will you say anything to Tom?"

Randy briefly chewed his lower lip. "Not directly," he replied. He chuckled when he saw her crestfallen expression.

"But fear not, I believe I have some skills when it comes to matchmaking," he claimed.

Diana blinked but allowed a grin. "Should I be worried for your brother?"

"I'm more worried for Lady Helen," he said in a quiet voice. "Are you *sure* you want her stuck with my brother?"

"Shouldn't I?" she asked in alarm.

He shook his head. "He deserves a good wife as much as anyone," he replied. "But if he can't abide her attentions toward a babe, I'm not sure he deserves her."

Diana slapped his arm as she laughed. "Some day I'm going tell him what you said."

"Some day I'm going to tell *her* what I said," he replied.

CHAPTER 21
CATARACTS IN THE RIVER
CAUSE A KERFUFFLE

*L*ater *that night*

Once the dishes had been cleared and the ladies had departed for the parlor, the gentlemen remained seated around the dining table.

"The wind seems to be in our favor," Will said, his gaze directed on the bank of the river. Although the sun had set hours earlier, a nearly full moon provided enough light to illuminate the western shore of the Nile. The passing landscape featured a number of triangular silhouettes, natural conical mountains made from ancient volcanic activity. At night, they appeared as if they were pyramids.

"Mahmood mentioned the usual time to Luxor is about a fortnight," Harry commented. "Even going upstream as we are."

"Are there any stops along the way?" Tom asked.

Will nodded. "Nasir—he's one of the crewmen—said we'll stop at a couple of villages where we'll take on supplies. There is also another stop which features two temples."

"Dendera," David remarked with excitement. "I'm most anxious to see the Temple of Isis. It's on the roof of another temple. I've been reading about it in volume four of *La Descrip-tion de l'Égypte*," he added, referring to one of the books he had purchased upon their arrival in Alexandria.

"What about the Temple of Hathor?" Tom countered. "Isn't that the one with the zodiac on the ceiling of a temple?"

"Not any longer," Randy said, frowning. "Diana was quite distressed to learn that a thief used explosives to remove it about twenty years ago."

"He stole the ceiling from a temple?" Tom asked in disbelief.

"Yes, and he sold it to the king of France for a hundred-and-fifty-thousand francs," Randy explained, his disgust evident. "At least it's on public display in Paris, but..." He shrugged as he sighed his disappointment.

David sounded a low whistle. "Damn," he muttered. "I suppose that means we'll have to stop in Paris on the way home if we wish to see it."

Harry and Will exchanged glances of amusement. "The British Museum is not without its share of Egyptian artifacts," Harry commented. "Including the Rosetta Stone. Have you seen it?"

David nodded. "Of course. I have a set of prints of all three sections of it," he claimed. "I've been studying the Greek versus the Egyptian hieroglyphics in an attempt to sort their meaning. So far, all I have learned for certain is that the hieroglyphics surrounded by an oval are the name of a pharaoh—"

"A cartouche," Randy clarified.

"—long triangular shapes are knives, and wiggly snakes are either a depiction of evil or the enemy. The rest..." He lifted a shoulder. "I have some time to study it more thoroughly before we reach any temples."

Randy dipped his head, deciding it best he not mention that Diana had already memorized the translations on the stone. As to whether or not she had devised the meaning of the hieroglyphics, he didn't yet know.

A few days later
Having finished their afternoon play near the stern of *The Dendera*, Helen regarded her younger brother with a grin. "I do hope if I ever have a boy, he'll be just like you," she murmured.

The young crewman manning the rudder—a boy of probably only ten years of age—watched them, amusement and perhaps a hint of jealousy apparent on his face.

Bradley babbled incoherently, his attention suddenly captured by a bird that flew overhead. "Bird," he said.

Helen's eyes widened in surprise. "Bird, yes," she said, watching as the Steppe eagle circled before flying off to the north. "Let's go tell Father you've learned a new word." She rose from the deck, happy her wide skirts hid what her legs had to do in order for her to stand from a sitting position.

She leaned forward and lifted Bradley into her arms when a shout sounded from somewhere near the front of the ship. Glancing toward the stern with a look of concern, she noted how the young crewman's eyes widened before he scrambled to his feet and leaned hard against the control for the rudder. The vessel suddenly veered sharply. She struggled to keep her balance, but with Bradley settled on one hip, she couldn't counteract the motion, and the sense of falling had her emitting a shout of "oh!"

On his way toward the stern by way of the thin corridor that ran through the center of the ship, Tom had just emerged into the sunlight when he heard the captain yell and felt the deck shift hard beneath his feet.

Off to his right, he caught sight of Helen and managed to move close enough so she landed in his outstretched arms as she fell. Her hold on the babe never lessened, though, and Bradley was saved from falling onto the wooden deck.

A slight scraping noise along the outer hull and another sudden shift beneath his feet had Tom struggling to lift her until she was standing. He tightened his hold on her as more shouts could be heard by the other crewmen.

Her eyes wide, she glanced up at him and then at Bradley, whose huge grin was entirely at odds with what was happening.

"Are you... are you all right?" he asked in alarm.

She nodded, although her mouth still formed an 'o' from her momentary disorientation. "I was sure I was about to land on the deck," she replied.

Instead, she was in Thomas Forster's arms, much as she had been the night he had kissed her in the gardens during the Morganfield ball. He was even staring at her in a similar fashion, as if he was memorizing every feature of her face and her eyes.

She couldn't help but do the same to him, her gaze sweeping the planes of his face, where shadows emphasized his cheekbones and the hint of a beard. His brows were furrowed with worry, and for the first time, she realized there were dark gray rims around the gray-green irises of his eyes.

How hadn't she noticed those when she had first met him in the Morganfield's ballroom?

She had certainly noticed the shape of his lips, though, the firm pillows emphasized by the arch of his lower lip and the two pointed hills that formed his upper lip. She thought to use a fingertip to trace their outline, and then wondered if he would pull it into his mouth to kiss and suckle it, or if he would simply pull it away so his lips could meet hers in a kiss. A kiss of reunion. A kiss of possession. A scorching kiss that would leave her walking on air, because at the moment she was sure she would be unable to do so of her own accord.

Although she would have welcomed a repeat of the act of intimacy they had shared in the gardens, she also knew it would be entirely inappropriate given what was happening to the ship, for the deck seemed to jerk beneath her feet once more.

Tom's hold on her was solid though, which had her pressed so close to the front of his body, she could feel his warmth, the solidity of his chest, the smell of the scent of his cologne, the wash of his breath across her cheek.

She really should be more concerned about what had caused her to nearly fall down, but not now. Not when she was nearly hypnotized by his gaze.

Until he suddenly glanced away. Although Tom continued to hold onto her, his attention went to the crewman who manned the rudder. Slight of build and short—more due to his age than anything else—the boy's eyes were wide with fright. He shouted something in Arabic, and another one of the crew, Nasir, soon joined him.

"What's happening?" Tom asked when the ship once again shifted suddenly. He managed to keep his feet and to move them so Helen was close enough to the nearby wall so her back was pressed against it.

"Cataracts," Nasir replied, his upper body leaning out over the deck rail so he appeared about to go overboard. "Boulders... islands in the water." He motioned to the boy, and the ship once again shifted when he turned the rudder, this time with less effect.

Will appeared from the corridor, his look of worry and breathlessness a sign he had rushed from where he had been reading in the parlor. "Did you lose the rudder?" he asked in alarm. With his attention entirely on the two members of the crew, he didn't seem to notice Tom and Helen even though they were only a few feet away.

"No, my lord."

"What did we hit?" He joined the crewman at the starboard railing, his gaze directed along the bit of hull that was visible above the waterline.

"Cataracts," Nasir repeated. "Last one coming up," he added, waving for the boy at the rudder to turn it, and the ship once again shifted, this time only slightly.

When Tom returned his attention to Helen, he discovered her staring up at him with an unreadable expression. Meanwhile, Bradley was beaming at him in delight, a bare foot and pudgy knee pressed into his midsection. A dimple at the base of one cheek made the babe appear almost comical, and Tom couldn't help the chuckle that erupted. "You are obviously unaware of how close you came to being dumped on your little bum, young man," he remarked.

A peel of laughter sounded out of Bradley, and the babe said, "Dada dada dada," as he waved his fisted hands about and bounced up and down on Helen's hip.

Tom blinked. He released his hold on Helen and quickly stepped backwards, his face heating with embarrassment. "Uh..."

Helen tore her gaze from Tom and glanced at Bradley before she said, "Thank you, sir." She dipped a curtsy. "Your timing was perfect. To keep me from falling on *my* bum," she added sheepishly.

Bowing his head, Tom screwed his face into a wince. "I... I... would not have let that happen, my lady," he stammered. "If you'll excuse me?" He took another step back, bowed deeper, and disappeared into the corridor.

Disappointed by his sudden departure, Helen leaned her back against the cabin wall and audibly sighed. He had held her for so long, as if he thought she might collapse should he let go. At no point did she wonder at his motives, nor feel as if he was taking advantage. If anything, he seemed as shocked as she had been by the sudden shift of the deck beneath their feet.

Of the scraping sound on the hull.

If not for Bradley making his presence known with his babbling, Tom might still be with her. Holding her. Mayhap even stealing a kiss.

"Children are to be seen and not heard," she said on a sigh, surprised by the annoyance she felt for her little brother. When she glanced down, she noted his good mood had been replaced with one that seemed to match hers. He was staring at her with furrowed brows, the expression completely out of place on one so young.

He made a sound of protest, a fist impacting her shoulder as he said, "No."

Helen gave a start, ready to scold the babe for his behavior. His expression was so comical, though, she found she couldn't keep a straight face. "Had to go and ruin the moment, didn't you?" she whispered. "*Brothers*," she added with disgust.

"Were you injured?"

Helen gave a start. The Earl of Bellingham was regarding her with a look of worry. "Oh, I'm quite fine, my lord. Your nephew was quick on his feet," she replied. "Saved me and Bradley from falling."

Will's reaction indicated his surprise. "I'm glad to hear it," he replied, his gaze darting to the corridor to see that Tom was already in front of his cabin door, about to go inside.

"What happened to have the ship shifting about so suddenly?" she asked. "And what was that awful sound?"

Returning his attention to Helen, Will sighed. "Seems we had to avoid some boulders in the water," he replied. "Nasir is going to check the hull when we stop at Benin Hasan for supplies. Make sure there isn't any damage."

"Is there some danger of us sinking?" she asked with worry.

His attention having gone to Bradley—the boy was once again grinning—Will shook his head. "Doubtful. These are well-built ships," he said, chucking Bradley on the chin with a forefinger. The babe giggled and coo'd. "They ride high on the water, so they're usually perfect on a river," he added, his expression changing when he returned his attention to her. "But apparently there are some stretches along this river where there are islands and rocks to avoid."

"Dada dada dada," Bradley said happily, grabbing Will's forefinger.

He chuckled in delight. "You have me confused with someone else," he said before he carefully extracted his finger. "If you'll pardon me, Lady Helen, I'm going up to the bow to speak with the captain."

"Of course, my lord. Thank you for alleviating my concerns," she replied. She curtsied to his bow and watched him disappear into the corridor. When she glanced around, she discovered she was once again alone but for her baby brother and the boy at the rudder. His attention wasn't on her, but rather on the stretch of river behind them. Bradley, however, was watching her intently.

"You really must learn how to address men who are not your father," she said on a sigh.

"Mama mama mama," Bradley replied.

Helen rolled her eyes. "Sister," she corrected him.

"Bird," he countered, one pudgy finger directed upward.

Her gaze going to the sky, she watched as an egret circled overhead. "Bird," she repeated softly.

A moment later, and she, too, made her way into the corridor and to her cabin, passing the earl when he paused in front of another cabin door.

The entire way, Bradley said, "Mama mama mama."

CHAPTER 22
TALK ABOUT A YOUNG WOMAN

*M*eanwhile

Watching from his barely-opened cabin doorway as Helen made her way to the parlor near the front of the ship, Tom huffed a breath of disappointment. The babe, still perched on her hip, was now saying, "Mama mama mama," his words directed at Helen. He carefully closed the door the rest of the way and banged his forehead against the polished wood surface.

He was about to do it again when he realized he wasn't alone. Whirling around, he discovered David regarding him with a lifted brow.

"I was set to ask you what all the excitement was about out there, but now I'm wondering who it is you're spying on?" David said, the book he had been reading landing on his lap as he straightened on his bed.

"I wasn't spying," Tom replied on a sigh. "Merely... watching to be sure someone was all right. We had a bit of a fright out there near the stern."

"Felt as if we collided with something," David remarked.

Scoffing, Tom headed to his own bed and sat on the edge of

it, his elbows resting on his knees. "Cataracts," he said. "Uncle Will is back there with Nasir," he added, waving in the direction of the stern. "I think the boy who handles the rudder wasn't paying attention, or perhaps the captain didn't warn him soon enough when he spotted the obstacles in the water." He chuckled softly. "The rudder on his ship is certainly responsive, though."

"I'm surprised the women weren't screaming," David said, swinging his legs over the edge of his bed. He mirrored Tom's pose and regarded his older cousin with a look of expectation.

"What?" Tom asked.

"Who were you watching to be sure they were all right?"

Tom closed his eyes and sighed. "Uh, Lady Helen. She was carrying Master Bradley when the ship shifted. I thought she might... might have been injured, is all."

"Was she?" David asked, obviously suspicious.

"No. She's fine."

David continued to stare at his cousin. "So... no chance she fell into your arms?" he asked with an arched brow.

Tom gave a start. "How did...?" He narrowed his eyes.

Barely able to contain his glee, David said, "I *knew* it. You are in love with her."

"I am not."

"Did you kiss her once you had her back on her feet?"

"No!"

"Liar."

"I couldn't kiss her. She was holding the babe," Tom claimed.

"But you wanted to," David accused.

Tom was about to say, "Yes," but clamped his mouth shut. "She's..." Here he stopped and swallowed.

"She's what?"

"Well, married, probably, given she has a babe."

David made a sound of disbelief. "We wouldn't be addressing her as 'Lady Helen' if that was the case," he argued.

The grimace Tom displayed was a mix of anger and pain. "No, we wouldn't," he agreed. Even if she was a widow, they would be addressing her by her married name.

David furrowed his brow, about to put voice to what he knew about Master Bradley when there was a knock at the door. "Come," he called out.

The door opened and his father appeared on the threshold. "Everything all right in here?" Will asked, his gaze darting between the two young men.

Shrugging, David said, "Yes. But what was all the commotion about out there? I heard shouting."

"There were some cataracts we had to go around," Will replied. "Although the captain has some directional control with the sails, his ship relies on the rudder for quicker turns." He turned his attention to Tom. "May I have a word with you?"

Tom swallowed and slowly stood. He directed a glance of worry at David before following his uncle out the door and to the stern. When Will indicated one of the metal chairs, he sat down and asked, "What's this about?"

Will settled into an adjacent chair. "You tell me."

His eyes widening in alarm, Tom opened his mouth to claim innocence but finally sighed. "If you're referring to finding me with my arms around Lady Helen—"

"I am."

Tom dipped his head, surprised that in all the excitement, Will had even noticed them. "I was merely helping to keep her on her feet. She... stumbled when the ship shifted, and she was carrying the babe and..." He shrugged as if defeated. "I didn't want her to fall, sir."

"Good," Will replied.

Blinking, Tom stared at his uncle. "Good?" he repeated.

Will shrugged. "You saved her from falling. Saved the babe from injury," he stated.

"I suppose I did," Tom agreed, although he didn't show any emotion at the admission.

"So... why didn't you escort her to her cabin? You left rather abruptly."

Tom tugged on his ear. "I... I didn't wish to... compromise her, sir."

Will sighed and settled back in the chair as he crossed his arms over his chest. "You like her," he stated.

Suspicious of his uncle's motives, Tom furrowed his brows. "I suppose. I mean... I don't *dislike* her."

Arching a brow, Will sighed again. "I know I told you boys to be on your best behavior on this trip—"

"I have been, sir."

"—but that doesn't mean you have to *avoid* her."

"It's rather hard given the tight quarters," Tom countered.

"You can talk to her."

"I tried, but that babe..." He displayed a grimace.

Will angled his head to one side. "What about the babe?"

"He's always about," Tom complained.

Will blinked. "You sound as if you're jealous of him."

Tom knew his face was reddening with embarrassment. "I'm not."

"Hmph. Well, I was on my way to speak with the captain when I stopped at your cabin," Will said, not adding that Helen had passed him in the corridor. The memory of hearing Master Bradley's 'mama, mama, mama' nearly had him grinning. The boy certainly knew what to say when he wanted his mother. "I'm going there now," he said, rising from his chair. "Just... be friendly with her."

Tom inhaled to respond but closed his mouth and watched as his uncle disappeared down the corridor.

"Friendly?" he had almost repeated. How could he pretend

friendship when he wanted nothing more than to take her into his arms again? Feel the warmth of her body as it pressed against the front of his. Capture her lips with his and kiss her until he had to take a breath. Slide his hands across her back, along her sides. Mold his hands over her breasts. Undress her and kiss every inch of her soft skin before claiming her as his own.

The thought of sexual congress with Helen Tennison had his cock reacting, and he shifted uncomfortably in the chair.

Just knowing she was sleeping in a cabin directly across from his had him groaning.

This trip up the Nile was going to be the death of him.

CHAPTER 23
AN INCIDENT AT DENDERA

A *week later, near Dendera, West Bank of the Nile*

"I could grow used to this sort of living," Randy said, as he watched Mahmood dock *The Dendera* at the port near the ship's namesake village. Another of the crew had already set out to arrange transportation to take them to the nearby temples.

"Oh, dear. Does this mean you won't want to go back to living in Oxfordshire?" Diana asked, her arms crossed as she watched the crew tie the ropes up on the dock.

"I said I could grow used to it, not that I would wish to do it," he replied. "I fear I'm growing fat. All this food and no exercise."

Diana arched a brow.

"Well, only some exercise," he amended, immediately understanding the meaning of her gesture. "The very best kind. It's my favorite time of the day," he whispered.

Her cheeks pinking with his words, she dipped her head. "Mine as well."

Randy puffed out his chest. "I am glad to hear I'm favored over your study of ancient temples and artifacts."

"I didn't say that," she teased.

He pounded his chest with a fist and feigned offense before he regarded her mode of dress, not surprised she had donned her breeches, white shirt, and boots. She and David had spent the night before strategizing over how they would explore the temples at Dendera.

Not having read the volume of *La Description de l'Egypte* which included the findings at Dendera as they had been doing, Randy didn't feel the least bit left out. He had listened intently, though, determined to learn what he could.

He feared they would be disappointed. Due to shifting sands, it was possible the temples—or at least their entrances—would be mostly buried in the desert. Remembering Diana carried a small shovel in her satchel, he supposed he could offer to help dig their way in if that were the case.

When he lifted the bag to carry it up on the deck, he found it far heavier than usual. "What have you stuffed into this?" he asked. "It must weigh almost as much as you do."

She blinked.

"I didn't mean it like that," he quickly amended. "It's just heavier than usual." He pulled the strap on over his head and shoulder so it rested against the opposite hip.

"Flasks of water and a couple of torches," she replied. "Unlike most temples I've been in, this one still has its roof. We'll need light once we're inside."

Nodding his understanding, Randy waited until Diana had stepped onto the dock before he followed.

*M*ahmood led the way toward the village of Dendera, shouting orders in Arabic to his crew while he was still within earshot. Behind him, his passengers paired up, the men offering their arms to the ladies. Flasks of water were either stowed in reticules or hung about their necks.

When it was apparent Bradley would be staying behind with the captain's daughter, Tom paused until Helen was abreast of him and held out his arm to her.

"Good morning, my lady," he said.

Although she was tempted to rebuff his offer—she was still smarting over what had happened on the back deck the week before—Helen placed her hand on his arm and said, "Good morning, Mr. Forster," rather glad when she caught him wincing at the use of his formal name. She was about to say something about the fair weather, but their guide began speaking.

"Dendera, which has also been called Tentyra, is home to several temples," Mahmood said as he adopted a leisurely pace, the bottom of his robe flapping in the breeze. "The largest was dedicated to Hathor, the goddess of motherhood, birth, and rebirth. She was also known for celebration and joy and the renewal of the cosmos," he explained, lifting his arms and spreading his hands to indicate the heavens. "Music, dance, beauty, and love," he added.

"It seems fitting a goddess would be in charge of so much," Tom murmured, his comment meant for Helen.

She huffed softly. "Yes, we women usually are."

He seemed about to agree with her, but his mouth clamped shut when Mahmood continued talking, the captain cum dragoman unaware of the conversation behind him. "Hathor is easy to identify in the carvings and paintings you will see on the walls of the temple, for she has the head of a cow or the horns of a cow," he explained, using his fingers on either side of his head to illustrate his point. "Not much is left of the other temple, one dedicated to Isis. She is the goddess known for her power and magic. She was the mother of Horus and a wife and a sister to Osiris, as well as a healer."

"A wife *and* a sister?" Tom repeated under his breath.

"The women really did have to do everything," Helen whispered.

Ahead of them, a line of hantours approached. "Ah, our carriages are here," he said, grinning broadly. "I will tell you more when we are at the temple."

"How far is it?" David asked, a hand held to his brow as he surveyed the southeastern horizon.

"About two miles," Mahmood replied. "It will not take long with these horses, though," he added, indicating the dark brown Arabians. "However, there are only four hantours for our party of ten," he warned.

"I'll ride with you two," David said, his attention on Tom and Helen.

The other three couples stepped into the buggies while Mahmood sat next to one of the drivers on the front bench. A moment later, and they were racing off across the desert.

Tucked between David and Tom in a hantour, Helen was glad she had elected to wear a smaller bonnet and bring along a parasol. There would not have been room for her wide-brimmed hat given the tight quarters of the carriage.

"What are you most looking forward to seeing today?" she asked, her query directed to David.

"Everything," David replied. "Especially if we can go inside. Carvings. Paintings. Columns. Diana packed her sketchpad and paints in her satchel and intends to document as much as she can while we're in there."

"From what I've read, it sounds as if this temple is one of the best preserved of all that have been discovered," Tom offered.

"Why wouldn't we be able to get inside?" Helen asked in alarm.

"The entrance might be blocked by sand," he replied.

"Oh," she said on a sigh of disappointment.

"I rather doubt Diana will allow that to deter her, though," David remarked. "She probably has a shovel in that satchel of hers."

"What about a lantern? Won't it be dark inside?" Tom asked. He hadn't noticed Mahmood carrying a lantern as they made their way toward the village.

Helen huffed. "If you dare say Diana has one of *those* in her satchel—"

"Torches," David stated. "She... has a couple of torches and a tinderbox to light them."

"In her *satchel*?" Helen asked in disbelief.

David nodded. "And a couple of flasks of water. I saw her packing it last night. She's been anxious to study this temple for the past week."

When Helen didn't say anything in reply, Tom asked, "What's wrong?"

She lifted her reticule from her lap, a difficult maneuver given how crowded they were in the hantour. "My father is always amazed at how much women can stuff into our reticules, but I do believe Diana's satchel has mine beat," she commented.

Tom chuckled, reaching over to heft her embroidered fabric bag in a gloved hand. The drawstring closure was made of a loop of ribbon that when pulled tight caused the top to close into a series of gathers. "It's far heavier than I would have thought," he remarked.

"That's intentional," Helen replied.

"Intentional?" Tom repeated.

"Should I ever be accosted by a footpad or an unwanted suitor, I will use it to beat him off," she claimed with not the least bit of humor.

Although David barked a laugh at hearing her response, Tom sobered. "I do hope you have never considered using it on me," he whispered.

Helen inhaled softly. "I have not, nor would..."

The hantour suddenly swerved and the Arabian let out a whinny of protest as he came to a stuttering halt and attempted to rear up. A shout from the driver sounded before the buggy tilted dangerously to one side and he disappeared from the driver's seat.

"Hang on," Tom shouted, his arms going around Helen as the hantour fell all the way over onto its right side, Tom ending up closest to the ground. The harness on one side snapped, leaving the horse still attached and off-kilter. His whinnied complaints accompanied those of the driver, who had been forced to step off the bench as the equipage tipped over. His continued shouts sounded from somewhere out of their view.

Atop the other two in the buggy, David hung on to the back of the seat with one hand whilst bracing himself using the other on the top edge the driver's seat, the momentum of the equipage's fall forcing him to seek purchase with a boot near the bottom of the driver's bench. He was able to finally extricate himself from the carriage, stumbling as he did so, and he stepped on a booted leg in the process.

"Ouch," Tom mouthed. Still in the squabs but lying on his side, his arms remained wrapped around Helen's waist and shoulder. She ended up halfway atop and in front of him, her eyes wide with fright.

"Can you move your hand?" he asked in a strangled voice.

She quickly repositioned her gloved hand from where it had landed near the top of his thigh, her murmured apology sounding in a whisper.

"Are you injured? Are you able to move?"

Helen furrowed a brow, sure she hadn't seen Tom's mouth form the query. "I think so." Then she realized it was David who had asked the questions. "Are you all right?" she asked, directing her query to Tom.

He nodded. "David stepped on my leg is all," he said. "And you? Are you hurt?"

"I... I don't think so, but you'll have to let go of me," she whispered.

Unaware of how tightly he held her, Tom released his hold. "Apologies," he murmured.

A number of voices from outside made it apparent at least one other hantour had turned around and made its way back to join them. Now instead of a single horse's whinnying, there was another sounding its complaint.

David gripped her around the waist and pulled out of the hantour. When she was finally free of it, her skirts settled around where she was left seated on the ground.

Then she stared at what was causing the horses to rear and whinny.

A snake slithered sideways atop the sand, its scales gleaming in the morning sun.

Without thinking, she gripped her reticule by the drawstring ribbon and slammed it down on the creature, over and over until the loud *pop* of a gunshot sounded.

She reared back, a cry of fright sounding before she scrambled backwards.

In front of her, the snake no longer had a head, and the rest of its body stilled its movements.

She heard a lady's scream and a man's shout before strong hands pulled her away from the carnage, her hand still holding onto her reticule. When she turned around, she was once again in Tom's arms. He had managed to climb out of the equipage after David had pulled her out, and he had paid witness to what she had done to the snake.

"Are you all right?" Tom asked, his eyes wide with fright.

"What *was* that?" she asked, attempting to turn her head but unable to do so given how he held her.

"A snake," he replied. "A viper of some sort."

"No. That... that *sound*."

Tom furrowed his brows. "A gunshot. Your father shot it," he explained, before Harry joined them, his manner frantic.

"Did it bite you?" he asked, his manner suggesting more than just fatherly concern. Stella appeared at his side, one of her hands in front of her open mouth as her eyes widened in shock.

Helen shook her head. "I don't... I don't think so," she replied. "Mother, I am fine," she added.

"It would have hurt," her father said. "A sharp pain." He lifted the arm that still held onto the reticule, pushing up her sleeve to examine her skin for puncture marks.

"No, Father. I am fine. Truly," she insisted, rather glad Tom still held her, for her legs suddenly felt rubbery. "My gown is..." She used a hand to brush away some of the dust from the skirt, pulling it out to see that the fabric hadn't torn. "Surprisingly undamaged."

Stella already had a hanky out and was brushing away the desert dust from the back of her gown. "As long as you're not damaged," she murmured.

Diana appeared on the other side of Helen. "Take a drink," she urged, holding a flask to her lips.

Helen did so, wincing at the metallic taste of the water. "Oh, that's awful," she said.

"Can you walk?" Diana asked.

Tom let go his hold on her, and Helen stood of her own accord. "I... I think so."

"So nothing broke or bent or twisted when you tipped over?" she went on, her attention going to the overturned hantour. Although the wheels appeared intact, the harness was ruined. The horse, long since released from the yoke, was being led away by the driver.

"What about you?" Diana asked, turning her attention to Tom.

He blinked, obviously surprised by her query. "I am fine. I'd be better if David hadn't tromped on me, though," he replied, holding out his leg to show the boot print left on the side of one of his Hobys.

"Apologies, Cousin," David said, pulling out a handkerchief. He leaned down and wiped off the dusty print.

"Much obliged," Tom said, realizing he still had a hand at the back of Helen's waist. "Oh, forgive me," he said, directing his words to Harry as he released his hold on her.

"I appreciate you seeing to her," Harry replied quietly. He moved to stand next to where the remains of the snake still lay in the sand. He bent and picked it up, making an odd sound in his throat. "Horned viper," he commented, arching a brow as he studied the markings.

Mahmood rushed up, quickly assessing what had happened. "Do you wish to keep it, my lord?"

Harry frowned. "Would one of the drivers like it for their dinner?" he asked.

Nodding, Mahmood reached out and took the snake from him. He passed it off to one of the drivers, who seemed especially pleased and bowed several times to Harry before returning to his hantour.

With the other two hantours having returned so their occupants could discover what had happened, Will conferred with Mahmood.

"If everyone is all right, we can still go on, can we not? Three to a hantour?" Will asked.

Mahmood nodded and yelled out instructions to the other drivers. The one holding onto the Arabian mounted it and rode bareback in the direction of the village. Meanwhile, the men lined up and lifted the overturned hantour back onto its wheels, experimentally pushing it to ensure the axels were still working.

"He will return with another harness and a different horse,"

Mahmood explained to Will. "By the time we are done at the temples, there will once again be four hantours for our use."

"I appreciate it," Will replied. He directed the others to return to their carriages and finally joined Barbara in theirs. David sat next to the driver while Helen joined her parents. Tom ended up in a hantour with Diana and Randy.

"How is she?" Randy asked.

"I think the gunshot was more upsetting for her than the snake," Tom replied. He chuckled softly. "I should never wish to be the target of her ire. She is wicked with that reticule," he added.

"Best you remember that," Randy warned, arching a teasing brow.

Diana failed to hide a smirk as the hantour jerked into motion.

A few minutes later, the Temple of Hathor came into view.

CHAPTER 24
A TOUR OF THE TEMPLE OF HATHOR

few minutes later
"There it is," Diana said, her gaze directed at the flat roofline of a structure that was slowly coming into view from behind a massive mud brick wall.

Framed with the angled pylons common to other Egyptian temples, the Temple of Hathor featured a figure-carved fascia atop six columns. Six stone panels, also carved, ran across the front of the columns, although several were mostly hidden by a sand dune. Two rectangular pillars framed the opening.

To the north, a gateway made up of two sandstone pillars topped with a broken lintel jutted from the sand, its surface etched with hieroglyphics.

"The capitals look odd," Tom remarked, referring to the tops of the columns on the front of the temple. "Rather an unusual shape."

"Those are supposed to be Hathor, but her face has been etched away," Diana explained. "The protrusions on either side of her face and in the front of her headdress are the cow ears," she added. To the untrained eye, the conical features might have been mistaken for an unusual hairstyle.

"By whom?" Randy asked.

"Christians. They attempted to erase any images of what they believed to be pagan gods," she explained. "And then they adopted the temple for their use."

"It obviously benefited from being buried in the sand," Randy commented as their driver directed the horse to pull their hantour into a line next to the one holding their aunt and uncle.

David had already stepped down from the driver's bench, hurrying to stand atop a slight sand dune. The hill obscured the lower portion of the right side of the front façade and appeared to block the entrance to the temple.

"The doorway is accessible," he called out. Given the height of the temple, he appeared rather small where he stood on a mound of sand.

Randy stepped down from the hantour, hoisting Diana's satchel over one shoulder before assisting her to the ground. He knew better than to offer his arm, for she was already practically running toward the temple, her hurried steps encumbered by the sand.

When Tom took off in pursuit, Randy chuckled and followed in their footsteps. "They seem to forget that *I* am the one carrying the bag with the torches," he said when he joined their guide.

"They will not need light for the front part of the temple," Mahmood remarked. He pointed at the façade. Hieroglyphic carvings were evident on the three left side panels that fronted the columns, their height not quite half the height of the entire temple. The columns continued up to support the front of the roof.

"Ah, I did not know if we would be able to go *inside* the temple," Mahmood replied. "When I was last here, the sand blocked most of the opening. Someone has been here and cleared it." His last words were quieter, as if he was talking to himself.

"Do you think someone else is in there now?" Randy asked, alarm sounding in his voice at the thought that Diana and David had already gone beyond the columns. Even as he asked the question, Tom had disappeared from view.

Mahmood shook his head. "If anyone else is here, they have been here for some time." He waved to the area around them, where the sand remained undisturbed and no other means of transport was visible. He turned and waited until a driver hurried up carrying several torches.

Randy's eyes widened at seeing the ragged-wrapped rush stalks. From the scent, he realized they had been soaked in some sort of animal fat. "But you knew there was a possibility we might encounter someone."

Mahmood shrugged. "I am not without a weapon, and I always pack a few rushlights in the box behind the driver," he replied, grinning.

Although it appeared dark beyond the rectangular entrance, light spilled in from around the richly decorated columns.

The voices of the others sounded hollow in the cavernous structure, the sandy stone floor amplifying their footsteps.

"We won't need the torches right away," Mahmood said. "The hypostyle is well-lit, but it is darker toward the back and in the crypts below."

"Crypts?" Randy repeated, removing his eye-glasses. He tucked them into a waistcoat pocket.

Mahmood nodded. "There are many. The passageways are very small, though. They are long and thin. Difficult for a man to explore."

Randy displayed a look of relief. Diana would insist on going down there to explore, though. "How does one go below?" he asked.

"There are stairs from trapdoors in the main temple floor. Near the walls," the guide replied. "There are stairs up to the roof, too." He indicated the torches. "We will light these when it becomes necessary." He waved for everyone to follow, and he entered the temple.

A round of 'ooh's and 'ah's sounded from their party as they surveyed the rows of round pillars filling the hypostyle. Their capitals were like those on the front of the temple, the heads of Hathor but with her features removed.

"Diana?" Randy called out.

"Here," she replied from somewhere to his right. He quickly joined her, understanding immediately what had her attention. The front wall as well as the two side walls were covered in carvings, some of the original paint still intact. She was slowly gazing at the front wall from left to right, as if memorizing it.

"The Romans were definitely here," she murmured.

"Oh?"

She pointed up to an area near the opening. "Latin," she said, pointing to a man's name etched in between the hieroglyphics. She dropped her finger down to where 'Leonardo 1820' was clearly carved into the limestone, and not far from it, in a flat area devoid of Egyptian carving, was a phrase in Greek. "It's a poem."

"That basically says 'I was here and saw all,'" Randy murmured.

His gaze swept up the wall to his left and then to the ceiling, which appeared black. He was about to mention it when Mahmood cleared his throat.

"We are in the hypostyle of the Temple of Hathor," he announced. "Built to honor and worship the goddess." He waved a hand to one of the pillars, a series of colorful carvings surrounding it all the way to the top. Most of the columns—twenty-four in total—were similarly carved and painted, the colors still vibrant, but a few appeared unfinished. Nearly all the capitals had been vandalized to remove Hathor's facial features. "You will not see as many carvings, reliefs or paintings in any of the other temples on your travels as you will see here in this one."

"Why would that be?" Will asked, his attention on one of the walls.

Mahmood lifted a shoulder. "It's as if the priests demanded everything of our history be recorded for posterity. Perhaps because they feared our history would be lost due to foreign rule."

"Foreign rule?" Harry repeated, turning from where he was studying one of the pillars.

"The later pharaohs were not Egyptian," the guide replied.

"The Ptolemaic dynasty," Diana murmured. "Which would explain why this temple is in such good condition."

"What's that, my sweet?" Randy asked.

"It's possible this temple was built only a couple of thousand years ago," she replied, her voice louder.

Barbara sounded a scoff. "Only?"

"Considering the pyramids we saw were *four*-thousand years old, then yes," Randy remarked.

"Oh, I see your point," his aunt replied thoughtfully.

"Let us go further into the temple," Mahmood suggested. "And to the snail—the staircase of light that leads to the roof."

Murmurs of curiosity followed his announcement, and everyone lined up behind the guide as he headed into the inner hypostyle, pausing between two columns. They weren't in very good condition. "This was probably the front of the temple in an earlier version," he announced, pointing to the columns on either side of him. From the worn appearance, it was evident the columns had been exposed to wind. "This temple may have been rebuilt or simply enlarged by later pharaohs." He turned and continued between two rows of three Hathor-topped columns.

Instead of heading into the offering hall, he turned right and then stepped through an opening in the wall on the left. He took a sharp right on the other side of the wall, where light appeared at the end of a corridor. The walls on either side were decorated in bas reliefs and looked as if they were covered in soot.

Ahead, a series of shallow stairs led up toward the source of light—a small window in the temple wall. The surface of the stairs looked as if something thick had been poured onto it and allowed to drip down.

"We know not why these stairs are this way," Mahmood remarked as he ascended the first section before turning to the left and disappearing up the next set of stairs. "But they are here for ceremonial purposes," he added, continuing his ascent. "This set for going up to the roof and there is another for going down."

"There's another set of stairs?" Harry asked, urging Stella to go in front of him. She did so, followed by Helen and Tom.

He had hovered near his daughter ever since their arrival at the temple, as if he feared she might require assistance after her ordeal with the snake.

"A long, straight set of stairs is on the other side of the temple," Mahmood replied. "The stairs we are on were used for religious ceremonies, especially during the festival to welcome the new year," he continued as he turned yet again to the left to climb another set of shallow stairs. "The reliefs you see on the walls depict the pharaohs making their offerings to the gods."

"These are astronomical symbols," Diana remarked, pausing to study a series of hieroglyphs.

"Indeed. This temple was probably used for astronomical observations," Mahmood agreed. "The roof provides an excellent location from which to see the entire sky at night."

"This must be where the zodiac was removed," Randy said, pausing to look straight up. Indeed, where the rest of the ceiling was black, a large area of the sandstone appeared especially rough and newly exposed.

"Damned frogs," David cursed.

"Penton!" Barbara scolded, using his title to good effect.

"Apologies," he replied.

When they finally emerged onto the sandstone-walled roof, the sudden bright light had the women opening parasols and Randy and Tom pulling out their eye-glasses.

"What is that?" Helen asked, pointing to the southwest, her attention on a rectangular ten-columned structure with short walls. The columns were topped with capitals of Hathor, but it no longer had a roof.

"The Kiosk of Hathor," Mahmood said, moving toward it. Only one wall of the structure had an opening. "Probably used for rituals involving Hathor and the sun disk," he added, pointing to the carvings in the sandstone. "A statue of the goddess would have been on display here during the New Year's Day festival. It is shown being carried by the priests in the reliefs on either side of the stairs we just climbed."

"What was considered the New Year?" David asked.

"Early summer," Mahmood replied.

"The roof was probably wood, which is why it's no longer here," Diana remarked, her gaze sweeping the carvings, many eroded from years of exposure to wind.

"And that one?" David asked. He was already heading for the only other structure atop the roof, one with a short set of stone steps in front of it.

"The Chapel of Osiris, which depicts the resurrection of his mummy," Mahmood replied. "The reliefs are of Isis, who was both his sister and his wife—she is the one who used her magic to bring him back to life so he could father the god Horus," he explained. "There are other underworld deities depicted here as well."

Harry grinned when Stella displayed a look of disgust.

"They had to maintain the purity of their bloodlines, my sweet," he whispered.

She scoffed. "As if they were horses."

The other side of the rooftop vantage provided an unimpeded view of the gateway to the north, the village of Qena to the west, and a smaller structure that barely showed above a sand dune.

Mahmood pointed to it. "Probably a mammisi," he said.

"A birth house," Diana interpreted for those who looked in her direction.

"Let us go down the other stairs," Mahmood suggested. "But we will require our torches, as it will be dark, and you must be careful as these stairs are as uneven as the others we climbed."

Using the tinderbox, Randy lit one of the torches Mahmood carried and one from Diana's satchel. He gave it to Will before lighting the other. Meanwhile, Mahmood had used the flame from the one torch to light the others before he disappeared into the stairwell leading down.

The rest of their party followed, Randy allowing Diana to carry the torch he had lit. "Should I light the other?" he asked.

"Let's wait. We may need it if this one goes out before I'm finished," she replied, her gaze on the walls on either side of the stairs.

Once they were back on the main level of the temple, Diana hurried to join Mahmood. "How can I go down below?"

He gave a start. "You wish to go into the crypts?"

"I do."

"They are not tombs," Mahmood stated. "Merely storerooms." He glanced over at Randy, who shrugged. Although he was tempted to forbid her from exploring the crypts, he knew she would be angry with him if he denied her the opportunity. "Is there any chance anyone—or anything—is already down there?" he asked.

Mahmood shook his head.

"I wish to go down, too," David said.

The guide sighed and led them to the Throne Room where a trap door was located in the floor. "Allow me to open this one and another in the Flame Room"—he pointed across the temple—"but the other doors are hidden under some sliding blocks in the perimeter walls. Only the priests knew of their location." He lifted the heavy door, which revealed the top step of a thin staircase that led into inky blackness.

About to go down, Diana was prevented from doing so when David held a staying arm in front of her. "Allow me, my lady," he said. He took Tom's torch from him, eliciting a sound of protest from his cousin, and he headed down the steep stairs. Once he was through the opening in the floor and the flame from his torch wasn't in danger of burning her, Diana followed him down.

"Am I a fool to wish to go down there?" Harry asked of no one in particular. "I am rather curious."

Mahmood lit another torch and handed it to him. "They are long, slim chambers," he warned, holding his hands out to indicate a width typical of a corridor. "Very deep."

"Understood," Harry said. He descended the stairs.

"Anyone else?" Randy asked.

The rest of the party shook their heads.

Mahmood disappeared for a moment to open another trap-door in the floor of the Flame Room. When he returned, he cleared his throat. "Allow me to take you into the sanctuary of Hathor," he said, waving in the direction the three-walled inner room near the back of the temple.

He lit another torch and handed it to Tom, who held it aloft as they made their way past openings into the chambers that lined the interior of the temple. Straight ahead was the sanctuary, but before they entered, a high-pitched squeaking sound had Helen pausing.

"What was that?" she asked.

Directly behind her, Tom paused and slowly swept the torch through the air in an effort to light the area around them.

"What was *what*?" Stella asked, from directly in front of her daughter. A gust of air had her gasping. "Oh!" she cried out. "I felt something touch my cheek."

Barbara and Will quickly joined her, Will waving his torch about in an effort to determine what might have startled the countess.

The sound of flapping wings had them gasping.

"There is no need to be fearful," Mahmood said calmly. "It is merely a—"

"Bat!" Stella yelled.

The sound of more flapping wings had Helen backing up until she collided with Tom. Her exclamation of surprise had him placing a protective hand at her waist. "I've got you," he whispered.

"Oh!" Barbara turned, ending up pressed into Will's side as he wrapped an arm around her waist while making sure to keep the flame from his torch away from everyone.

"Shh," he said as loudly as he could manage. Although Stella allowed another whimper, the movement in the air around them seemed to cease.

"We have merely disturbed the bats that use this temple as their cave," Mahmood said in a quiet voice. "There is nothing to fear from them."

"Are there any down below?" Randy asked, thinking of his wife and cousin.

"I do not believe so. The trapdoors are kept shut. Let us continue."

"I think I would prefer to go back to where those large columns are," Stella said. "Where it's lighter."

"As would I," Barbara said, hooking her arm into Stella's. The two took off toward the light at the front of the temple.

Will sighed. He was about to join the women to provide protection, but it was Tom who offered to do so. "Allow me," he said, handing the torch to Mahmood.

The four who remained behind watched them go before Mahmood led them into the sanctuary. Like all the other walls in the temple, these were covered in hieroglyphics. A gilded wooden structure meant to house a statue of Hathor was in the middle.

"Here the pharaoh is offering Hathor a copper mirror, a sacred emblem of the goddess," Mahmood said, waving to one of the images. The light from his torch illuminated the illustration, but when the sound of a bat reached them again, he sighed. "I apologize. They are usually not this active," Mahmood said.

"I think we have seen enough today," Will said.

The guide nodded his understanding. "I shall go down to see how the rest of them are doing in the crypts." He headed toward the first trapdoor while the other four made their way toward the entrance.

Tom offered his arm to Helen and was relieved when she accepted. Perhaps she had forgiven him for what had happened the week before.

Once they were back in the hypostyle, Tom and Will saw to extinguishing their torches and resumed their study of the carvings on the walls and columns.

CHAPTER 25
CRYPTS ARE CREEPY

*M*eanwhile, down below

When Diana finally reached the bottom of the stairs, she was surprised to discover David hadn't moved very far. "What's wrong?" she asked. Although it was warm, it wasn't nearly as hot as when they had been inside the pyramid at Giza. The air held a slight odor, although it was not unpleasant.

"I thought to wait for you to tell us what we're seeing," he whispered. "And which way to go."

"Why are you whispering?"

"Because of the echo," Harry answered for David. He joined them, the light from his torch and the other two making it possible to see most of the corridor in front of them. A number of passages led off of it.

As if to reinforce his comment, his words echoed off the hard surfaces.

"Understood," she replied, keeping her voice low. She lowered her torch to better illuminate the stone floor. "There's very little sand here," she commented.

"You were expecting some?" Harry asked.

"More sand would indicate a number of visitors in here. Perhaps the trapdoors have remained undiscovered for a long time."

"How many of these chambers do you suppose there are?" David asked, holding his torch high. The stone ceiling didn't include any decoration.

"If they're all this size... mayhap ten or twelve," she guessed.

"Mahmood said the trapdoors are usually hidden," Harry said. "Maybe they haven't all been discovered."

"They're covered with moving stones," Diana murmured. "But you must know which stones to move."

"I do wish I could read these symbols," Harry commented, holding his torch to illuminate a series of bas relief carvings along the wall.

Diana furrowed a brow at seeing a depiction of a pharaoh making what appeared to be an offering of jewelry. "Since we're below the Throne Room—"

"Are we?" David asked. "That staircase was... not straight," he commented.

"True." She continued down the corridor, studying the carvings. "These are in relief rather than etched," she commented.

"So?" David replied.

"It's far more difficult to carve in relief than simply cut into the stone," she replied. "It's like a story that just keeps going."

"Or a series of stories," Harry murmured.

"I believe these are pharaohs making offerings to the gods," she said before she turned and went down one of the passageways, the light from her torch showing it was a dead end. The carvings continued on both sides of the wall, though, and she continued to study them.

Meanwhile David headed down another, parallel passageway. When he turned around at the end of it, he let out a shout of surprise.

Harry, who was still out in the main corridor studying one of the walls, stiffened while Diana rushed from the end of the passageway she had been studying. "What was that?" she asked in alarm.

"I have no idea, but I think we are not the only ones down here," Harry whispered.

"Why do you say that?" she asked. Despite trying to remain calm, she could feel her heart race and hear her pulse in her ears. She glanced in both directions, expecting to see the light from David's torch. "David?" she called out.

"In here!" he responded from somewhere farther down the corridor. "Don't move. I'm coming to you."

She listened intently, sure she heard footsteps, but not from where his voice was coming. Light flickered from somewhere off to her left, and she was about to head in that direction when David's face suddenly appeared to her right.

Apparently Harry saw him before she did.

"Dammit, Penton, you nearly scared me to death," Harry scolded.

"David," Diana whispered. "You look as if you've seen a ghost. Where's your torch?"

"Umm. I dropped it. It... it went out," he stammered. "There's someone else down here. I saw a light go by the end of the crypt I was in."

"It could have been me," Harry reasoned, "Although..." He allowed his comment to trail off when he realized he hadn't made it down as far in the corridor as David had.

Diana's eyes widened, her gaze going beyond David to where the glow from another torch spread from the end of one of the passageways. "It wasn't you, my lord," she whispered.

David whirled around and nearly backed into her.

"Careful, or you're going to get burned," she warned, holding her torch higher. She immediately regretted the move, for something dark squeaked and sailed over her, casting a shadow on the ceiling.

"What was that?" Harry asked.

Determined not to panic, Diana listened intently. "Flapping wings," she murmured. "A bird or... or a bat," she reasoned.

"I wouldn't mind a bird," Harry commented. "Not particularly fond of bats, even if they do usually eat fruit."

She turned around and gave him a quelling glance. "I rather doubt he could survive down here. He obviously came through one of the open trapdoors," she said. "Probably saw our torchlight."

"Or his light," David whispered hoarsely, pointing down the corridor in front of them.

Straight ahead, the silhouette of a man wearing a robe appeared from the darkness.

"Who is that?" Harry asked, his labored breathing sounding loud.

"There you are," Mahmood called out. He had turned around, his torch now in front of him so he was no longer in silhouette.

"Mahmood?" Diana guessed.

"Yes. I've been looking for you. I could hear voices, but..." His gaze raked over David and he sighed. "Your torch has already gone out?" he asked, apparently sorting what had occurred.

"I uh,... I might have accidentally dropped it," David stammered. "When I saw you. Or your light as you walked by."

A squeaking sound preceded the reappearance of the bat, which flew over their heads in the direction of the stairway. "I have seen quite enough," Harry announced.

"Can we get out of here?" David asked.

When Diana's torch flickered, she nodded. "Although I would love to see more, I fear my torch won't last much longer."

"I will lead us to the stairs," Mahmood said, following the direction the bat had taken.

"I'll go last," Harry offered.

They were halfway up when Diana's torch finally flickered out. Behind her, David cursed.

"Take mine," Harry offered, holding his torch to the side for David, who was in front of him.

"Please keep it, my lord. It's lighting the steps for me," David replied.

"All right."

At the top of the stairs, Harry's torch flickered out as he emerged through the trapdoor. "How is that for timing?" he asked rhetorically.

"A clear indication it's time to get out of here," David remarked. "I'm hungry."

Mahmood chuckled softly. "I will close the other trapdoor and meet you at the front of the temple."

When Diana joined Randy where he stood studying the graffiti on one of the walls, he quickly wrapped his arms around her and kissed her forehead. "Am I glad to see you," he murmured.

"What's happened?"

Randy lifted a shoulder. "Bats," he replied. "They caused a bit of a stir up here."

She nodded. "Yes," she replied. "One did the same down in the crypts, but it was Mahmood who frightened us even more," she added, grinning. She opened the satchel hanging from his shoulder and stuffed her torch inside. "Then my torch went out halfway up the stairs. I thought your cousin was going to suffer apoplexy."

His eyes rounded before he suddenly barked a laugh. "Let me guess. David's went out first?"

She nodded as the two made their way to the exit. They paused to allow Tom and Helen to proceed them, his brother having offered his arm to Helen for the walk back to the hantours.

The two glanced at one another and grinned conspiratorially.

CHAPTER 26
A CONVERSATION CONTINUES

few minutes later
As promised, the driver of the fourth hantour had returned with a horse and harness and was parked along with the others. Couples paired up for the return ride to the dock and the enticement of a late luncheon.

With Diana and Randy in one, Will and Barbara in another, and Harry and Stella in the third, that left three of them to ride in the fourth.

Rather than go with Tom and Helen, David elected to sit with the driver of the hantour carrying his parents.

After Tom assisted Helen into the last hantour, he glanced around to discover he would be riding with her—and no one seemed particularly bothered by it. Especially not her parents. Even after what had happened on the journey to the temple.

"You don't mind if I ride with you, my lady?" he asked.

"Why would I mind?" Helen countered. She displayed a look of hurt.

He climbed up and took a seat next to her. "I feared you might have thought me bad luck, over what happened earlier."

Helen sounded a huff. "What happened had nothing to do with you. Now Penton..." She sighed.

"What about David?"

"He was the one who pulled me out of the carriage and left me on my bum," she complained. "Right in front of that snake."

"Oh, I'm quite sure he didn't mean for that to happen. He was probably concerned you might have been injured. As was I," he replied.

She dipped her head, glad when the hantour jerked into motion and headed back toward the river. "Thank you for seeing to me. For making sure I could stand."

"Of course, Helen. I..." He paused, as if he thought better of what he was about to say.

"What?" she prompted.

"I would have been devastated had you been bitten or if you had broken a bone," he claimed.

"Devastated?" she repeated.

He nodded. "Of course."

She stared at him, her blonde brows furrowing. "Last week...when we were at the back of the boat—"

"I was a fool to leave you as I did," he blurted.

Blinking, Helen inhaled softly. "Thomas," she said on a breath.

"If we'd been alone, I would have..." He clamped his mouth shut and seemed to have trouble breathing.

"You would have... what? I beg you tell me."

Dipping his head, he leaned closer and said, "I would have kissed you."

"So why didn't you?"

Tom gave a start, obviously not expecting her response. There were so many others that seemed more appropriate.

I would have slapped you.

I would have stomped on your boot.

I would have screamed.

I would have pushed you overboard.

The examples continued to run through his head as he stared at her. "I... I didn't think—"

"That's just it, isn't it?" she countered. "You didn't think. You had me in your arms. You had me up against a wall. You could have had your way with me—"

"My uncle was there," he interrupted, trying to keep his voice low lest the driver understand English. "The crew. They would have seen us," he argued. "Bradley was right there, too. What would *he* think?"

Helen scoffed. "Bradley is just a babe. Besides, he sees my parents kiss one another all the time. In fact, they're so in love with one another, it wouldn't surprise me if they had another baby."

Tom's eyes rounded. "Aren't they too old?" he asked in alarm.

The sound of disbelief had him on alert. "Hardly," she replied, one hand going to her hip.

He had seen his aunt do the same and knew he was in for a scolding if he didn't say something to save himself. "It's just hard to imagine having a much younger brother in the family is all."

"Oh, Alexander doesn't mind," she claimed, referring to her older brother. "Especially now that he has one of his own. Besides, aren't *you* a much older brother?"

Tom chuckled softly. "You have me there," he admitted, although George was no longer a babe. He did the math and realized his youngest sibling was nearly fifteen years of age.

"What about you?" he asked, relieved when her hand left her hip to clutch the top of her reticule. Although he had expected to see it was ruined from how she used it to beat the snake, the evidence of its use as a weapon wasn't visible.

Helen lifted a shoulder. "I wouldn't mind another brother. Mayhap a sister," she mused.

He reached over and gripped her gloved hand. She allowed him to bring it to his lips so he could kiss the back of her knuckles. "Please don't be angry with me."

Her eyes widening in surprise, Helen said, "I am not. At least, not any longer," she whispered.

Daring a glance at the driver and noting all the other hantours were ahead of them, Tom leaned over and kissed her on the cheek. Emboldened when she allowed it, he placed a hand on the side of her face and nearly had his lips to hers when the driver shouted something and their hantour slowed.

A quick look around had him realizing they were already at the river. "We're back to the dock," he said on a sigh of disappointment.

"Father says another day on the river, and we'll be in Luxor," she replied.

"Uncle says we'll stay in a hotel for a few days while the crew restocks the ship for our return trip to Cairo," he murmured.

"I'm looking forward to it," she replied. "I can finally take a real bath."

The thought of Helen Tennison in a bath had Tom imagining all sorts of possibilities.

Him helping her to wash.

Him gliding a wash cloth up her shin and over her knee.

Him watching her breasts as they barely broke the surface of the water, her pert nipples hardening when they were exposed to the cooler air.

Him climbing into the bath with her, although he couldn't picture exactly how they would sit and still fit without all the water gushing over the sides.

Him wrapping her in a bath linen and pulling her into his arms.

Him carrying her to a soft bed where he would make love to her and hold her for an entire night.

"Are you coming?" Helen asked.

"I am," he replied on a sigh of satisfaction. He blinked several times, suddenly remembering where they were. "Um, right away," he added, before struggling to step down from the equipage with a cock still hard from his daydream.

Swallowing, he offered his arm and the two headed for the ship and the late luncheon waiting for them up on the top deck. "May I help you up the stairs?" he asked.

Helen angled her head to one side. "I should like to go to my cabin first." She pulled her skirt out and winced at seeing the ground in desert dust. "I really need to change my gown."

"Of course," he replied, giving her a bow as he struggled to tamp down another arousal at the thought of her undressed.

She curtsied and turned to head down the corridor.

The sight of Bradley running into her arms before they even had a chance to get to their cabins was like being dunked into a cold water bath.

CHAPTER 27
CONVERSATIONS NEAR KARNAK

he following afternoon

Anticipation was in the air as *The Dendera* drew closer to El-Karnak, the closest village to the columns and pylons of the huge Karnak temple complex visible from the south bank of where the the Nile curved sharply to the west.

Grinning when he saw that nearly all his passengers were up on the deck watching their approach, Mahmood joined them.

On the table, David had Volume III of *La Description de l'Égypte* opened to an illustration of the entire Karnak site. Next to him, Tom was leaning over to study the drawing. "It's practically a city unto itself," he murmured.

"You are right to be impressed by this temple, for it is not just one, but many," he said, waving a hand in the direction of the ruins. The setting sun cast the sandstone blocks in a golden-red wash. Against the blue sky, the effect was magical.

"That would make a most impressive painting," Randy mused.

Diana glanced in his direction, a grin teasing her lips. "I

already have it in my mind's eye," she replied. "But I have to decide how large a canvas to use."

"If I promised it could hang in the dining room of Gisborn Hall, would you make it six feet wide?" he asked in a low voice. "Maybe even eight feet?"

She gave a start. "What, pray tell, is hanging there now that has you wanting such a large depiction of Karnak to replace it?"

"A naval scene, I think. Apparently it's been there since my father's uncle's father's grandfather won it in a game of cards."

Grinning, Diana was about to reply when Will leaned toward him and said, "Gisborn won it from my three times great-grandfather. The ship was captained by him over a hundred and thirty years ago."

Randy blinked. "Are you joking?"

"I am not."

"Then why isn't it hanging in the dining room at Devonfield House? Or at Ellsworth Park?" Randy asked, referring to Will and Barbara's estate near Gisborn Hall.

"Why, indeed?" Will countered.

Diana tittered. "I shall do a large painting and hope it does not offend your mother," she whispered. "For if you recall, she is his sister," she said, indicating Will, "So her three times great-grandfather was the same man."

Randy blinked.

Will barked a laugh and turned to his wife. "What say you, my beautiful countess?"

Barbara blushed. "I do believe a painting of a naval scene will be perfect in the dining room at Ellsworth Park. It will be far better than that atrocious portrait of who-knows-who is hanging there now."

"Very well," Diana said. "But don't expect me to paint it before we return to England. It would be most difficult in such small quarters as these," she added.

When he saw they were done with their conversation,

Mahmood continued his talk. "The Egyptians called this temple complex *Ipet-isut*, meaning 'The Most Select of Places'. Unfortunately, it is not as preserved as Dendera, nor as colorful. But what it lacks in color, it makes up for with over one-hundred columns, several monoliths, and a number of statues," he explained. "Now, we shall go there in the morning after you have eaten your breakfast. We must take water and some food, for there is much to see." He paused a moment. "If I may suggest the ladies wear shoes that are not mere slippers. Wear boots if you have them, for the terrain is uneven."

"I know what *I'll* be wearing," Diana murmured, referring to her breeches and boots.

Randy chuckled softly. "I would expect nothing different, but I must tell you the gown you are wearing right now is especially fetching on you." Although she had worn it many times during the fortnight they had spent on the river, the sky blue sprigged muslin set off her blonde hair and blue eyes to good effect.

Diana lifted a brow, fairly sure he meant she would be even more fetching if the gown was off of her.

"Will we walk from the boat?" Will asked, noting how the *dhahabîyeh* continued its trek on the river and was nearly past the site of the temple. Even as he asked the question, the main sail dropped and the boat noticeably slowed.

"Indeed. We are nearly to the dock. There is a path that will take us to a sphinx and then to the first pylon," Mahmood replied. "From there, we will walk through the center of everything, but we must take care not to trip or turn an ankle."

"Bradley is staying on board tomorrow," Harry stated, his comment directed to Stella.

"I would not think to take him," she said. "Although he missed Helen terribly yesterday."

Tom displayed a grimace at hearing the countess' comment, but when he noticed Helen glance his way, he quickly recovered to ask, "Will we require torches? Or a shovel?"

"No. Very little of any roofs remain, so the sun will be providing our light," the captain replied. "As for shovels, there is far more sand filling the inside of these temples than we can ever hope to remove."

Leaning toward Diana, Randy said, "Your satchel will certainly be lighter."

She nodded. "I'm taking my sketchpad and measuring tools, though."

"Enjoy your dinner," Mahmood said, the same moment the sun set completely and the boat came to a halt at the dock.

CHAPTER 28
A COUSIN LEARNS THE TRUTH

The following morning

By the time breakfast had been consumed and everyone who was going to the temple had stepped onto the dock, it was nearly ten o'clock.

The married women paired up with their husbands for the walk to the Karnak temple complex, the uneven terrain forcing them to hold on to their men even though there was a path of sorts to follow.

The only unmarried lady, Helen, walked up from the river on the arm of David, who offered his arm before Tom had even come out of his cabin to join the party for the day's excursion. She wore a stylish hat, but also carried a parasol.

"Thank you, Lord Penton," she said, happy for the escort.

"Oh, please, called me Penton," he insisted. He had chosen a short top hat with a wider brim for the tour, warned that they were to be exposed to a good deal of sun.

"All right," she replied. "Are you looking forward to exploring this temple? You seem especially happy for all these adventures."

"Oh, I am. I may never have the chance again to risk life and limb as we've been doing on this tour."

"Oh?" she responded, his words unexpected.

"When I return to England, I shall be remaining in London to assist my grandfather with the business of the Devonfield marquessate," he explained. "I may go to Oxfordshire to collect my things, but I shall quickly return to London. I look forward to the challenge."

"It must be very satisfying to have something to look forward to," she said.

He made an odd sound in his throat. "Said as if you don't. Have something to look forward to, I mean," he clarified.

Helen swallowed back the sudden lump in her throat. "I don't, not really," she said.

"Not... marriage?"

She allowed a soft sigh. "I am not betrothed, my lord," she replied, trying to keep her words sounding light.

"Do you wish to be?"

Helen nearly stumbled on the edge of a sandstone block. "Well... of course."

Glancing back, David saw that Tom had ended up at the very back of their party, and from the way he meandered on the path, he didn't seem particularly inclined to want to keep up with everyone else.

"Do you trust me?" David asked, returning his gaze to Helen.

"Uh... I suppose," she replied, startled by the query. She dared a glance behind her, wondering what had had the viscount's attention.

"Tell me, do you have any thoughts about my cousin Thomas? As they relate to marriage, I mean?"

Helen's eyes rounded. "Penton," she said in a scolding whisper. "I don't believe it's any of your concern, my lord."

"Good," he replied.

"Good?" she repeated in confusion.

"I have some experience with... betrothals of convenience," he continued in a conspiratorial voice.

Gasping, Helen nearly stopped in her tracks. "Are you... are you proposing?" she stammered, struggling to keep her voice to a whisper.

"Not exactly," he replied, daring another glance back to catch Tom staring daggers at him. "Stay close to me today. When I say something clever, remark upon it or giggle and act as if we are to be married."

Helen blinked several times. "But... why?"

"Do you wish to wed my cousin or not?"

"Penton!" she once again scolded. She was about to say more, but clamped her mouth shut. "Is it that obvious?"

"That he wants you to be his wife?"

She gave a start, not expecting *that* particular take on it. "Does he?"

A look of confusion crossed David's face. "He stares at you all the time. Acts like a lovesick puppy dog, especially when you're in the company of the baby."

Helen inhaled softly and swallowed. "I've caught him staring, but I hardly know why he would be jealous of Bradley," she murmured.

"He's jealous of..." Here he stopped and dipped his head. "Forgive me. It is none of my concern as to who... well, may I just ask if you are a widow, perhaps?"

Confusion had Helen's brows furrowing. "No. I've never been married. I've never even been betrothed," she said in a quiet voice. "Why would you even think so?"

David didn't answer her question, merely asking another of his own. "And Bradley?" he pressed.

Her brows rose in anticipation of the rest of the query. "What about him?"

"Well, did... forgive, my lady, but how do you account for him?"

"Account for him?" she whispered. Understanding suddenly dawned on Helen, and she lifted a gloved hand to her face as she let out a gasp of surprise and then nervously laughed. "Oh, Penton, you're a terrible tease," she accused. "You really had me going there for a moment."

Now that it was his turn to be confused, David appeared dumbfounded. "I... I don't follow," he murmured.

Helen giggled again, this time not bothering to cover her mouth. She leaned in close, lowered her voice to a whisper, and said, "Silly goose, he's my little brother."

David's look of confusion slowly cleared. "As in...?"

"My father's spare heir, yes," she affirmed, a brilliant smile lighting her face. She giggled again.

David's look of startlement was followed by a bark of laughter, which had the others turning to stare at him. "Oh, my lady, you have managed to surprise me as I have not been since... well, since my days at university," he claimed.

Helen suddenly sobered. "You mean... *everyone* thinks Bradley is... is my son?" she asked in a hoarse whisper, remembering the conversation she'd had with Diana when they were at the pyramids.

Lifting a shoulder, he said, "Well, I certainly did and so does Thomas." He glanced over at her. "So... this shall make our day even more fun," he added, a grin suddenly splitting his face.

"Aren't you going to tell him? *I* should tell him," she replied, almost letting go her hold on him.

"No," David replied, placing a staying hand over hers. "Let him stew. We can wait until later. Father says we'll be spending the next few nights in a hotel in Luxor."

Helen glanced back at Tom. "How could he think that of

me?" she asked in a quiet voice, her momentary humor dissipating.

Although she wasn't expecting a response, he said, "You simply have to forgive us. We men aren't always so... perceptive."

Knowing he spoke the truth, Helen merely rolled her eyes and was glad they had made it to the front of the temple.

*D*avid glanced back at Tom again, noting how his cousin narrowed his eyes when their gazes locked. *The machinations I must perform for those in love,* he thought ruefully. Turning his attention back to Helen, he said, "Don't hold it against him, my lady. I think he truly feels affection for you, but he may believe you have a beau back in London." Entirely too amused by the situation, he struggled to keep a straight face.

CHAPTER 29
TOURING THE TEMPLES AT KARNAK

*D*espite the short walk from the river, it was almost eleven when they stood in the partial shade of the first pylon of the temple complex. Off to their right was a sphinx featuring the head of a ram atop a lion's body, the base and part of the statue beneath the sandy ground. It wasn't nearly as large as the one they had seen in Giza, and part of the nose was missing.

"As you can see, this Temple of Amun-Re is half-buried in the desert, the height of the sand requiring us to guess at how far down the original floor of the temple might be," Mahmood explained as they regarded the limestone entrance.

Due to the uneven terrain, the married women continued to hold onto their husbands when they would usually go off on their own to examine an artifact or column. Taking her cue from them, Helen continued to hold onto David's arm as the guide began the tour.

"Why is the right side so much higher than the left side?" Barbara asked, referring to the pylon. The angular sides were symmetrical but looked odd given their different heights.

"This may have been the last part of the temple to be

added," Mahmood replied. "But we believe it was never finished." He waved them past a pair of columns, the one on the right of the entrance still standing while its mate lay collapsed in two lines on the left, the column drums still aligned with one another. "I know it appears as if a giant has knocked it over, but it probably fell over due to its base being on land that was at one time quite marshy," he explained. "We will first go into the grand forecourt. Follow me."

After they passed through the rectangular opening of the first pylon, the second pylon—or what was left of it—was visible straight ahead. The ruined condition suggested it had been made of mud bricks rather than limestone or sandstone. Given the height of the sand that had collected in the forecourt, only the top halves of the columns on either side of the courtyard area were visible. The sand varied in depth from one side to the other, the winds having caused a sand dune effect.

"This great forecourt would have been the closest the peoples of Egypt could come to their gods," Mahmood explained. "Although they are probably buried, we would expect this area to include some rooms for storing items for the processionals during the festivals," he added.

"What are those capitals supposed to be?" Barbara asked, clinging to Will's arm as she pointed to the colonnade on the left. It was almost a mirror image of the one on the right, except that colonnade was interrupted by the entrance to a smaller temple.

"The columns are meant to depict papyrus stalks with closed buds," Mahmood replied. "A very simple design."

"They're far more decorative than Doric capitals," Helen remarked, earning a look of approval from David. Studying one of the columns on the left, Tom pretended not to notice.

"Not as garish as the Corinthian capitals of the Roman temples," Stella said thoughtfully.

"I could imagine these in our parlor," Harry remarked. "In fact—"

"Not in the parlor, darling. Mayhap in front of the town-house, though," she countered. "We could start a new fashion in Mayfair. Egyptian columns."

He chuckled. "Never. I happen to adore the Greek columns we have," he said, arching a teasing brow.

Despite the shadow of her parasol, Stella's blush was apparent to anyone who was looking at her.

"I do wonder what's buried beneath all this sand," Diana murmured, her furrowed brows indicative of her thoughts. Letting go of Randy, she headed in the direction of the smaller temple off to the right, grimacing when she realized it was the Temple of Ramesses III. She and David had studied the crude map the French had drawn of the area in preparation for that day's tour, and she had expected to find it in better condition. Inside were the remains of two colonnades that had at one time lined the walls, and straight ahead, where the rest of the temple should have been, lay a pile of rubble.

"One day this may be rebuilt," Tom murmured from where he stood next to her.

She glanced over at him. "It will have to be dug out of the desert first," she replied on a sigh.

"Are you thinking to do it?" he asked.

Scoffing, she regarded him for a moment with a thoughtful expression before she finally shook her head. "No. I think the Egyptians should see to their own temples," she said.

They turned around when Mahmood called for their attention.

"If you will follow me," he announced, before leading them through the opening in the second pylon. Their path took them on a downward slope. Here the depth of the sand was less, so the height of the columns was far more impressive than in the forecourt.

Even more so were the twelve columns on either side of the center aisle, each topped with an open capital featuring the feathery blossoms of flowering papyrus. Beyond those columns on either side were row after row of shorter, smaller columns. They were topped with the closed-bud capitals.

"Now we have entered the hypostyle," he announced proudly, his arms held out.

"These are huge," Randy said in awe, as he stared at the greater columns.

"Thirty-three feet in circumference," David stated. "Their capitals are eighteen feet in diameter, and it's said they can support a hundred men."

"Oh, I wouldn't wish to go up there," Tom murmured.

"I wouldn't want you to," Helen said, her face reddening when he glanced with surprise in her direction. "They're entirely too tall," she added, earning her a nod from Tom.

Randy angled his head back. "And they are carved all the way to the top," he marveled.

"Painted as well," Stella said, awestruck. She was circling one of the columns, as if she was studying all the carvings.

"They were indeed," Mahmood confirmed. He pointed to the underside of the architraves. Between each capital atop the columns were painted hieroglyphics, their colors still vibrant. "But it is not yet known what is written up there or on the columns."

"You cannot read them?" Barbara asked in surprise.

"I cannot, my lady," Mahmood admitted. "Not all of it. I do know that every place you see an oval shape around a series of hieroglyphics, it depicts the name of a pharaoh."

Barbara's eyes widened as she returned her attention to the column to which she was standing.

"The smaller columns have a circumference of seven-and-twenty feet," Diana stated. She had pulled out her sketchpad and a pencil from her satchel, prepared to begin drawing the one in front of her.

"How many columns are there in this part of the temple?" Harry asked of their guide. "It's like a forest," he added, for despite the midday sun, the columns provided shade where they stood.

"One-hundred-and-twenty-two is the number of the smaller columns," Mahmood replied. "Although calling it a marsh of papyrus plants would be a better analogy than a forest of trees, for we believe that is what the builders intended," he explained.

"So these larger columns here in the middle must have supported a higher roof?" Will guessed.

"Yes. The central nave," Mahmood confirmed.

"Is there any thought as to how deep these columns go? How tall they really are?" Tom asked, as if he was determined to gain Helen's attention.

Mahmood waved for him to follow, and the two moved toward the outer wall and the last row of columns. Between two columns, the sand was considerably lower on this side of the hypostyle, and it appeared as if someone had dug a channel between the columns and the wall deeper than even Tom was tall. The carvings on the exposed sandstone suggested they continued well below the bottom level of the deep channel. "Mayhap sixty or seventy feet tall," Mahmood said. "Until the sand is removed to the original floor, we will not know."

"Seventy feet?" Tom repeated in awe. He shook his head. "How would they have even erected such tall columns?"

Mahmood shrugged. "Using the same techniques they did to build the pyramids," he suggested.

"Up there, above the architraves," Diana said, pointing to some vertical pillars with crossbeams that formed rectangular openings above the largest columns. "Were those windows?"

Mahmood glanced up to where she indicated. "Indeed," he agreed. "Those are the window frames of the clerestory." In some of the openings, the grills were still intact.

"So it would have been light here in the temple," she mused, her gaze going to the last two great columns at the back of the hypostyle. Not only were they devoid of carvings, their surfaces weren't nearly as smooth as the others in the hall.

"They are unfinished," Mahmood confirmed, noting her gaze. "But they give us a hint of what was involved in building such a temple."

"Indeed," Diana murmured, before she continued her survey of the temple.

Several in their party had already ventured beyond the third pylon, where a complete obelisk and the base of another stood.

"The obelisks of Thutmosis the First," Diana said before she displayed a huge grin. "I wasn't sure they would still be here," she remarked.

"Why not?" Randy asked.

"I feared the French might have transported them to Paris," she whispered.

"Ah," he replied.

"At one time, there may have been six obelisks in this area between the third and fourth pylons," Mahmood said. He indicated the area to the right, where a line of mounds of rubble indicated another series of pylons perpendicular to the ones they had passed through. "That was once another entrance to the temple out there," he explained. "And this is where they intersected. Imagine the spectacle of the processions during the annual festivals. It would have been quite grand."

Barbara glanced up at Will. "Rather hard to imagine given the current state of this courtyard," she murmured.

He chuckled. "Still, you have to be impressed that another

monolith is still standing here," he said, his attention on the Obelisk of Hatshepsut. The base of it appeared to have been protected by a series of walls around it that had partly crumbled.

Meanwhile, the base of its mate stood nearby. The top half of it lay on the debris of a temple dedicated to Wadjyt, or the Eye of Horus. Noting the pyramidal shape at the end of the monolith and where it had landed, David chuckled. "It poked out the Eye of Horus," he jested.

Mahmood was not amused, and Diana seemed ready to scold her cousin-by-marriage for his comment.

Despite his height, Will couldn't see over the top of the downed monolith. "This is solid granite," he remarked in surprise.

"Pink granite," Mahmood affirmed.

"It must weigh..." He shook his head, about to say 'a ton' when he realized it would have weighed more.

Far more.

"Over three-hundred tons," Mahmood stated. "Quarried and brought here by boat."

"Is that possible?" Stella asked, her query addressed to Harry.

The earl shrugged. "You've seen enough pyramids to know that it is," he replied.

She was about to argue and realized he had a point. The blocks for those structures might have been limestone, but they were sometimes larger than the monolith.

Mahmood continued the tour, pointing in the direction they had been going. "The farther we go, the more treacherous our journey, so please be careful."

Seeing she wasn't currently clinging to David's arm, Tom hurried to offer his arm to Helen. She gave him a passing glance before placing her hand on it.

"Do you find it interesting?" he asked.

"Very much so," she replied. "And you?"

"Well worth the trip and a few mosquito bites, I think."

The two of them picked their way among the rubble, Helen occasionally having to grip his forearm when her half boots threatened to slip on the smoother rocks.

"Diana must be thrilled by all this," she said.

"I think she and David memorized everything they could," he remarked. "If someone decides to excavate this temple, my brother may lose her," he added, although his self-conscious grin betrayed his tease.

"What will she do when you return to England?"

He shrugged. "Probably look for Roman ruins," he replied. "We certainly have evidence enough of them on our property."

"You do?" she asked in surprise.

"Coins, mostly," he replied. "We find them when we till the soil for planting in the spring. Not many, but it can be like a scavenger hunt when we find one or two. We never find more than that, but who knows what she'll unearth?" He paused before the top half of a statue. "She probably wishes she had her shovel so she could dig this out," he remarked.

"Would you help her?" Helen asked.

Tom nodded. "If I had a shovel, yes," he replied. From the look on her face at hearing his response, he knew he had answered correctly. "I apologize for not coming out of my cabin in time to escort you this morning," he added.

"Oh, it's quite all right. Penton saw to escorting me," she replied.

"Has he already proposed marriage?"

Helen blinked as she turned to stare up at him. "No," she hedged.

Tom displayed a look of relief. "He made quite a spectacle of himself in Greece with his pretend betrothal to Miss Jane Fitzsimmons," he murmured. "Now Mrs. Michael Henley."

Her eyes widened despite the viscount having admitted to being part of a fake betrothal. "Did he throw her over?" she asked with worry.

He shook his head. "Broke it off so she could wed Diana's brother, Michael," he replied. "They arranged the betrothal during the Morganfield ball," he added, arching a brow as if to emphasize his point.

Helen inhaled softly. "The night you kissed me," she said, her attention on her mind's eye.

"Indeed," he responded.

He was about to say more, but Mahmood called out, "We have just gone past what was the fifth and sixth pylons. In this courtyard, there are ruins of several small temples. I will take you into a special one."

The group followed him to the remains of a granite-walled structure located past a pair of granite pillars. Although the sides of the doorway and most of the walls were standing, the lintel and part of the roof were missing.

"This chapel was built by Philip Arrhidaeus," Mahmood said as he led them into the two-room structure. An opening at one end and a few openings in the roof provided plenty of light for them to see the interior.

"Who?" Tom asked.

"He said Philip Arrhidaeus," Helen whispered.

At Tom's blank expression, David sighed. "Philip the Third," he clarified.

"Who?" Tom pressed, his query meant for his brother.

"Of Macedonia," Randy whispered.

"Alexander the Great's half-brother," Diana stated from the other side of Randy.

"Shh," Barbara scolded.

Will grinned when he noted how Diana had a leather-gloved hand covering her mouth in an attempt to stifle a grin at the expense of her brother-by-marriage.

"Note the ceiling," Mahmood stated, his gaze lifting.

They glanced up to where the ceiling was still intact to discover a field of carved white stars with red centers on a background of blue.

"And this was the altar," Mahmood said, his hand resting on a misshapen rock. The corners had broken off, but carvings were still evident on some of the surfaces.

"Wasn't he the one who wasn't very bright?" Tom asked. "Suffered seizures and was executed?"

Three of their party turned to look at him in surprise. "There is some writing to suggest he was mentally deficient," Diana confirmed.

"Unstable, don't you mean?" David countered.

"But he is recognized as having ruled after Alexander's death," Diana said.

"Probably had some help," Tom mused.

Mahmood sighed. "Let us continue our tour. We are nearly finished."

"We are?" Helen asked in surprise.

Their guide chuckled. "You will wish to have your luncheon somewhere in the shade of a column or statue," he said. "Unfortunately, the site of the Sacred Lake does not have water in it, or I would recommend it." He pointed in the direction of a square, flat area, the outline made evident by the foundations of a temple on one side and rubble along two of the other edges. "When you have finished eating, I will take you to the Khonsu Temple and then back to the ship." He pointed in the direction from which they had come and then to the west.

"Let's head back to the hypostyle," Will suggested. Exposed as they were to the sun, he knew most in the group were growing uncomfortably warm.

Pairing up, they picked their way back over the rubble and sandy terrain, past statues half-buried and columns that no longer held up roofs to smaller temples jutting from their sandy base.

Once they were back in the hypostyle, they settled next to one of the largest columns where a basket containing their luncheon had been left by one of the crew.

Tom made sure he was seated next to Helen.

CHAPTER 30

BABOONS AT THE TEMPLE
OF KHONSU

An hour later

Located to the west of the Temple of Amun-Re, the much smaller Temple of Khonsu seemed in far better condition than the temples they had toured earlier that day. The gateway, its tapered sides and lintel heavily carved, still had its transom, a sun disk carved in relief at the center. The pylon behind it was also symmetrical, a sign it had been finished, and the frame around the entry was intact. There were vertical niches built into the angled front, but no statuary occupied the four spaces.

"We believe this was constructed during the rule of Ramesses the Third," Mahmood announced as they approached the pylon indicating the entry to the temple. In front of it, a sphinx similar to the one they had seen in front of the Temple of Amun-Re seemed to act as a guard. "There is some thought that it was one end of an avenue of sphinxes which connected Karnak to the Temple of Luxor," he said, pointing to the west. "A road lined with these statues would be nearly two miles long."

Will glanced to the west. There was no sign of a temple, but he knew from his days at sea that anything at a distance of two miles would not have been visible above the horizon. "Then where are all the sphinxes?" he asked in alarm. Even if the French had found a few and relocated them to Paris, nearly two miles of sphinxes suggested there had been hundreds of them.

"Under the sand," Mahmood replied. "Although there are places between here and there where you can see them or part of them as if they are trying to emerge from the desert." He turned and waved to the temple gateway. "Although there was a wall around this temple at some time in its history, only this remains to show us the way in. Follow me."

While he spoke, most in their party had moved to examine the sphinx, but when it was time go inside, the women once again paired up with their husbands. Although Tom hurried over to offer his arm to Helen, David beat him to it, saying, "My lady?"

Helen nodded. "Penton," she acknowledged, placing a hand on his arm. Although she had seen Tom's attempt to offer his arm from the corner of her eye, she pretended ignorance and gave David a brilliant smile.

Except Tom wasn't having it. Before she could put voice to a protest, he had stepped up to her other side and gently pried her parasol from her hold, offering his free arm as he angled the parasol over her head.

Surprised, she managed only a scoff before Mahmood resumed speaking.

"Here we find a forecourt in fairly excellent condition," he said, his arms outstretched. Like the forecourt of the Karnak complex, this one featured columns with closed-bud capitals on either side. Sand had drifted inside, but it wasn't nearly as deep as that in Karnak, probably because the temple was fairly intact. "You will find inscriptions here we think may have been added by Herihor, a general and high priest of Ramesses the Eleventh."

Diana inhaled softly. "Can you read them? The inscriptions?" she asked in surprise.

"I cannot. The histories of these temples are mostly passed along in spoken form. I am merely telling you what I learned from my teacher."

He continued walking into the next section of the temple, the hypostyle hall. Far smaller than the one in Karnak, the hall featured eight columns. What they saw in the sanctuary beyond the hall caught their attention, though.

Two carved baboons.

"Are those monkeys?" Stella asked in awe. Although the bases of the statues were covered by sand, the statues themselves were not.

"The god Thoth, actually," Mahmood replied. "The god of wisdom is depicted as a baboon," he explained. "The statues are probably leftover from an earlier temple. One of the last pharaohs native to Egypt, Nectanebo, is credited with restoring or rebuilding this one as well as others throughout Egypt," he explained.

"Why a baboon?" Helen asked, still flanked by David and Tom.

"Baboons are known to stand in the sun and raise their arms every morning. To warm themselves. They shout as if to greet the sun, to greet the sun god, Ra, and because they are considered a very intelligent animal, they are Thoth's representation here."

"We've certainly heard them," Tom remarked.

"You have?" Helen asked, turning to regard him with a quizzical expression.

"When we were sailing through the Strait of Gibraltar," he replied. "Did you come a different way?"

She shook her head. "We were on a steam ship," she replied. "But we went through the strait in the late afternoon, so the baboons would have finished warming themselves."

Tom nodded his agreement. "You are fortunate they did not wake you... or the babe... whilst you slept," he commented.

"Most fortunate," she agreed, glancing up at David to see him smirking.

Diana had already pulled her sketchbook from her satchel and was doing a quick drawing of the statue when Randy joined her from where he had been examining the walls. "You'll want to take a look at the inscriptions," he murmured.

She glanced up. "Did you find more graffiti?" she asked, grinning. It had become almost a sport for him to search for and read whatever inscriptions he could find from those who had visited the temples in the past.

Randy shook his head.

Intrigued, she tucked the sketchpad under her arm and moved to the wall, her brows furrowing as she moved from block to block, studying each before finally scoffing in frustration.

"These stones..." she said, her attention on the walls. "Some of these inscriptions are upside down, or half-missing," she murmured, her gloved hand tracing places along the seams where the carvings were unmatched.

"Indeed. The blocks used here were from other temples," Mahmood explained.

She huffed a sigh of disappointment.

"It became a common practice in the last dynasties," he added sadly. "They simply reused parts of old temples to build the new ones."

Nodding her understanding, she asked if they could see the Colossi of Memnon, two massive stone statues near Luxor. "I know they are not truly of Memnon, but rather of Amenhotep the Third," she added.

Surprised by her statement, Mahmood arched a dark brow. "You are familiar with their story?"

"If you are referring to the story told to the Romans, then I am," she replied.

He chuckled. "I cannot promise they will sing," he warned, referring to an odd effect that sometimes happened in the morning hours.

"I don't care if they do," she replied.

"Then I will arrange for transport and take you there on the morrow."

Randy dipped his head to hide his amusement. "When you told me the story of those statues, I thought you did so because you had seen them with your own eyes," he claimed.

"How could I have?" she countered. "I've never been to Egypt before."

"Well, I know that now," he replied, still grinning. "I admit I have had the desire to see them ever since you told me your tall tale."

"It's not a tall tale," she argued.

Instead of responding, Randy turned his attention to their guide. "When will we be able to tour the Temple at Luxor?" he asked.

Mahmood displayed a huge grin. "If we see the Colossi of Memnon in the morning, then we shall tour Luxor in the afternoon," he said. "But first, we must sail there. 'Tis not far. Mayhap an hour to the dock in front of your hotel."

"Hotel?" Stella repeated.

Nodding, Mahmood said, "You will stay there three nights before we continue our journey."

"Will we be able to take a real bath?" Barbara asked, her query resulting in a chorus of questions from the others.

The guide held up a staying hand. "Baths, yes," he affirmed. "You will find your accommodations most civilized in Luxor."

Will chuckled as Harry joined him near the temple entrance. "So, do we continue up the Nile or..." Harry asked with a shrug. In all their plans, they had never discussed continuing the trip farther than Luxor.

"Let's discuss it over dinner," Will suggested. "I have a feeling if you were to ask Diana, we would be in Egypt for another year," Will claimed.

Harry chuckled. "Helen might be in agreement," he replied. "She seems quite happy on this trip." He glanced over to where his daughter was still flanked by Tom and David. "All this attention from handsome young men. She doesn't usually receive it in London," he added.

Will nodded. "If I was a betting man—"

"My money would be on your son," Harry interrupted.

Blinking, Will furrowed his brows. "David?" he said in surprise. "I would have thought Thomas," he murmured.

Harry chuckled. "Should I be concerned about either one?"

Shaking his head, Will's attention went back to the three as they regarded the statues of the baboons. "No," he replied finally, deciding not to mention that he didn't expect David to take a wife until he was older.

The two stepped away from one another as their wives joined them, and soon the entire party headed back to the boat.

An hour later, they arrived in Luxor.

CHAPTER 31
LUXURY IN LUXOR

*L*ater *that night during dinner in the hotel*

Having bathed and dressed for dinner, Barbara and Will headed down to the hotel's dining room to discover the rest of the family and the Tennisons already seated at a rectangular table. Their animated conversation and the glasses set before them suggested they had been enjoying drinks before dinner. Although he was not at their table, Mahmood sat with one of his crew at an adjacent table.

The men all stood and waited until Barbara was seated before they sat down. "Forgive us for not waiting, but we have been plotting," Harry said, his comment directed to Will.

"For tomorrow or beyond?"

"Tomorrow. It seems we would all like to see the Colossi of Memnon," Harry replied.

"What are these Colossi of Memnon?" Barbara asked.

"They are giant statues. Two of them, and they are not far from here," David replied. "It is said that due to a crack in one of them, it sings in the mornings."

"Tell them the story you told me," Randy said, directing his request to Diana. "The one about the Romans."

Suddenly on the spot, Diana's cheeks bloomed with color. "Uh, all right," she agreed. "The Romans—we're talking over fifteen-hundred years ago—used to take elaborate holidays to Egypt. The wealthy ones would sail down to Alexandria, where they could see the lighthouse. After that, they would visit the pyramids at Giza, then board a boat, and cruise up the Nile."

"Two of the Seven Wonders of the World," Randy interjected.

"Exactly. And they must have had some sort of guide book or learned from someone what they should see whilst in Egypt, because they obviously saw the Colossi of Memnon. Those statues are absolutely covered in Latin graffiti. Even the Emperor Hadrian saw them," she claimed.

"Oh, do go on," Barbara encouraged.

"Well, imagine you're a wealthy Roman citizen," Diana continued. "You sail across the Mediterranean for an exotic Egyptian adventure, seek out all the sights, attend some amazing Egyptian festivals, and drink copious amounts of beer."

"Oh, I don't think I would drink the beer," Stella murmured, much to her husband's amusement.

"So of course you're going to see those two huge statues. Listen to them singing in the morning," Diana mused. "Believing them to be statues of Memnon."

"Memnon as in the hero from the Trojan War?" Tom asked in disbelief. "The king of Aethiopia? The one who was slain by Achilles?"

"Yes," Diana affirmed.

Tom frowned. "Are they not of him?" he asked in confusion.

She shook her head. "They are of the pharaoh Amenhotep the Third," she stated. "The Romans thought they were of Memnon because he shared one of his names with a name found inside the Tomb of Ramesses the Fifth and Sixth, so they thought the tomb was his as well."

Randy leaned forward. "Think of the timing. We're talking about a *thousand-year* difference between their deaths and when the Romans would have visited these statues," he said with excitement.

"The Egyptians must have known the Romans had it all wrong," David claimed, his brows furrowing as he sorted the timeframe.

"Yes!" Diana agreed enthusiastically, nodding her head for emphasis.

"So... why didn't the Egyptians correct the Romans?"

Chuckling softly, Diana dipped her head. "Would you? You had all these rich Romans—including emperors—giving you their gold coins. Why correct their mistaken assumptions?"

"So history wouldn't get it wrong?" David replied rhetorically, obviously annoyed. After a moment, he scoffed. "The Egyptians were probably laughing behind their backs," he guessed.

"No doubt," she agreed.

"How far away are these statues?" Barbara asked.

They all turned to Mahmood, who had been listening intently to their conversation

"Only two miles from here, my lady, but first we must cross the river. We shall hire a felucca—a sailing vessel—to make the crossing. I shall inquire as to carriages we might take on the other side. What time would you like to go?"

"If we wake up early, we can be back before the heat is too high," Harry suggested.

"Breakfast at seven o'clock. Leave at eight?" Will countered.

When their party agreed, he turned to the guide. "We'll need to pay you extra, for I have reason to believe this wasn't part of your original itinerary for us."

"You may pay me after I know the costs," Mahmood replied. "We will have time to visit the Temple of Luxor in the afternoon—it's very close. Have you decided if you wish to continue up the river for another fortnight, or if you wish to return to Cairo?"

Will and Harry exchanged quick glances before turning to their families. "We'll discuss it over dinner and give you an answer on the morrow," Will replied, earning a nod of approval from Harry.

*T*wo hours later
With their bellies full and the ladies having departed for the hotel's parlor for hibiscus tea, the men leaned back. "Do we continue up the Nile or head back to Cairo?" Will asked.

"If we continue, what would we see?" Tom asked.

David was quick to respond. "There are temples at Edfu, Kom Ombo, and Philae—that's about a hundred and twenty miles from here."

"It would seem a shame to turn around now," Randy argued. "I would understand if you would all wish to go back, but I happen to be on my wedding trip with my wife," he said.

"We are well aware," his brother deadpanned.

Randy directed a grimace at Tom. "Father always said 'happy wife, happy life', and I am in agreement. Diana and I will continue even if you decide to go back. We can make arrangements to meet you in Rome in a couple of months," he explained.

"Everly, what say you?" Will asked.

Harry chuckled softly. "I admit I have been very surprised at how well my countess has faired on this trip. Not a peep of complaint. And Helen and Bradley seem entertained by the adventure—"

"They do indeed," Will said, chuckling. "Too bad he probably won't remember it." His quick glance in Tom's direction had him catching his nephew's brief grimace.

"I told my man of business I would send word should I be gone longer than six months—"

"Only six months?" Will repeated in surprise.

"I realize now I should have guessed my ladies would enjoy this more than I expected," Harry admitted. "Who knew they wouldn't mind sleeping under mosquito netting and eating strange foods and seeing shriveled up mummies?" he added rhetorically.

"We really haven't seen any of those," David complained.

"We are not bringing any of those back with us," Will stated, his attention on his son.

David scoffed. "I was only teasing," he claimed. "Besides, I would rather not suffer a mummy's curse," he added.

"Nor would any of us," Randy agreed.

"So... do we go on or go back?"

"Go on," the rest said in unison.

Will chuckled softly. "Well, that was easier than I thought it would be."

They finished their drinks and headed to the parlor to join the women. Given the plan for an early departure in the morning, they were soon off to bed.

Not necessarily to sleep, though.

Randy's announcement they were to continue up the Nile to Philae was met with a shriek of delight from Diana. She showed her appreciation by riding him to a rather satisfying release. His last thought before he dozed off was 'happy wife, happy life.'

CHAPTER 32
A COLOSSAL MISTAKE

The following day

As Mahmood had promised, a felucca was waiting for them at a dock directly in front of their hotel. Manned by only two men—one at the bow and one at the stern—the boat featured two sails and was large enough to accommodate their party of ten.

Ten because Bradley, dressed in a white gown and bonnet, joined them for the trip to visit the Colossi of Memnon.

Mahmood was the last to board the ship, ensuring there were five adults seated on each side of the vessel. As the sails filled with the morning breeze and the felucca began the trip across the Nile, he announced the hantours he had arranged to take them to the statues would also be taking them to Medinet Habu.

"To the Temple of Ramesses the Third?" Diana asked in surprise.

"Indeed. It is only three miles from the statues," he explained. "The area around it is the ruins of an abandoned Coptic village and church. However, the paintings, especially those on the ceilings and between the columns, have survived. I think they are worthy of your attention."

"I'm going to have to find another sketchbook," Diana whispered. "I only have a few blank pages left in this one," she added, patting her satchel.

Randy winced. "We'll ask at the hotel," he said.

Across from them Bradley was seated on Helen's lap, and she was angled so he could watch the water. His excitement was evident when he suddenly attempted to leave her lap—and the felucca.

"Bradley!" she scolded, following his line of sight to discover what had him so excited.

"Croc'dile!" Bradley said happily, his chubby fist waving toward the water.

A quick glance at the dark green shape swimming alongside the hull confirmed her brother's assessment. Inhaling sharply, Helen wrapped her arms around him and quickly moved to the center of the deck, nearly tripping on her skirts. Tom and David were both up from their seats along the starboard side of the boat, reaching out in an attempt to keep her on her feet. She ended up in David's arms.

"A crocodile!" Stella confirmed, quickly rising to join Helen in the center of the deck.

The sudden shift in weight had the captain shouting a warning, and shouting again when Harry leaned out in an effort to confirm this wife's claim.

"There is nothing to be afraid of," Mahmood said, his hands held out, palms down, in an effort to calm the group. "The crocodiles will not come aboard," he assured them.

"What about at the dock?" Barbara asked in worry.

"We will keep them away."

Meanwhile, Helen had regained her feet and was left staring at Tom when David released his hold on her, Bradley perched on one of her hips.

"Bach'lor," he said, a pudgy finger finger pointing at David.

"You remembered!" David said in delight. At Helen's look of surprise," he added, "I've been trying to teach him some new words," he said proudly.

Bradley pointed his finger at Tom and said, "Dada."

"I think not," Tom replied, a look of horror on his face.

Helen blinked twice, turned, and thanked David for his help. Then she carefully returned to her seat. Meanwhile, Stella plucked the boy from her hold and settled him on her lap, where one of his thumbs caught his attention before ending up in his mouth.

Directing a look of disdain at his cousin, David returned to his seat. Tom sighed and settled back onto his for the remainder of the short trip.

An hour later
"They're huge," Randy murmured, turning to help Diana down from their hantour. Once she was on the ground, his steps were hurried as he made his way toward one of the two seated statues that loomed ahead of them. Water nearly surrounded the bases of the statue, a sign they had been built on the floodplain of the Nile.

"I told you they were," Diana whispered. Dressed as she was in her breeches and boots, she was able to keep up with him. "Sixty feet tall."

"How much graffiti will we find, do you suppose?" he asked, ignoring the shallow lake to get as close as possible to the base of the statue on the right.

"A hundred and seven inscriptions," Diana replied absently, joining him to stare at the rectangular base.

"How do you know that?" he asked in surprise, his gaze immediately going to some inscriptions on the front of the statue's leg. Some carvings even continued down onto the foot.

"Jean-Antoine Letronne wrote about them in his book, *La statue vocale de Memnon considérée dans ses rapports avec l'Égypte et la Grèce*," she replied. "Father acquired a copy when I was twelve."

Randy didn't bother asking if she had read it. She probably had it memorized.

"Will it sing for us?" Stella asked. She wasn't far from them but had opted not to wade through the water. Standing on his own two feet, Bradley was clinging to her skirts.

"I don't think it does that anymore," Harry replied. "The Romans rebuilt the upper part of the one on the right after the top broke during an earthquake."

"Oh, so that's why his face is in such poor condition," she remarked. "The other seems in better shape."

When the breeze picked up, Bradley began coo'ing. "Seems we have our own singing monument," Helen remarked, grinning for the first time since they had boarded the felucca that morning.

Barbara tittered at the boy, but her gaze was on the two statues that stood in front of them. "They are certainly colossal," she said. "What are they made of?"

"Quartzite sandstone," Mahmood replied. "Back when it could sing—one of the cracks in the sandstone was the source of the sound—the Greeks said it was calling to his mother, Aurora, the goddess of the morning sun."

"Why are they so far apart?" Will asked.

"Amenhotep the Third's temple was here. From what was written by the Romans who came here, it is said the temple was larger than even Karnak," Mahmood claimed. "These statues of him flanked the entrance to the first pylon."

Will furrowed his brows. Although a few trees and some uneven ground could be seen above a shallow lake behind the statues, the expanse of otherwise flat ground showed no evidence of ruins. "What happened to it?"

"This is a floodplain," Mahmood said with a shrug. "The foundations were probably made of mud brick. After a few earthquakes, it is not surprising the temple would have collapsed and its remaining blocks carted off to be used for other temples," he explained.

"Such a shame," Barbara murmured, tittering when she realized a cow was grazing near the water's edge behind the statues. "I didn't know you had cattle here," she remarked.

Mahmood's brows furrowed before he spotted what had her making the comment. "That, my lady, is a water buffalo. But we also have cows."

"Oh," she murmured.

Will offered his arm and they moved closer to the other statue at the same time Diana and Randy were making their way to it. "She is obviously thrilled to be here," he commented.

"I rather imagine she would be more thrilled to actually discover something new. Or old, rather," Barbara replied.

"Thank you for not balking when I told you we would be continuing our trip south," he said.

She reacted with surprise. "Why would I balk?" she asked. "This has been very diverting and far more interesting than Oxfordshire," she added. "And I haven't been having to run a household."

He chuckled. "I promise we'll still go to Rome on the way back."

"I am looking forward to it," she replied.

When the rest of the party had seen enough, they returned to the hantours for the trip to the Temple of Ramesses III.

"Ｗhat do you know of this temple?" Randy asked Diana when the driver of their hantour halted the horse in front of the temple.

"Vivant Denon was the first to describe it in recent times,"

Diana replied. "That was at the turn of the century, when Napoleon's savants were here. Then there was a Franco-Tuscan Expedition about twelve or thirteen years ago. Jean-François Champollion was part of that."

After the other hantours had joined theirs and everyone had assembled, Mahmood led the way to the first pylon. "These ruins you see around you are from a Coptic settlement that may have been home to over eighteen-thousand inhabitants," he explained. "Houses, narrow streets, and the remains of religious buildings can all be found here." He turned and faced the pylon. "By now, this must appear familiar to you. However, wait until you are inside."

Like the pylon at the Khonsu temple, the tops of four niches, two on each side, could be seen above the sand that had collected over time. The opening was clear, though, and they made their way into the forecourt. All the visible walls were carved with hieroglyphics, many the same as what they had seen in other temples. Some were done in relief while others were etched. The most arresting differences were the colossal statues of Ramesses III on one side and uncarved columns on the other.

"Again, you will see familiar scenes, as if whole sections of other temples were copied onto the wall of this one," Mahmood said, waving them past the second pylon and into a peristyle hall. Although there was a carpet of sand covering the floor, it wasn't as deep as in the other temples they had toured, so more of the walls were visible. So were the columns, these in the shape of the pharaoh.

"This place is massive," Randy remarked, gazing up to discover that the painted symbols on the ceiling and at the top of the columns still retained their brilliant colors.

Diana was quick to examine as much as she could.

"I would say it's Greek to me, but I cannot help but think

you're able to decipher these symbols," David said, joining her at one of the walls.

"Most of it is unintelligible to me," she admitted. "But look at this." She pointed to a series of carvings inside an ovoid outline. Several more ovoids appeared on the wall, all vertical and some containing the same symbols. "What could be so important as to always be outlined?"

David shrugged. "A name?" he guessed. "Someone important."

"A pharaoh's name. It's called a cartouche," Diana agreed. "Maybe a god, but they seem to be drawn with their bodies and headdresses." She waved to an area where a figure of the god Horus appeared to be accepting an offering from a man.

"And the symbols not in the ovals?" he asked.

"The rest of the words of their language, I would surmise," she reasoned.

"Have you any clues?"

She arched a brow. "Snakes are enemies, and these..." She pointed to a series of elongated triangles. "Are weapons. Knives."

"Agreed. What about the animals? The birds?" he pressed.

"Animals and birds," she replied. Her forefinger traced one. "A sparrow," she said before pointing to a large outline of what appeared to be a bird of prey. "An eagle."

David stepped back and took in the entire wall, his brows furrowed as if he was about to disagree. "All right," he hedged. "What about these wavy lines?" He indicated a series of serpentine lines that were parallel to one another.

She gave him a quelling glance. "Water," she replied.

Blinking several times, David scoffed. "So... you're thinking this language is very literal."

"Well, it would seem so," she replied. "Except..." her attention went to another series of the symbols. "The one that looks like a sistrum could be something having to do with loving something... or someone, and this sideways lotus flower I think is for fertility." She glanced over at him and saw his gaze was on the departing backs of Tom and Helen. "Are you jealous?"

David gave a start. "What?"

"Are you... jealous. Of Tom?"

His eyes rounding in shock, he said, "No, of course not. What would I be jealous of?"

Diana gave him a quelling glance before returning her attention to the hieroglyphics. Her brow furrowed when she noticed one shaped like a wishbone with a crossbar at the middle. When she stepped back and studied the others around it, she murmured, "to love."

"What?"

She shook her head. "Nothing."

Glancing around, she realized the others had already moved on. "Come, let's see what we're missing."

The two climbed a ramp that led through a columned portico to a third pylon. The large hypostyle hall beyond no longer had its roof, and most of the original carvings had been etched away and replaced with Christian symbols.

"This is where a church was once located," Mahmood explained. "The Egyptian gods are thought of as pagan gods, so any depictions of them have been removed."

"Such a loss," Randy said on a sigh.

"Two years ago, the Epigraphic Survey was published from work done here to document all these wall carvings," Mahmood continued.

"Epigraphic Survey?" Randy repeated.

"A rendering of all these scenes," their guide clarified, waving an arm to indicate the carvings. "We believe it includes a list of all the pharaohs who ruled Egypt."

"Incredible," Will breathed, his attention going to the statuary.

"Indeed," Barbara said. She glanced over to discover Tom

staring at Helen's back, his face displaying an expression of pain. "Oh, dear," she whispered.

"What is it?" Will asked, turning to follow her line of sight.

"You tell me. Your nephew seems terribly upset with Lady Helen, but I cannot for the life of me decide what has him so vexed."

Will arched a brow. "With her? Or the baby?"

Barbara did a double-take. Helen was holding Bradley so his head rested over her shoulder, his closed eyes suggesting he was sound asleep. For a moment, she wished she was the one holding him. "You think he's jealous of Master Bradley?" she asked.

"I'm not sure what's going through his head," Will admitted. "But after the incident on the felucca this morning, I have to believe something happened between them."

The sound of Mahmood's voice interrupted their conversation. "If you are finished here, let us travel back to the hotel for a luncheon and then I shall take you to the Temple of Luxor. I fear after this one, you may be disappointed," he warned.

"I rather doubt it," Diana murmured, taking Randy's proffered arm.

He grinned. "You've liked them all, haven't you?"

She nodded. "They might appear all the same, but there is something unique to every one of them," she said, arching a brow.

"You have the right of it," Mahmood said, overhearing her comment.

CHAPTER 33
A MUMMY MAKES THE DAY

ater that afternoon

When Mahmood mentioned that the Temple of Luxor was very close to the hotel, he was sincere in his claim. After a light luncheon of kebabs and mashed fava beans, Bradley went off with Mahmood's daughter to spend the afternoon in the hotel's parlor. The rest of the group took their leave of the hotel and made their way along the riverfront, their path taking them past a colonnade.

"This is the Temple of Luxor," Mahmood announced. "Unlike other Egyptian temples which are oriented east-west to honor the sun god Ra, this one and the Temple of Karnak are oriented north-south along the east bank of the Nile. We are on the outside of it. You will note that over time, a good bit of rubbish has accumulated here, as have other buildings, including a mosque, Roman barracks, even a pigeon tower," he explained. "Someday perhaps it will be cleared out, making it easier to see it as my ancestors would have seen it."

"What are these columns from?" David asked, stopping to examine a carved column topped with a closed-bud capital.

The column didn't seem particularly tall since a good third of it was underground.

As were all the other columns in the double-rowed colonnade.

"The sun court of the temple," Mahmood replied.

Sounds of disbelief greeted his comment.

"The wall is missing here," he explained. "As are the roofs. But I insist we enter at the front, where we can can still find one of the obelisks."

Knowing the other obelisk had been gifted to the French and moved to Paris a few years earlier, David grumbled a curse, his gaze taking in the debris field around him. Off to the left, a weathered old man sat cross-legged next to a number of dark items lined up on a tarp. When he smiled, only a few teeth showed. Curious, David made his way to the display of strange objects.

"What are these?" he asked, his brows furrowing at seeing the various shapes. Some items were only a foot or two in length while some were much longer. Some were nearly black while other appeared to be wrapped in fabric.

"Mummies," the man replied. "You want?" The rest of what he said was in Arabic.

David blinked, "Mummies?" he repeated. Upon closer inspection, he realized the smaller items were—or rather had been—baby crocodiles. Some were wrapped in yellowed linen while others were a blackish green. Then he realized the larger bodies, also wrapped in linen but much darker in appearance, were human. "Mummies," he murmured.

He gave a start when he realized his cousin, Tom, was at his elbow. On the other side of him, her arm on Tom's, stood Helen, her attention on the mummies.

"Don't look," he said, his comment directed to Helen.

But it was too late, for the young lady inhaled sharply. Instinctively, Tom wrapped an arm around her shoulders and pulled her so she was facing him. "Don't faint, don't faint, don't faint," he whispered frantically.

Helen raised her face to stare at him. "I won't faint," she assured him. "I was just... unprepared, is all." She attempted to turn her head to look behind her, but he lifted a gloved hand to her cheek to prevent her from doing so.

For a moment, their gazes locked, and it was as if they were back in the Morganfield's garden, her in his arms and their lips mere inches from one another. They might have reenacted the kiss they shared, but the moment was broken when Diana appeared next to them.

Her worried gaze first on Helen and then on the display of mummies, Diana asked, "Are you unwell?"

Her attention still on Tom's eyes, Helen shook her head. "I am quite well," she replied in a quiet voice.

"All right," Diana said, although she didn't sound convinced. By the time she took a good look at the vendor's display of mummies, Randy was by her side.

"He's selling these?" he asked in surprise. He made an odd sound in his throat. "Is... is that a cat?" he asked, pointing to a flat mummy wrapped in yellowed linen. The shape was that of a cat's profile, so it appeared to have only two legs.

"Cat, yes," the old man replied, grinning enthusiastically. "You buy?"

Randy shook his head, his eyes rounding when he realized what the other mummies were.

The sound of Mahmood's shout had them turning to see him, the earls, and the countesses quickly approaching.

"Don't let Mother see," David said, turning so his back was to the display. Still holding onto Helen, Tom turned around, as did Randy and Diana, as they attempted to form a human shield.

Will was tall enough to see over them, his look of curiosity soon changing to disgust. Harry glanced over David's shoulder before he dropped the arm Stella was holding and said, "I have to look, my love."

Stella stayed where she was, her gaze on her daughter and Tom. "Did you suffer a shock, my dear?" she asked.

Helen's eyes widened when she realized she was still in Tom's hold. She quickly stepped away from him. "I did, Mother, but I'm much better now," she said.

"Apologies, my lady," Tom said to Stella. "I didn't think she should see the mummified cats."

Stella angled her head to one side, her gaze sweeping the line of bodies behind Tom. "And the humans?" she asked, the edges of her lips turned up as if she was teasing him.

"Humans, my lady?" he repeated, his brows rising nearly to his hairline. He turned around and gulped. "I... I hadn't noticed them, my lady," he said, his face displaying a grimace when he turned to face her.

"Are those mummies?" Barbara asked in awe. She had moved to the end of their line and simply walked around Randy to stand at the end of the display, her hands going to her hips.

"Aunt Barbara," he gently scolded.

"It's not my first time seeing a mummy," she said, not taking her eyes from the morbid display.

"It's not?"

"Of course not. There was an entire line of them on the dock at Cairo. I think they were loading them into some crates to ship them somewhere."

"Ew," David replied.

"I rather imagine they were intended for museums," Diana murmured. "But they should have been left where they were found."

Randy regarded her with worry. "Why did you say it like that?"

She arched a blonde brow. "Desecrating the dead like this?" she countered. "Never a good idea."

"I didn't think you were superstitious," he chided.

"I am not. But others are, and that's all it takes for someone to think they've been cursed."

"Ah, you have heard of mummy curses?" Mahmood asked.

She lifted a shoulder. "I have read a number of books," she replied.

"I have spoken with Ahmet," he said, waving to the vendor. "If you wish to purchase one of his mummies, I can interpret for you." From his manner, it was apparent he hoped they wouldn't partake. He lowered his voice. "However, I can tell you they cost much less in Cairo."

Chuckling but not in a humorous way, Randy made a sound of disgust.

"How are these crocodiles mummified?" Harry asked from where he was crouching next to the line of baby crocodiles, his manner entirely serious.

Mahmood sighed. "They are buried in the sand and left to..." He seemed to struggle for the right word.

"Desiccate?" Harry offered.

"Yes. Very different from how the pharaohs were mummified."

"How were they mummified?" Helen asked.

"Mr. Salman explained it to us when were were at the pyramids at Giza," Tom whispered.

"Another dragoman gave us an explanation, but it was entirely too brief," Helen added, as if she hadn't heard Tom's comment. "He provided no detail at all."

Everyone turned to look at her with surprise. "Ew," David said again.

Mahmood cleared his throat, directing his attention to Will. "Should I tell them?"

Will lifted a shoulder. "They already know the worst."

Dipping his head, their guide held out one hand, his fingers extended. He used his other hand to count off each step. "First, the body is washed in water from the Nile. Next, the brain is removed followed by the other internal organs and placed into canopic jars for preservation."

"Ew."

Ignoring David's comment, Mahmood continued. "They cover the body with natron for forty days."

"What is natron?" Helen asked.

"A sort of mineral salt," her father replied. "They would have found it in dried out lake beds. Then used it to help dry out the body," he explained.

Mahmood nodded in agreement. "The dried body would be anointed with oils and resins and then wrapped in linen."

"With jewels," Diana interjected.

"Amulets, yes," Mahmood agreed. "Then a final layer of resin..." He pointed to one of the human mummies. "Which makes it dark after a time, and then they would be placed in a sarcophagus."

"Sounds quite involved," Barbara remarked. "How long until the funeral?"

Mahmood chuckled. "The entire process took seventy days, so... then it would be placed in a tomb and sealed for the journey to the afterlife."

"Well, I think we've seen enough," Will said, his comment directed to their guide. "Might we go into the temple now?"

"Of course," their guide replied as he headed toward the single obelisk in front of the pylon. "I insist you take care as you navigate the ruins here," he said. "There is a good deal of rubble. Much debris." He pointed to what appeared to be a hill to the south. "It has built up over the centuries from those who lived here."

Harry hung back with the vendor, and he pointed at one of

the crocodile mummies. "I wish to buy that one," he said, pointing to one without a linen wrap.

The old man held up a few fingers, and Harry pulled some coins from his waistcoat pocket. When the vendor waved for him to choose one, he extracted his handkerchief and wrapped it around the back of one of the crocodiles before lifting it. "It's very light," he remarked before straightening. "*Shukran*." He slid the mummy into his top coat pocket so only its tail poked out before he hurried off to join the others as they faced the first pylon.

From the way rubble and sand had been removed from part of the area, it was apparent where the missing obelisk had been located. Its mate was still standing in front of the left side of the pylon, where sand remained piled up quite high. Also in front of the pylon were the top halves of a pair of statues, elaborate crowns with balls on top still atop their heads. The bottom half of their bodies were buried in the sand.

"This temple honors the gods Amun, Mut, and their son, Khonsu," Mahmood stated.

"Which pharaoh is this?" David asked, pointing to the statues.

"We think Ramesses the Second. Like the other Theban temples around here, this one was built with Nubian sandstone," Mahmood explained as they made their way past the pylon and into what remained of the forecourt. Some of the space was now taken up by a mosque. "This is the Abu Haggag Mosque, built twelve-hundred years ago and still used today." He turned and waved to a spherical structure mounted on a column. "Pigeon tower," he said. "Pigeons are a favorite food here. They are quite tasty."

As if the birds had heard his comment, several appeared from inside and flew off.

Up ahead, a grand colonnade of two rows of columns all intact and topped with the open lotus flower capitals, indicated where the hypostyle hall might have been, but with the walls on that side missing, it was hard to imagine the original layout. Another colonnade, the one David had remarked upon when they had been walking to the temple, came next. On their left, parts of walls and columns jutted up from the ground, their bases somewhere down below.

A pair of statues, only the top halves visible above the ground, were next to and in front of a partial wall. Although carvings covered most of it, some of the rock face had broken away. "Amun and Mut," Mahmood stated, indicating the statues.

The group moved to study the double statue. Although Mut was missing her nose and Amun's cheek was gone from one side, their other facial features and headdresses were still quite clear.

"Take time to look at the rest and know that much is buried beneath us," he said.

Breaking off into smaller groups, the older couples headed towards the sun court while Diana and Randy regarded the top half of the sanctuary.

David wandered off to the grand colonnade, leaving Tom and Helen together at the statues.

"Thank you for trying to... to protect me earlier," Helen stammered.

"You're welcome," he replied. He cleared his throat. "I noticed you didn't bring Bradley this afternoon."

She shook her head. "He's with the nanny," she replied. "Although it was good for him to be outside earlier, he was quite tired."

Tom turned to her and then glanced around. When he was sure no one was watching them, he took her hand and led her around to the other side of the statues. Sandwiched between the wall and the backs of the statues, another wall protecting them from being seen from the courtyard, they stood staring at one another until Tom finally said, "I... I wanted to speak to you about..." His face screwed in a grimace.

"About?" she prompted. When he didn't respond, she sighed. "Did you bring me back here to kiss me?"

His eyes rounded. "Uh, well, I wouldn't object to doing so," he admitted.

She blinked. "You wouldn't object?" she repeated, her words making it sound as if she was offended.

He shook his head. "No. I quite liked kissing you. I thought about it many times since. How I might do it differently."

"Differently?" she repeated, her confusion evident.

"Longer," he clarified. He lifted a shoulder. "And I like holding you," he said, reaching out with a hand to place it at her waist. When she didn't push it away, he tightened his grip on her.

"I like it when you hold me," she replied, stepping close enough so they nearly touched, her skirts pressed against his pantaloons. "As you were doing earlier."

He hesitated before wrapping his other arm around her shoulder, his gloved hand pressing against her shoulder blade. "I wanted to ask you if..."

When he didn't continue, Helen sighed and suddenly lifted onto her tiptoes, her lips touching his as one of her hands went to his shoulder for support.

For a moment, she felt only his breath on her cheek, heard only the sound of birds, and felt only the heat of his lips on hers. When his tongue invaded her mouth, she tasted him and moaned softly.

He pulled his lips away to inhale a breath, but he pulled her closer. When he resumed the kiss, it was as if he had been a starving man, as if he couldn't get enough of her.

Consumed as she was in the kiss, it was all Helen could do to hold on, both of her hands gripping his shoulders until his arms tightened their hold on her and she was fully pressed against the front of his body.

Heat suffused the front of her bodice even as she realized she could feel his heartbeats against her breasts. Or maybe it was her own heart, the pulse sounding loud in her ears as he deepened the kiss.

When she finally had to end the kiss to take a gulping breath, she stared up at him.

His eyes were glazed over, and for a moment, he didn't appear to know where he was. When they cleared, he visibly swallowed, released his hold on her, and stepped back. "Apologies," he whispered.

She blinked. "For what?" she asked.

But he had already disappeared, leaving her by herself behind the statues of a god and his lover.

When she emerged back into the sunlight, she turned and regarded the Amun and Mut with a frown. "A lot of help you were," she murmured on a sigh of frustration.

When the group returned to the hotel, she did so on the arm of David.

CHAPTER 34
A YOUNG LADY'S BOLD LETTER

*L*ater that afternoon

Although she had marveled at the statuary and flower-topped columns at the Temple of Luxor, Helen couldn't shake the sensation that something was wrong.

Tom hadn't said a single word to her after their kiss behind the statues. He had, in fact, gone out of his way to avoid her ever since their return to the hotel.

Perhaps he simply couldn't abide being in the company of Bradley, for she had agreed to look after the toddler while her parents took a walk along the river. Given his penchant to either stand in one place and gawk or run willy-nilly with no regard for his safety, Helen had opted to keep him on her hip as she made her way to the parlor, hoping his nappy wouldn't dampen her skirts.

By the time they returned to their hotel for dinner, she was at her wit's end.

Her mother had been happy to take Bradley from her, and Mahmood's daughter had been ready to change his nappy and put him down for an afternoon nap once they went down to spend time in the shaded gardens before dinner.

While others headed to the gardens, Helen changed into a different gown but remained in her room. Fighting back tears, she sat at the room's small escritoire. Pulling a sheet of parchment from her stationery box, she considered what to say before she dipped a quill into the ink pot and began to write.

> *Dear Thomas,*
>
> *I write to you because my every attempt to speak with you has been interrupted, and I find myself experiencing a sort of frustration that I fear might erupt at a most inopportune time or in an inappropriate place.*
>
> *From our brief time together at the Morganfield ball, I was left with the impression that you liked me. That you might even feel affection for me.*
>
> *Your kisses both then and today would certainly suggest your regard was more than a passing fancy.*
>
> *Perhaps time and distance had caused your regard to fade, or perhaps there is another who has taken my place in your thoughts, for your behavior towards me this past fortnight has been most bewildering. I know you watch me, for I catch you doing so. Sometimes you seem ready to say something and other times you seem almost disgusted by the very sight of me. Your hasty departure earlier today was most unsettling. i feel as if one of those awful mummies has cursed us.*
>
> *What, pray tell, has happened?*
>
> *Have I done something (of which I am unaware) that has caused you to regret our words that night? I ask again—is there another who has replaced me in your thoughts?*
>
> *I am prepared for whatever is your answer. I will be sorry if I have fallen out of your favor, but I know in my heart that I have done nothing (knowingly) to earn your disregard.*
>
> *Could you see to meeting with me in private? To face me and tell me how you truly feel, so that we may proceed without the*

awkwardness that has become so apparent that even my father has begun to wonder?

Tonight, after everyone is abed, at say eleven o'clock, come to my bedchamber. You needn't knock—I shall leave the door unbarred so that we may discuss our situation in private.

If you do not come, I will assume you are no longer interested in courting me. Yes, I will suffer for a time, for I have held you in my heart ever since that night, but I will also know it is better to know your thoughts than to wonder what I have done wrong.

Sincerely,

Helen

As she reread her letter, the words written in her even penmanship, Helen began to question what she was doing.

Cornering Thomas Forster. Forcing him to face her.

If he showed up at her door, they would finally have the opportunity to talk—or rather whisper—to determine his thoughts on their future. If he didn't show up, she would know his regard for her had indeed changed to one of indifference, and she would simply be forced to stop thinking about him. She would be forced to endure another Season in London. Forced into a marriage with a widower or a young buck for whom she had no feelings at all.

A loveless marriage.

A tear streaked down her cheek at the thought of spending the rest of her life like that. Living with someone but feeling alone.

Perhaps there would be children she could love. Perhaps that would be enough. But after growing up with parents who openly displayed their affection—or at least didn't do a very good job of hiding it—she could hardly imagine a relationship so different for herself.

The tear fell from her cheek and landed at the bottom of her letter, blurring the 'en' at the end of her name.

"Hel," she whispered. Well, that certainly felt appropriate at the moment.

She lifted the parchment and gently blew on it before carefully folding it into an envelope. Taking up the quill, she wrote "The Honorable Thomas Forster" on the outside and set it aside.

Pulling a hanky from her pocket, she dabbed at her cheek and let out the sob she had been attempting to stifle.

Now was not the time for tears.

Tonight she would have her answer.

One way or the other.

Her gaze darted to the window, and she hurried to look out on the gardens below. Her parents were lounging at a small metal table, her father's head bent as he wrote of his latest findings in his journal. A sheet of parchment separate from his book displayed a drawing he had done of a hibiscus bloom, a nearby bush filled with the rose-red flowers.

At the other small table, Diana, Randy, Thomas, and David were playing a game of whist. The earl and countess were nowhere to be seen, but Helen knew Barbara wished to spend the afternoon shopping.

This was her chance.

She stepped out of her bedchamber and hurried to the other side of the hotel's open courtyard, counting the doors until she reached the one she had seen Tom come out of that morning. Trying the handle, she was relieved when it easily opened. Once inside, she glanced about, nervous because she wasn't sure where the best place would be to leave her note.

In the middle of the floor, as if it had been shoved under the door? Atop the bureau? On the bed?

She glanced at the small bed. Like hers, it was shoved against one wall and was surrounded by a fine netting that hung from the ceiling. The edges of the netting were draped open to show the bed had been made up by a servant.

After placing the letter on the middle of the pillow, Helen hurried out the door, carefully closing it behind her before she headed for the stairs.

She wasn't aware she was being watched as she exited the hotel to join the others in the gardens.

CHAPTER 35

A FLEDGLING RELATIONSHIP IS DISCUSSED

*M*eanwhile, at the end of the walkway

"Well, that was rather odd," Barbara said, suddenly halting her climb to the second floor. She carried a hat box in one hand while a reticule dangled from the other. Her attention was directed down the carpeted walkway leading to the rooms they had let.

"What was odd?" Will asked from behind her, his gaze darting about as if he was on alert for a footpad.

"Lady Helen," she whispered, before resuming the climb until she was beyond the top stair. She stepped aside to allow Will to join her. "She's gone down the other set of stairs, but I am quite sure I saw her come out of one of *our* rooms."

Encumbered with a number of boxes under his arms, Will rushed ahead of his wife to their room, using an elbow to push down on the door handle. "Do you suppose she was merely waiting for someone to answer the door?" he asked, dropping the boxes on their bed so he could take the hat box from her.

"She was most definitely *in* a room," Barbara whispered.

He glanced around. "But not ours?"

She shook her head and poked her head out of the room. "Two doors down."

"Tom's room," Will said. He hurried to stand before the door and knocked. He waited a moment but finally opened it and glanced around. Not seeing anything out of place, he carefully closed the door and rejoined his wife. "Well, she was probably just looking for him," he said.

Pulling her gloves from her hands, Barbara gave him a curious glance. "I think there's something going on with those two," she said, after he had shut the door.

"Going on?" he repeated.

"Surely you've noticed."

Will screwed up his face in a grimace. "Maybe."

Barbara scoffed and turned to regard him with disbelief. "I thought he liked her."

"Oh, he does," Will said. "He loves her."

She blinked, obviously not expecting such a definitive answer. "You seem terribly sure of his regard," she accused.

"Well, I'm his uncle, and..." Here he shrugged. "I may have paid witness to something... before we left London," he stammered.

"Paid witness to *what*?" she asked in alarm.

Will held out a hand, intending to lead her to one of the room's settees. "You're probably exhausted from our long day. Why don't you have a seat, and I'll see to having some drinks delivered," he suggested.

She wasn't to be deterred, though, one fist going to a hip. "Paid witness to *what*?" she repeated, obviously annoyed by his attempt to avoid the conversation.

Inhaling deeply upon realizing she wasn't to be distracted, he let out the breath in a *whoosh*. "He kissed her. Or she kissed him. It was dark. Rather difficult to tell who started it, actually. But they were both willing participants, I believe."

"Where?"

"In the Morganfield gardens. During that ball we attended the night before we left London."

After a moment, Barbara began tittering, a brilliant smile replacing the look of suspicion she had displayed only the moment before. "Oh, this is interesting," she murmured, her face displaying a look of awe. She suddenly sobered. "So... why is Tom avoiding her?"

Will winced. "You noticed that, too?"

She scoffed again. "I'm not blind, Will. We've both seen him watching her. I've seen her watching him. And then, when they look as if they're actually going to look at one another at the same time—"

"They both turn red," Will finished for her.

"Indeed," she agreed. "So.. why does he offer his arm one day and then go out of his way to stay so far away from her the next?"

Will lifted a shoulder. "Maybe he doesn't like Bradley. She had her brother with her at the temple this morning," he remarked.

"I was rather surprised they didn't leave him with Mahmood's daughter for the entire day," Barbara said thoughtfully.

"Me as well, but Lady Helen does seem rather fond of him."

"She probably wants one or two of her own by now," Barbara commented. "If she wasn't here in Egypt, she would be about to start her third Season. Poor girl," she added in a whisper. Finally taking a seat in one of the settees, she sighed and then suddenly gasped as she watched Will sit next to her. "What is it?" he asked.

She shook her head. "I thought the timing of our two arrivals was coincidental, but perhaps..." Here she stopped and sighed.

"What are you thinking?" he prompted.

"Do you suppose Everly planned this trip so they would arrive in Egypt at the same time as we did?" she asked.

Will chuckled. "No," he replied. "I don't know how he could. Besides, it's a good time to be here in Egypt. There are apparently a number of Englishmen on their way to or from India at any given time. The weather is not too hot. The rainy season is about over," he reasoned. "But I could ask him if you'd like. Except... what exactly would I be asking?"

Barbara gave him a quelling glance. "Did you time your trip so your daughter and my nephew could secretly court one another?"

Once again chuckling, Will said, "Did you hear how ridiculous that sounded? I rather doubt Everly is even aware of his daughter's regard for Tom. Or visa-versa," he argued.

"His attentions are rather concentrated on plants and such," she agreed. "I don't know how Stella puts up with him."

About to defend the earl—he had paid witness to Everly's regard for his countess while the two were examining a row of columns, the man stepping in front of her to kiss her forehead when he thought no one was looking—Will instead said, "So what are we going to do about our nephew?"

Barbara's eyes widened as she considered the query. "Nothing, I suppose," she whispered.

"I can have a talk with him," he suggested. "Discover if he's changed his mind or is merely hiding his regard for Lady Helen."

Nodding, Barbara rested her head against the back of the settee. "You do that, darling. But before you do, could you see about those drinks you mentioned? I am parched."

Chuckling, he stood and made his way to the door. "I'll be back in a moment."

As he headed down the walkway to the stairs, he paused before Tom's door. Glancing around to be sure no one was about, he once again entered the room. Not sure what he was looking for, he slowly made his way inside, looking for any sign of something that didn't belong. Something out of place.

He realized why he had missed the letter resting against the pillow on the bed the first time he had been in the room—the netting surrounding the bed had hid it from view.

He didn't touch it, but he could read the feminine writing from where he stood.

Expecting the envelope to be addressed with simply the word, 'Tom' or 'Thomas', he was surprised to see it was more formally addressed.

The Honorable Thomas Forster.

Not a love note, then.

He displayed a grimace at the thought Lady Helen was breaking off whatever relationship they might have had. He reached out and plucked the note from the pillow and held it up in front of the light from the window. Although he couldn't make out many words, what with the way the parchment had been folded, the ink had nearly bled through in one spot.

The backwards script of a time.

Eleven o'clock.

Not about to unfold and read the missive, Will quickly returned the note to the pillow and left the room, gently closing the door behind him.

Something was going to happen at eleven o'clock.

Either Helen Tennison was meeting Tom or he was to meet her, or she was planning to break off whatever the two had in the way of a relationship.

Perhaps he did need to have a discussion with someone.

CHAPTER 36
A MISSIVE IS DISCOVERED

*L*ater that afternoon

Returning to their rooms to change for dinner, Tom was accompanied by David and his aunt and uncle. Their last game of whist had been won by Barbara, his aunt replacing Diana and Will replacing Randy when the newlyweds announced they wished to return to their room when there was still one hand left to play.

"I shouldn't take long," Tom said, just before David disappeared into his own room.

"We'll meet you downstairs in the parlor," Barbara said before disappearing into her room.

Tom entered his room and glanced around, happy to see the bed had been made and that the hotel's laundress had delivered his other clothes at some point since their departure that morning.

He pulled a white shirt and cravat from the pile and placed the rest of the clean clothes atop his trunk before moving to sit on the bed to take off his boots.

Tom gave a start when a note slid down his pillow.

He chuckled softly at seeing the name written on the

outside. Thinking it merely a missive from the hotel or a bill from the laundress, he tossed it aside and continued undressing. He took the time to wash his face and upper body, humming softly as he scraped a razor over his cheeks and upper lip.

About to pull on a pair of pantaloons, he instead sat down on the bed and opened the letter. Even before he had it unfolded, he knew it wasn't from the hotel.

Especially when he read the opening lines.

> *Dear Thomas,*
>
> *I write to you because my every attempt to speak with you has been interrupted, and I find myself experiencing a sort of frustration that I fear might erupt at a most inopportune time or in an inappropriate place.*

For a moment before he continued reading, Tom experienced a combination of embarrassment, both for himself and for the young lady. But what could he do?

By now he had decided there was no other man in her life. No way to account for her having a son. If he had any hope for a future with her, he would have to discover the truth of Bradley's existence. Find out exactly what had happened.

He finished reading the missive before taking a look at his pocket watch. Dinner would over by ten o'clock. After such a long day and with no excursions scheduled for the following day, everyone would be abed by the time she had listed in her letter.

Eleven o'clock.

For some reason he couldn't sort, he felt relief at knowing that at eleven o'clock or shortly thereafter, he would either be betrothed to Lady Helen or be forced to forget her.

But first, he had to get through dinner.

CHAPTER 37
AN ASSIGNATION LEADS TO
A CONFRONTATION

*L*ater that night

Although dinner had not been especially long and drawn out that evening, it had felt as if the minutes had ticked by entirely too slow for Helen.

She wondered if they had for Tom.

From the manner in which he had caught her eye as they entered the dining room, she knew he had read her letter. As to his thoughts on the matter, he gave nothing away during the animated discussion of that day's discoveries.

Animated until tiredness seemed to overtake them. If the men stayed for a glass of liquor prior to going to bed, she and the other women wouldn't know of it until their men joined them, for none of the ladies opted to take tea in the parlor after dinner.

Her heart beating too fast and her increased breathing making her feel light-headed, Helen glanced at the timepiece that hung from a gold chain around her neck.

Ten-fifty-five. At least, it was as close as it could be given the lack of clocks with which to synchronize it. She had opted to believe the hotel's clock in the parlor and had reset her timepiece while they waited for the Bellinghams and their party to join them for dinner earlier that evening.

The jeweled chronometer had been a gift from her sister-in-law, Margaret, for her twenty-first birthday. The gemologist and Helen's brother, Alexander, had adorned the gold watch casing with a row of emerald gems along the outer rim and at the end of the winding mechanism, making it easy to wind the watch every morning and every evening. Given Bradley's tendency to grab at the jewels, she kept it hidden under her bodice during the daytime.

She stood from the bed and moved to the cheval mirror in the corner of the room. The moonlight streaming through the room's only window was enough by which to see her reflection. Her long blonde hair was brushed out but still wavy from the bun in which it had been wound all day. Dressed in her best night rail, her blue satin dressing gown left open in the front, she appeared almost ethereal in the silver light.

What would Tom think when he saw her though?

She had thought to simply wear what she had for dinner that evening. At half-past-ten, she was still wearing the emerald dinner gown, earning her compliments from both Diana and Barbara. She had caught Tom watching her at least twice during the evening meal, but he hadn't said a word to her.

She was sure he had read her letter. There had been that slight lift of his head, as if he was acknowledging her concerns and would explain himself later.

Before that, she had imagined her letter accidentally falling behind his bed when the counterpane was pulled aside. Lying on the floor under his bed, never to be found or read by anyone until...

Helen gave a start when she sensed movement behind her. Whirling around, she found herself face to face with Tom.

"I didn't hear you knock," she whispered.

He shook his head. "I didn't," he replied. "I… I almost didn't come. For… obvious reasons."

A rock seemed to fall into her stomach, and Helen lifted a hand to press against her middle. "Obvious?" she repeated, fighting back tears.

"I feared I might be discovered. You would be ruined, and…" Here he paused and bit his lip. "Well, I suppose that's no longer a concern," he said before allowing a long sigh.

Helen stared at him for a moment, her brows furrowing in confusion. "No longer a concern?" she repeated. "Whatever are you talking about?" She faced the door, thinking perhaps he meant that someone had indeed seen him enter.

"Helen," he said softly. "I wish you would have told me that night."

She blinked. "Told you what?"

He ran a hand through his hair, his frustration obvious. She quickly lifted a hand and smoothed away the furrows left behind, watching as he closed his eyes and seemed to shiver beneath her touch.

"I can do math," he said.

"I never thought you couldn't," she countered.

"Bradley is a year old."

"One year and a month," she corrected him.

"Which means he was born a year ago January," he said.

"He was."

"Which means…" He paused and dipped his head. "He was already… on the way… the night we kissed. At the Morganfield ball," he struggled to get out. "In September."

"Yes, that's correct," she said, her blonde brows furrowing in confusion.

"Who… pray tell, who is the father?"

Helen once again blinked. "Well, Father, of course," she replied.

Tom inhaled sharply. His subsequent groan and a sound of disgust was loud in the quiet room. "Oh, God," he whispered.

"Tom, whatever is wrong?" she asked.

He scoffed. "You don't *know*?" he asked, disbelief evident in his voice.

Helen swallowed, wondering if he had heard some rumor suggesting her mother had been involved in an *affaire*, which would suggest Bradley's father was someone *other* than her father. Given her parents amorous behavior, she knew it was rather unlikely, though.

Which left only one other consideration.

"Well, if you're saying my mother is too old to be having a babe, then let me be the one to inform you that Queen Charlotte was still having babies when she was nearly forty."

It was Tom's turn to blink, and he did so several times. "Your... your *mother*?"

Helen nodded. "Who did you think...?" She widened her eyes as realization dawned on her, and she stepped back as her mouth dropped open in shock. "Thomas Forster!" she scolded.

"Bradley is... is your *brother*?" Tom asked, only a moment before her open hand made contact with his cheek.

Hard.

The slap was so loud, Helen winced at the thought it might have awakened everyone in the hotel. From the expression on Tom's face, she didn't know if she had truly hurt him or simply knocked some sense into him.

Either way, she was fairly sure it had worked.

CHAPTER 38
AN UNCLE AND A FATHER CONFER

a few minutes earlier, outside the door to Helen's room

Steeling himself for the worst, Will lifted his hand, intending to knock on Helen's door. If Tom was inside, he wasn't sure what he was going to do to his nephew, but a dressing down would be the very least of it.

He began imagining all sorts of appropriate punishment for the young man.

A night spent alone in one of the temples with only a mummy for company.

Leave him in the desert with only a dromedary to find his way back to civilization.

Make him spend a day in Bradley's company with nothing more than a single nappy and a bottle of milk.

He shook his head upon thinking of the last scenario. Knowing Tom as he did, he was fairly sure the young man and the babe would make a day of it, and they would both come out of it better for having spent the time together.

Will had thought he had made it clear to all the boys on this trip that they needed to be on their very best behavior. The fact that Tom wasn't in his room—Will had stopped there first

—meant it was likely he was in Helen's room. Nearly fifteen minutes had passed since the 'eleven o' clock' he had read through the paper when holding her letter to the light.

'Eleven o'clock' was no doubt the time intended for an assignation.

An assignation he now realized had been initiated by Lady Helen.

Will lowered his fist and considered what he was about to do, giving a start when the door to the next door room suddenly opened.

"Bellingham?" The whispered word was said by Harry. From his manner of dress and bare feet, it was apparent he had hurriedly pulled on a dressing robe, although he was wearing a pair of pantaloons.

"Everly," Will replied, nodding to the earl. "I, uh,..." He rolled his eyes. "I suppose you're wondering why I'm standing outside your daughter's room," he whispered.

"Actually, I am not," Harry replied, a long sigh following his words.

"You knew...?"

From's Harry's expression, Will realized whatever Helen's father knew, he had learned only moments ago.

"How did *you* find out?" Harry asked.

About to admit to finding Lady Helen's letter on Tom's pillow, Will was prevented from doing so when a strange sound came from beyond the door.

Thwack!

"What the hell?" he asked in a hoarse whisper.

"It sounded like... like a slap."

"A slap? Or a... a spank?" Will countered.

Harry's face screwed into a grimace. "Across the face," he said, with the confidence of someone who had suffered the same fate. He even used a hand to rub one cheek as if in sympathy.

Will nodded. "I may have experienced something similar once a long time ago," he admitted.

"Oh, I deserved it," Harry said. "It actually confirmed for me that Stella would make the perfect countess."

"Same," Will agreed. He once again lifted his fist to knock on the door but paused when Harry placed a staying hand on it. "What?"

"I don't know about you, but I only learned from Stella a few minutes ago that my daughter told her she intended to take matters into her own hands regarding a certain young man," Harry explained.

"Thomas?" Will guessed.

"Indeed. Until this trip, I had no idea she was the least bit interested in him as a potential suitor, though. What do you know about it?"

Will cleared this throat, dipping his head as he tried to decide whether or not to tell Harry what he knew.

"What?" Harry prompted.

Will let out a long sigh. "I may have paid witness to a... uh,... particularly passionate kiss they shared during the Morganfield ball. In the gardens," he stammered.

"The night before you left England?" Harry guessed.

"Indeed. I was going to interrupt and admonish him, but..." He sighed and ran a hand through his hair. "I knew the two of them wouldn't be doing more than kissing that night. And I knew we would be gone from England in a few hours, and..." He shrugged.

"You did the same with your countess, did you not? When you went off in a naval ship?" Harry asked, his query sounding like an accusation.

Will nodded. "I might have done more. I did more," he admitted. "Which is why my oldest son is not my heir," he whispered.

"Helen is the reason we made this trip," Harry blurted.

"Oh?"

"Well, not *the* reason, but she suggested it a few months ago. I hadn't been on an expedition for a very long time, and she had the idea to come to Egypt," Harry explained.

"Did she say why?"

"She didn't, but..." Here he chuckled softly. "If I remember right, she and Stella had just returned from Lady Devonville's parlor when she brought it up."

Will stiffened. "My stepmother," he murmured. "She and Barbara have been corresponding regularly. Cherise would have known of our itinerary for Egypt."

"Which explains why Helen insisted we be in Cairo the day we arrived," Harry commented thoughtfully. "She helped with all the arrangements and all the details. Knew who I should contact about accommodations. She no doubt planned this... this assignation," he added, waving to the door.

"She'll make an excellent wife for any deserving man," Will said. "An exceptional mother, too, given how good she is with your spare heir."

The two glanced at the door, as if they thought it would open at any moment. "If she *did* slap him, then she's probably apologizing to him," Harry theorized. "Hopefully."

"Or he is," Will said.

"Which means they're probably forgiving one another..."

"Probably kissing," Will guessed.

"She's no doubt concerned about the red mark she left on his cheek."

"Serves him right," Will stated.

A moment of silence passed.

"So... what would be next, do you suppose?" Harry asked.

"Well, I admit, I'm still a bit confused," Will said softly. "I've caught Tom staring at her. I've seen her watching him. Half the time, he seems amenable. But when she has Bradley in her company..." He lifted an eyebrow.

"I think I might know why *that* is," Harry murmured thoughtfully.

"Oh?"

"If you saw the girl you had been kissing in the gardens more than a year ago, and she had a babe in her arms or clutching at her skirts... even in the company of their parents, what would *you* think?"

Will furrowed a brow. "Well, truth be told, I thought Lady Helen was the mother of Master Bradley at first. That her husband was somewhere else... or that he had died," he whispered. "At least, I did until Barbara explained Bradley was *your* son."

Harry chuckled softly. "Poor Thomas."

"Poor Lady Helen," Will said, glad to learn what his wife had told him was true. He glanced at the door again, contemplating if he should knock or not. "What do you suppose they're talking about now?"

"Uh... probably their future. If there is to be one. Marriage, children..." Here Harry's dark brows suddenly furrowed. "*Making* children."

He reached up and was about to pound on the door when it suddenly opened.

His fist almost impacted Tom's nose.

CHAPTER 39
GUILT AND UNDERSTANDING

A *few minutes earlier, inside Helen's room*

For the split second after he felt the sting of Lady Helen's slap, Tom experienced a combination of relief and gladness, eye-opening startlement and empathy.

The first two were understandable, of course. How could he have been such a fool to think that she, an earl's daughter, could be a ruined woman, even before he had met her? The sense of relief he felt at learning the truth was so profound, he wanted nothing more than to pull her into his arms and shout out loudly of his regard for her.

As for the empathy, he was sure her hand felt the same painful sting as his face was still experiencing. He reached for it, careful to hold it from the back side. He saw her eyes go round with fear, felt her pull against his hold as he turned her hand over.

She gasped when he lowered his head until he his lips made contact with her palm, the kiss as gentle as he could manage.

"I'm so sorry," she whispered, her breaths loud in the quiet.

"It is *I* who am sorry," he said, letting go of her hand to wrap his arm around her shoulders to bring her closer. "I was a fool to believe you were a ruined woman. That you had feelings for someone else."

Although she felt stiff beneath his hold, she slowly relaxed, and he added his other arm to pull her forward until she was pressed against his chest. He lowered his face to kiss her forehead.

"You truly thought Bradley was my son?" she asked, finally giving into his hold and raising her hand to his cheek. It was too dark to see if she had left a mark with her slap.

"How could I not?" he asked. At hearing her scoff, he added, "You are so good with him, Helen. I've never felt such jealousy of a man I've never met," he admitted. "I believed you were his mother because... because you are the perfect mother."

From the look she displayed, he knew he had surprised her with his words. "In fact, I am wondering what I will have to do in recompense to ensure you are the mother of my children." He tightened his hold on her when he felt her inhale sharply.

Despite the dark, he could make out her look of awe and finally let out the breath he had been holding.

"Children?" she repeated, her whisper so quiet he had to lean down to hear it. "*Your* children?"

"And yours," he said.

The words were barely out of his mouth before he closed the distance between their lips and kissed her thoroughly. That she allowed him to do so, that she returned the kiss so eagerly, had his heart swelling in his chest, pounding hard against his ribs. When they finally parted, he left his forehead pressed to hers. "I almost wish we had one right now."

Her eyes once again rounded. "We could make one if you'd like," she offered, waving to the bed.

Tom chuckled, partly from hearing the enthusiasm in her

voice and partly to keep his hardening manhood from making itself apparent.

There had been a moment earlier, when he had first slipped into the room and spotted her standing in front of the cheval mirror, that had him reacting as he had the first night they had met at the ball. Despite her wearing a chaste night rail and dressing robe, he had imagined her as his new bride. Imagined he was joining her for their first night together as a married couple. Imagined what it would be like to remove the garments and smooth his hands over the bare, soft skin of her body. Kiss her on those sweet lips. Kiss the soft rounds leading to her pert nipples and suckle them until they were red and ripe with need. Kiss her along the tender flesh of her thighs.

He might have imagined more at that moment, but Helen had finally realized he was in the room with her, and reality had returned him to the here and now.

The wrong reality.

Thank the gods.

Bradley wasn't her boy. He was her brother.

"Believe me when I say I would like nothing more in this world than to make love to you," he whispered.

"But?" she prompted.

He glanced towards the door. "I fear the sounds I would make when I experience euphoria with you would be heard by everyone in this hotel. And maybe half of Cairo," he added, his manner serious.

Helen began to giggle, and she buried her face in his chest as if to stifle the sound. "What makes you think you would be a loud lover?"

Grinning, Tom leaned down again and kissed her forehead. "My brother married Diana last September, and believe me when I tell you, we all know when he's making love to her."

"Well, they are incandescently in love with one another," she said, grinning.

"As I hope we will be," he murmured.

"I will know we are if you're as vocal when you are making love to me," she countered.

"You minx," he accused.

She inhaled sharply and stared at him.

"What is it?" he asked, quickly sobering.

"My father says that to my mother. Frequently."

"Which is probably why there is a Bradley," he said dryly. He once again grew serious. "Truth be told, my father says it to my mother, and I've heard my uncle say it to my aunt on many occasions whilst on this trip."

He watched as she stared at him, as if she couldn't decide if she should put voice to her thoughts or keep them to herself. "Tell me what you're thinking," he urged.

Helen stiffened in his hold. "How many other... *minxes* will there be, do you suppose?"

Tom blinked, at first not understanding her query. "Other minxes?" he repeated.

"Mistresses?" she clarified. "Ladies of the evening?"

He shook his head. "I don't employ any, nor do I intend to in the future," he said. "Why would I if we're going to be making love so... vocally?" he added, allowing a teasing grin. "And frequently?" He sighed with relief when she settled back into his hold.

"Even when I am round with child?"

"Oh, especially when you are round with child," he whispered, leaning down to kiss her forehead and eyelids. He made a sound of frustration in his throat. "If I don't leave this room right now..."

"Then what?" she prompted.

"I'm going to end up holding you in my arms until we both fall asleep, and when we're discovered in the morning—"

"Who would discover us?"

"—by any one of my family or yours," he went on, ignoring

her query. "My uncle will string me up by my..." Here he clamped his mouth shut and grimaced. "Well, let's just say we won't be having all those children we want."

Helen sighed with frustration. "Oh, all right. Then be off with you," she said, giving him a gentle shove.

Tom bestowed another kiss on her forehead, then her lips, and finally on the back of both of her hands before he let go, bowed, and made his way to the door.

He opened it to discover both his uncle and the Earl of Everly standing on the other side of it, his uncle's arms crossed and their expressions suggesting he would not be long for this earth.

Lord Everly's fist barely missed the same cheek Helen had slapped only moments ago.

CHAPTER 40
CAUGHT BUT NOT

"My lord," Tom said, giving a start before he bowed slightly. When the earl didn't respond right away—he looked stunned from his interrupted attempt to knock on the door—Tom's nervousness took over. "I wondered if I might have a word with you, my lord. About your daughter," he continued, his anxiousness growing. "I wish to ask your permission to marry her."

Harry leaned to one side until he could see Helen. "Have you already asked her?"

"No, my lord. I wished to gain your permission first," Tom replied, sounding ever so reasonable despite the circumstances.

From the expression he had seen on his uncle's face, Tom knew he would be facing Will's censure soon enough.

He had a thought he might end up having to spend a night in a temple with only a mummy for company. Or that he would be left in the desert alone with a camel and be forced to find his way back to civilization.

Perhaps Uncle Will would think to leave him in the

company of Bradley all day, for he was fairly sure he and the boy could make a day of it. It might have been twenty years since he was that age, but he was fairly sure he could remember how to play.

Harry exchanged a quick glance with Will before he said, "We'll talk about it over breakfast." He turned his attention to his daughter. "Anything I should know, Helen?" he asked.

"I love him, Father," she replied. "I want him to be the father of my children. The sooner the better."

Harry sighed as he returned his gaze to Tom. "Did you already discuss the matter with her?"

"I did, sir. She tried to convince me we should start this evening, but I, uh, tempted Fate and declined with the hope she'll forgive me. I thought we had best wait," he stammered.

"Good man," Will and Harry murmured in unison. "Well, if there isn't anything else...?"

"Good night, Father. Good night, my lord," Helen said. She turned to Tom and stood on tiptoes to kiss him on the same cheek she had slapped. "I am sorry I slapped you," she whispered.

Harry and Will exchanged knowing glances.

"I deserved it, my sweet," Tom whispered. "Good night." He waited until the two earls had stepped aside and made his way between them, hurrying to his own room in an effort to escape any admonishments.

Meanwhile, Helen dipped a curtsy and shut her room door, leaving the two earls on the other side.

Harry made an odd sound in his throat as Will chuckled softly.

"Well, shall we tell our wives now, or wait until the morning?" Will asked in a hoarse whisper.

"I have some brandy if you'd like to join me for a drink?" Harry suggested. "I could certainly use one."

Will nodded. "I like your idea better."

The two headed down the hall to retrieve the brandy and then to the empty lobby below.

It was well past midnight before they went off to bed.

CHAPTER 41
A REVELATORY MORNING

The following morning

"Is there something you wish to tell me?" Barbara asked, when Will finally peeled an eyelid open and murmured a groggy "good morning".

Will managed to open his other eye before he groaned and placed a hand on his forehead. "There was, but I can't remember," he said through a mouth that felt as if it was filled with cotton.

"Who were you drinking with last night?" she asked. "And *what* were you drinking?"

Groaning as he moved to sit up, Will leaned over and bussed her on the cheek. "Brandy. Rather good brandy, as I recall." At her look of disbelief, he added, "With Everly."

The events of the night before—those that had happened after eleven o'clock—came crashing back. He began chuckling, the sound almost maniacal, which had his countess displaying a look of confusion.

"You sound positively mad," she accused.

"Helen slapped Tom across the face. They're getting married," he blurted.

Barbara blinked before her brows furrowed and a hand went to his forehead. "Oh, now I know you've gone mad," she said in dismay.

He captured her hand with one of his and brought it to his lips. Kissing the back of it, he made a purring sound and grinned. Despite his hangover, his morning tumescence was evident, and Barbara's eyes rounded as he moved atop her.

"William Stephen Slater, whatever in the world... Oh!" she cried out when she felt his hands gather her night rail up to her hips.

"I'm thirsty, my sweet, and only you can satisfy me right now."

Inhaling sharply, Barbara settled back into the pillow. "I suppose I shouldn't mind when you're this mad," she whispered, once again gasping. She felt more than heard his chuckle against her thighs, his whiskers scraping the tender skin in a most erotic manner.

"Mad for you," he murmured before his lips kissed her cunny. His tongue soon followed, darting between her folds and around the tight bud of her womanhood until she was wet with need. Until she was murmuring, "yes, yes, yes," and saying his name as if it had several syllables.

He left her on the brink of her release, though, chuckling again when she whispered, "no, no, no." He removed his nightshirt and sunk himself into her on a groan of satisfaction that might have been heard by everyone else in the hotel.

"Will," she admonished him before he straightened atop her and trailed the back of his fingers over her abdomen. The move sent her over the edge, the feather light darts of pleasure enough to set off a powerful orgasm that nearly forced a scream from her. He was quick to take advantage of how her body responded, pushing his manhood into her deeper with his every thrust until he, too, went over the edge and into an oblivion of pure pleasure.

He remained suspended over her for several seconds before his arms gave way and he nearly collapsed atop her. Rolling off her body, he landed on his back and let out a soft curse of appreciation before he passed out.

When Barbara finally caught her breath, she glanced over at him. He was snoring softly, a beatific grin lighting his face.

"That must have been some very good brandy," she whispered.

As for what else he had mentioned, she decided she would learn more over breakfast. Turning onto her side, she placed her head in the small of his shoulder and joined him in a happy slumber.

CHAPTER 42
A MOTHER AND DAUGHTER TALK

$\mathcal{M}$*eanwhile* Stella looked up from where Bradley rested in her arms to see her daughter standing in the doorway. Helen had paused, as if she dare not cross the threshold into the hotel's parlor.

"Your father was deep in his cups when he came to bed last night," Stella said. "When I asked what might be the matter, he mentioned your name and then passed out. Might you know anything about that?"

For a moment, Helen displayed a look of confusion. "Oh, I suppose he was celebrating," she replied, finally entering the parlor to take the upholstered chair opposite her mother's.

"Celebrating?"

"My betrothal."

Despite how Bradley had begun to stir in her arms, Stella went very still. "Betrothal?" she repeated in a soft voice.

"Yes. Thomas would like to marry me, but he won't formally propose until he has secured Father's permission, which I think might be happening at this very moment."

"Thomas?" For a long moment, Stella seemed lost in thought. "Thomas Forster?"

"Yes, Mother." Helen leaned forward, her face displaying concern. "Are you all right? I thought you would be pleased."

Letting out a breath she didn't know she'd been holding, Stella chuckled. "I am," she claimed happily. "Oh, I am, only... I wasn't aware he's been courting you. His behavior has been so... odd." Despite hoping to hear such news—almost expecting it —it still caught her by surprise.

Helen tittered. "He hasn't been, not really," she admitted. "So do not concern yourself with thinking you have been blind," she explained.

Stella kept her attention on her daughter as she considered whether or not she should admit what she had suspected. "Yet *you* do not seem especially surprised," she said suddenly. "What had him speaking of marriage so suddenly? Of deciding you were to be his choice for a wife?"

Although she had noticed Thomas' regard for her daughter —she had caught him staring at Helen a number of times—she still experienced a moment of disbelief despite what Harry had said the night before. Her daughter really was going to marry the son of an earl.

Straightening in her chair, Helen's face reddened. "I, um, I may have slapped him. Slapped some sense into him," she stammered. "I would have hit him with that carved sphinx we purchased from the street vendor, but I feared I might do permanent damage if I did. I do rather like his appearance the way it is."

Blinking several times, Stella made an odd sound in her throat. "I did that to your father once," she murmured. "You are correct in saying it is quite effective in securing their attention."

"I discovered that's very true, yes," Helen agreed.

"Tell me, what did Thomas do to deserve such violence upon his person?"

Helen seemed to think on her answer before she lifted a shoulder. "It was more what he had led himself to believe of me, despite knowing I wouldn't do such a thing."

Stella blinked, ready to be angry with Thomas. "What such a thing did he think you had done? That you hadn't... or didn't?"

Waving to her brother, Helen tittered. "It seems I'm guilty of being too attentive when it comes to Bradley. He believed I was his mother."

Blinking again, Stella scoffed. "He *what*?" she countered.

"I think he heard Bradley call me 'mama' once, and I do dote on him something awful, so I suppose he's not really to blame," Helen reasoned.

Glancing down at the boy, Stella watched as Bradley grinned in delight and said, "Mama," as he attempted to capture a foot in his chubby hands.

"Well, *finally*," she said as her face brightened. "You've been saying 'dada' for so long, I wondered if you would ever know to call me mama," she added.

"Dada, dada," he replied happily.

"You're definitely done feeding off me for the rest of the day," Stella said under her breath.

Helen laughed even as a tear streamed down one cheek. "He kissed me. At the Morganfield's ball, the night before they left London for Sicily," she said.

"Oh, did he now?"

"Indeed. We were supposed to dance the waltz, but he offered to take me for a walk in the gardens instead. The ball was such a crush that night, I welcomed any excuse to go out of doors."

"That's when he kissed you? In the gardens?" She thought of all the indiscretions to which the flowers in the Morganfield gardens had paid witness over the decades and chuckled softly.

Helen nodded.

"You didn't get caught," Stella stated.

"No," Helen acknowledged. "It wouldn't have mattered if I was. None of the young bucks in London had any intentions of courting me, so ruination wouldn't have changed anything," she said in a quiet voice.

"It would have changed *everything*, darling," Stella countered.

"How?" Helen challenged, straightening in her chair.

"We would have forced him to marry you before he left England."

"He wouldn't have been ready for marriage. And I wouldn't have wanted to marry a resentful man. Father wouldn't have forced the issue," she claimed, obviously with more confidence than she felt. "Besides, Thomas would have been long gone by the time the gossip spread, Mother," she added. "But I agree. It was better this way, even though I've been forced to wonder for some time if anything would ever come of that kiss."

Stella considered her daughter's words, realizing she had been rehearsing them for well over a year. That didn't mean she was particularly amenable with the idea of marriage to Thomas Forster, though. "Are you happy at the thought of marrying him?"

Helen nodded. "Incandescently so. Although I must warn you, I may end up living at Gisborn Hall in Oxfordshire."

"Oh," Stella murmured, her momentary thrill at hearing Helen was indeed happy with the arrangement quickly abating.

"Or we might take up residence in the Gisborn townhouse in Mayfair, should Lord and Lady Forster decide to live at Gisborn Hall. Which I think is more likely since there are apparently some archaeological sites there for Diana to explore."

Stella's eyes widened at hearing this last. "Oh, I do hope it works out that you can stay in the capital," Stella breathed.

"Well, you're friends with his aunt. Perhaps you can mention it to Lady Bellingham, and she can pass along the thought to Lady Gisborn when we return to England," Helen suggested.

"You know I will." She glanced down at Bradley again to discover he was sound asleep. "When will you marry, do you suppose?"

Helen shook her head. "It will be months before we're back in Europe, and the boys are planning time in Rome as their final stop on their Grand Tour," she explained.

Stella's eyes widened in delight. "Rome," she said on a sigh. "You should marry in Rome," she whispered.

Lifting a shoulder, Helen grinned but didn't mention that she didn't think she could wait that long. She was about to put voice to a query about how she might marry in Egypt when her Father appeared in the doorway. "Good morning, Father," she said brightly.

"Morning, darling," Stella said in a quiet voice as Harry made his way to her to place a kiss on her forehead. "I didn't realize you were awake."

"Morning to you two. Three," he amended when his attention went to his son. "I've actually been up for a while. There is a young man in the hotel lobby who would like a moment of our daughter's time—or rather the rest of her entire lifetime," he said softly.

"Oh!" Helen said, quickly rising from her chair.

"Don't rush, Helen. Make him wait for you," Stella admonished her.

"Yes, Mother. Thank you, Father." She curtsied and slowly walked out the door, her measured steps exaggerating her slow pace.

Stella exchanged a knowing glance with her husband when they heard the footsteps increase in frequency and fade on the carpeted corridor floor.

"I told you so," Harry whispered before he joined his wife on the settee.

Glad she agreed with him this one time, Stella said, "Yes, you did." She paused. "Did he happen to mention their desire for children?"

Harry glanced over at her. "He did."

"Are you going to make him wait?"

Knowing exactly what she meant, he shook his head. "Even if I told him to, it wouldn't matter," he murmured.

"Why do you say that?" she asked in alarm.

"Because if I know my daughter, *she* won't let *him* wait," he replied. "She is his now."

Stella grinned even as a blush suffused her face. "Like mother, like daughter," she said in a whisper.

"Minx," he accused.

But he didn't argue.

CHAPTER 43
A PROPOSAL

a few minutes later

Pacing across the hotel lobby, Thomas listened intently for the sound of footsteps on the stairs. His meeting with the earl had gone better than expected given how the evening had ended the night before.

Apparently the Earl of Everly had been too deep in his cups to remember he had discovered Tom in Lady Helen's hotel room the night before.

Or maybe he remembered and had decided it was an opportunity to see to it his three-Seasons-out daughter was finally betrothed.

Whatever the reason, the earl had assured him he would draw up a marriage contract and grant Tom the dowry he had arranged for his daughter.

"I'll set it aside for her and our children," Tom had assured his future father-in-law. "Should something happen to me."

The look of appreciation Harold Tennison displayed showed through the obvious discomfort of the hangover he was experiencing. "Good man," he had said.

The two had shook hands and the earl had taken his leave, promising to send Helen to meet with him.

Tom glanced around. Was a hotel lobby in Luxor, Egypt really the appropriate place in which to make his marriage proposal? He had half a mind to escort her to the nearby ruins of the temple and either stand in front of the statues of Amun and Mut or find a three-thousand-year-old column next to which he could make his promise of eternal love and affection.

Was it though? Eternal love and affection? If for the rest of his life he felt only half of what he had that morning, when he had awoken to the thought he might find Helen snuggled up next to him in his bed, then he was sure she would own his heart for eternity.

If he did propose somewhere in the Temple of Luxor and did so before the afternoon hours, they could be assured of some privacy.

At least privacy from fellow tourists and explorers. As for anyone else—or anything else—there were plenty of standing structures behind which they could hide.

The thought that some linen-wrapped mummy might pay witness to his proposal and haunt them for the rest of their lives had him thinking he might have to amend his plans.

The sound of a soft cough and the words, "Father said you wished to speak with me," pulled him from his reverie.

Tom whirled to discover Helen regarding him with curiosity. How had he missed her arrival? She managed to look resplendent in a gown he hadn't yet seen her wearing on this trip, one that would put shame to what any of the wives of the pharaohs might have worn back in the day. Even if their gowns had been as form-fitting as what was depicted in the hieroglyphics on temple walls, accentuating their bosoms and hips, they weren't nearly as snug as the bodice of Helen's gown. The thought of cupping her breasts in both his hands had him swallowing and clearing his throat before he could remember what she had said.

"I do," he replied. "But... not here, I think," he stammered.

She glanced in the direction of the front doors, where the reflection from the morning sun danced on the smooth waters of the Nile. "Perhaps you would like to take a walk along the waterfront?" she suggested.

He nodded. "I would," he agreed, not having considered the Nile as a backdrop for his proposal. Offering his arm, he grinned when she glanced up at him with the same expression he remembered from the night before. "Did you sleep well?"

She giggled softly as she placed her arm on his. "I admit to having tossed and turned a few times."

"Because of me?" he asked, momentarily thrilled that she might have been thinking of him at the same time he was thinking of her.

"Of course, because of you." She audibly sighed as they reached the well-worn path along the east bank of the river. In the distance to the right, the columns of the temple glowed a golden yellow, the morning sun well above the opposite bank of the river. "I admit to hoping you might return for..." Here she visibly reddened.

He swallowed. "For...?" he prompted.

"Another kiss," she whispered.

"I wanted to," he said, his chest puffing out at hearing her admission.

"Mayhap... more?" she pressed.

Nearly stopping mid-step, he made an odd sound in his throat. "More?" he repeated, his voice sounding strangled to his ears.

She seemed to think better of her query. "I knew you wouldn't, of course. You're far too honorable to have taken my virtue before settling affairs with Father," she said, her head falling to one side as she glanced up at him.

"Do you find fault with my honor?"

She quickly shook her head. "Not at all. In fact, I find it refreshing in a man of your age."

He regarded her with a quirked brow. "The young bucks in London lack honor, do you mean?"

"Some do," she acknowledged. "There are some who would ruin a young woman merely for sport."

Making the odd sound in his throat again, Tom frowned. "Is there someone I need to hunt for sport?" he asked, his manner conveying his sudden anger.

Helen inhaled sharply. "Not for me," she replied. "My older brother has obviously seen to deterrents on my behalf."

"As he should," Tom replied, his momentary anger quickly dissipating. Deciding they were far too exposed so close to the river, he led them onto a path that fronted the temple grounds.

Given how most of the Luxor temple seemed half-buried in sand and debris, it was difficult to imagine what it might have looked like when it was first built.

"The symmetry is all wrong here. The missing obelisk is far too obvious," Helen said, reaching up to trace one of the carvings on the side of the remaining obelisk with a gloved fingertip.

"It is," Tom acknowledged. "Back in 1830, the Egyptian ruler Mohammed Ali Pasha had them both gifted to France. One was removed and shipped off to Paris, but I rather doubt they will ever come back for the second."

"Why ever not?" She placed her hand back on his arm, apparently oblivious to the red stain left on her glove.

"Blunt. Diana said it cost two-and-a-half million francs to pay for the dismantling, shipping, and re-erection in the Place De La Concorde. The French had to pay for the relocation, of course."

Helen gasped. "So, not exactly a gift," she murmured.

He nodded his agreement as they passed through the wide

opening in the pylon. The pair of carved busts of the pharaoh Ramesses II flanking the opening appeared far different in the morning sun than they had the afternoon prior. He tried to imagine what they looked like below ground, but without an image or drawing to use as reference, he couldn't. A third torso topped the sand off to the right side of the pylon, its base still buried in the mound of sand fronting the pylon.

Leading her along the well-worn path into the temple, where sand had drifted to surround the base of most of the columns, Tom paused in between two columns along the grand colonnade where the bases were mostly exposed. He moved to stand in front of her and dipped his head. "You are right when you say I would not have done such a thing as attempt to take your virtue," he said, returning to their earlier conversation. Despite the lack of a roof above, the spacing of the columns made the area seem closed in. Intimate.

Her eyes rounding at hearing his claim, Helen appeared disappointed. "But... were you... *thinking* about it?" she asked, hope sounding in her voice.

He barked a laugh but quickly sobered. "I fear I am not as honorable in my thoughts as I have been in my actions," he admitted sheepishly. He swallowed again. "Actually, I have thought of it many times," he admitted. "What it would be like to... to lie with you."

For a moment, he wished he hadn't put voice to his thoughts, but now that he had, he was desperate to learn her feelings. What if she didn't feel affection for him? What if she had changed her mind since the kiss they had shared the night before? "Have I shocked you?" he asked.

"Not as much as you fear, I think," she replied, her voice so quiet he almost didn't hear her. "Have you had these thoughts since... since we were in Cairo?" she pressed.

Reaching out, he grasped her around the waist and pulled her against the front of his body, relieved that she allowed the impropriety. "Since the Morganfield ball, actually," he stated, as he rolled his eyes.

"Thomas," she said softly, a brilliant smile lighting her face. She rested the side of her head against his chest.

"I cannot help it. I rather enjoyed that kiss. I thought of it often whilst I watched my cousin Donald with his new wife, and now when I see how Randy is with Diana, well, I think I should like to start and end my days with such a kiss. With you."

Helen pulled her head away from his chest and angled it to one side. "Only at the start and end of each day?" she gently teased.

His gaze darted to one of the columns, its capital carved into the shape of a papyrus bud and its smooth surface a testament to the erosion caused by centuries of wind and sand. "Well, we could kiss in the middle of the day, too," he replied. "If you'd like."

"Mayhap before dinner?"

"Oh, I'm quite sure that could be arranged."

"And now?" she whispered.

He lowered his forehead to hers. "Only if you agree to marry me," he said. He suddenly squeezed his eyes shut. "Oh, that was a terrible proposal," he complained. "Can you ever forgive me?"

Helen giggled and lifted a hand to the side of his face. "Kiss me, and I'll allow you to try again."

He chuckled softly and barely touched her lips with his. The tentative nature of the kiss continued, their breaths held until he pressed harder. When she parted her lips, he took it as an invitation to press his firm pillows harder against her softer, fuller mouth. He slid his tongue between her lips, the tip brushing along the bottom edge of her teeth.

Although she seemed surprised—a tremor even passed through her body—she didn't pull away. Emboldened, he used his tongue to explore the inside of her mouth. When the tip darted across her teeth again, she inhaled suddenly. Her tongue finally tangled with his until he finally, slowly ended the kiss.

He straightened, grinning when he saw how her eyes seemed unfocused and her lips were red as the berries they had eaten that morning for breakfast. "Lady Helen Tennison, will you do me the honor of becoming my wife?" he asked.

Appearing a bit unsteady on her feet, Helen inhaled and let the air out in a *whoosh*. "I will," she replied, nodding her head slightly. "Whenever you'd like. The sooner, the better." She glanced around, stunned to discover they were still alone despite the sounds of traffic on the nearby road.

Chuckling, Tom kissed her again, a quick kiss, before he drew her into his arms and embraced her. "I don't think we can right now," he murmured. "But I can at least bestow a ring on your finger," he added, releasing his hold on her to pull a gold band from his waistcoat pocket. He held up the ring, its single lapis lazuli stone polished to a high sheen. "It's not a sapphire, but—"

"It's gorgeous," she breathed, yanking the glove off her left hand. "And *gold*." She watched as he slipped it on her fourth finger. "My brother will be so impressed," she added. "He makes jewelry."

"I have been to his shop," he acknowledged. "And as for the gold, I wasn't going to give you silver."

Admiring the ring on her finger, Helen glanced up and grinned. "I would not have minded, but this... this is beautiful." She stood on tiptoe and kissed him again. "Thank you, Thomas."

His grinned widened. "I do wonder if there is a way we could marry here in Egypt."

Helen tittered. "I don't think I can wait any longer," she claimed. "I want a baby. *Your* baby."

Tom sobered before his eyes widened. "Oh," he breathed. "I… I suppose we could… get started—"

"Right now?" she interrupted, her excitement evident.

He blinked. "Wouldn't your father kill me?"

She appeared uncertain for a moment before she shook her head. "I rather think he expects it."

"Oh?"

Lifting a shoulder, she said, "I might have mentioned I was in want of a child as soon as possible, which means you must be my lover in Luxor," she added, poking a forefinger into his chest. "And everywhere else we go."

"Oh. Well. Then I suppose we…" He stopped speaking as he considered what they might do. "I can ask if there's a room with a larger bed at the hotel," he reasoned.

"A larger bed?" she asked, her brows furrowing.

"Well, although I intend to hold you close when we're asleep, I wish for there to be plenty of room when I make love to you," he murmured.

She dipped her head. "All right."

"But first I think we should go to the ship. Speak with Mahmood. Perhaps he knows someone in Luxor who can marry us."

She nodded.

"And then we can share a bed… that is, if he doesn't kill me…"

He couldn't continue when she once again kissed him. When she ended it as suddenly as she started it, he continued, "Or a mummy doesn't curse us, or—"

"Thomas," she scolded, although she was still smiling.

"Is it too early to tell you I love you?"

It was Helen's turn to sober. "Oh, Thomas," she breathed. She was once again in his arms, her lips pressed to his as she stood on tiptoes and gripped his shoulders.

They might have continued kissing but for the sounds of voices near the entrance of the temple.

Familiar voices.

Tom sighed. He leaned down and once again bussed Helen on the forehead. "Seems we're no longer alone, my... may I call you my sweet?"

She glanced in the direction from which the voices were coming. "Of course. Just promise me you won't call me 'my pumpkin' or 'my sweet melon' when I'm round with child."

"I would never!" he exclaimed. He tried hard to hide his sudden humor at the thought of what she might do to him if he did, but he audibly chuckled. "I promise."

"Dammit," she cursed under her breath, which had his eyes widening in surprise. "Now you'll be thinking it," she claimed.

"I won't. I won't. I promise," he assured her, managing to display a serious expression.

When he turned to face the back of the pylon, he spotted his brother and Diana examining the carvings on the structure. Although he had seen Diana many times dressed as she was in breeches, boots, and a white shirt, a satchel hanging at her hip, it was still unexpected. The archaeologist was obviously planning a day of exploration in the ancient temple. "Shall we tell them our news?" he asked.

Before he had finished his query, Helen dropped her arms but entwined her hand with his. "Diana!" she called out, rushing to join her future sister-in law. With their hands joined as they were, Tom was forced to follow.

He caught Randy's attention and nodded when his older brother arched a brow.

Perhaps he could be of help in seeing to it Helen spent the night with him.

More importantly, though, he hoped he might help when it came to arranging a quick wedding.

CHAPTER 44
MARRIED—FOR ALL
INTENTS AND PURPOSES

A few minutes later

Finding *The Dendera* still docked where they had left it two nights ago, Tom and Randy were practically breathless by the time they spotted the captain directing a crewman who carried a wooden crate of provisions.

Mahmood listened intently to Tom's request, his soft chuckle at odds with the young man's earnest plea. "Today?" he asked when Tom finished explaining he wished to marry as soon as possible.

"Or... tomorrow?" Tom countered.

"Do you have a contract? A dowry for her?"

Tom blinked. "Her father is drawing one up. He has arranged a dowry for her. Five-thousand pounds, I think."

Mahmood arched a brow. "I had to give my bride three water buffalo and ten pieces of gold," he said.

Randy hid his amusement behind a hand. "Is there someone who can perform a... a civil ceremony?"

"Our weddings are religious traditions here," Mahmood replied. "Islamic. Or Coptic."

"There's no... Ministry of Justice? No civil means of marrying?"

Mahmood shook head. "The office in Cairo is governmental. No weddings. But I believe I remember hearing of a traveler whose marriage was performed by a priest here in Luxor," he mused. "An English-speaking man. Not fancy. No Crowning Ceremony," he added.

Tom and Randy exchanged uncertain glances, neither of them familiar with Coptic wedding ceremonies.

Glancing back to Nasir, Mahmood said something in Arabic. The man nodded and left the boat. When Mahmood turned back to them, he sighed. "When he returns with some hantours, I will take you to this man. But I cannot promise he can do what you require." He glanced up to discover Diana and Helen waiting on the dock. "If he can do it, you will need to ask your wife to change her clothes if she is to be there," he warned.

Randy winced. "I will," he said, turning around to discover Diana already heading toward the hotel.

"Will you be our witnesses?" Tom asked.

"I wouldn't miss it, little brother," Randy replied. "Do you have a ring?"

"I already gave it to her. That gold one I bought in Cairo," he replied.

Randy chuckled.

Mahmood rolled his eyes. "Have you a room at the hotel for the next two nights? We leave for Edfu in three days," he said.

Tom blinked. "I'll see to one right now, Captain. Thank you." He left the ship, Randy watching him go as he continued to chuckle.

Mahmood regarded him with suspicion. "Did you know they have been courting on my ship?" he asked.

Randy shook his head. "They weren't, I promise you," he replied. "But they have been in love with one another for well over a year," he added. When he saw the captain's look of surprise, he said, "It's a long story that started with a kiss in the gardens."

Mahmood's face split into a grin. "Now this I understand."

An hour later
The two hantours arrived in front of a modest mud brick home, the rectangular box featuring only a wood-framed front door and one window along with a set of stairs on the side that led up to the roof. A low mud brick wall surrounded the small abode, and three chickens roosted beneath a palm tree.

Randy and Diana exchanged quick glances, both reminded of how they had spent some nights in Athens on the roof of her family's mansion watching shooting stars. "You look especially lovely today," he commented.

She dipped her head. "It's not every day I'm going to witness a wedding," she replied. "And gain a sister in the process."

"Let's hope," he replied, helping her down from the hantour. Meanwhile, his brother was doing the same for Helen, their attention on the front door of the house.

Having ridden on the driver's seat of their hantour, Mahmood had already stepped down and was nearly to the door when it opened.

An older gentlemen garbed in a light robe, his hair white and his shoulders rounding forward, regarded them with curiosity before turning his attention to Mahmood. They spoke for a moment before a grin split the man's face. He waved them forward, and the four of them approached.

Randy held out his right hand. "Lord Randolph Forster, sir," he said.

"Reverend Thomas O'Malley," the man replied, a hint of an

Irish accent tingeing his voice. His eyes sparkled with delight. "Whose whelp might you be?"

Randy blinked. "Uh, my father is the Earl of Gisborn."

"Ah, the inventor," O'Malley replied.

"You know him?" Randy asked, his eyes rounding at hearing the reverend's comment.

"Never met him, but I know someone back home who uses one of his plows. You on your Grand Tour, I suppose?"

"Indeed. My younger brother, Thomas, wishes to marry Lady Helen Tennison," Randy explained, waving to the couple. "He gained her father's permission this morning. Lord Everly is drawing up the contract now for the dowry." He stopped speaking when he saw how O'Malley was shaking his head.

"I canna marry them."

Randy's face fell, and he audibly groaned.

"*Legally*," O'Malley added, mischief apparent in his expression. "But I can perform the ceremony. Do you have a ring?"

"I do." Tom held up Helen's hand and gave her an apologetic glance as he removed it from her finger.

"I think I might even have a marriage certificate around here somewhere we can have all of ya' sign, but ye'll have to do it all over again when you get back to England."

"We understand," Tom replied.

"Ye can't be havin' any babes before ya' do, or they'll be considered bastards."

"Understood," Randy said, directing an apologetic glance in Helen's direction.

"Well, all right then. We can do it in here if you like," he said, pointing into his house. "The Coptics get away with it, so I don't see why we canna."

"Thank you, sir," Helen said, her voice sounding breathless.

They entered the small house, where a desk overflowing with papers and a small bookshelf took up most of one wall. A leather chair was in front of it, the only other pieces of furniture in the room.

O'Malley indicated the chair and nodded to Mahmood to sit. "We won't be long, Captain," he said. He shuffled through some papers on his desk and pulled a parchment from one of the many cubbyholes. "Here we are," he said triumphantly. "Now I just need my book of prayer," he murmured, reaching for a small volume from the bookshelf. He waved them into another small room featuring a worn settee in a deep blue velvet and a low table. A silver tea set on a salver was in the middle of the table. "Was my mum's," he said absently. He raised the flame on a lamp and turned around. "Couple in front of me…"

Tom and Helen stepped up to face him. "My aunt is going to be rather upset with me that she's not paying witness to this," Tom whispered for only Helen to hear.

Helen winced. "My mother will be so relieved I'm finally wed, she'll forgive me," she replied. "I hope."

"…Witnesses back there," O'Malley said with another wave. "Are we ready?"

The four grinned and nodded.

Holding out the prayer book in one hand, O'Malley opened his mouth to begin when a commotion sounded in the front room.

"Where are they?" Barbara could be heard, her query directed to Mahmood.

She appeared on the threshold, Stella at her side. Behind them, Will, Harry, and David, all breathless, came to a halt.

"Ah, and these are…?" O'Malley asked, not the least bit surprised by the appearance of others.

"My aunt and uncle, the Earl and Countess of Bellingham, and their son, Viscount Penton."

"My parents, the Earl and Countess of Everly," Helen said, her voice quavering.

"Bellingham, did you say?" O'Malley asked.

"O'Malley? Is that you?" Will asked, his stunned expression turning to one of humor and disbelief.

"You *know* one another?" Harry asked.

"Reverend O'Malley was our chaplain aboard *HMS Greenwich*," Will replied. "Whatever are you doing here in Egypt?" he asked, turning his attention to the old man.

"Marrying your nephew, it would seem," he replied. "Shall we begin?"

"Yes, please," Helen said.

Tom squeezed her hand.

Clearing his throat, the reverend read the marriage ceremony from the Common Book of Prayer, and when it was time, Helen and Tom repeated the vows. Once O'Malley made the pronouncement they were married, there was a collective sigh as Tom turned and kissed Helen first on the lips and then on the forehead.

Diana embraced Helen before her mother could reach her, while Harry moved to shake hands with Tom.

"She didn't wish to wait," Tom blurted.

Harry chuckled. "I'm well aware," he replied, slapping Tom on the shoulder. He turned and regarded Randy with a quirked lip. "Are you the one to thank for this?"

Randy stiffened. "We didn't intentionally *not* tell you," he said. "It just happened so fast. Mahmood knew of Reverend O'Malley. How did you know where to find us?"

"Nasir told us. We noticed Helen with Diana, who was wearing a gown when I know she was dressed differently earlier in the day, and then we saw the hantours leaving from in front of the dock" he explained. "It was easy to sort what was happening."

O'Malley cleared his throat. "I need the bride and groom and the two witnesses, please," he said, placing the marriage certificate onto the low table in front of the settee. He added a pot of ink and a quill next to it, and he watched as they all took turns signing the document. When they finished, he added the rest of the information and signed it before handing it over to Helen.

"So… how long have you been in Egypt?" Will asked, taking a seat next to his former chaplain.

"Since I retired. I remained chaplain for many years after you left us," O'Malley replied. "There's always another war. After the Greek War for Independence, I took a trip up the Nile and settled here." He held out his hands to indicate his home. "Now there are Europeans coming through here all the time," he added. "Englishmen, diplomats…" He shrugged. "Tourists."

Will chuckled. "What does a reverend get paid for a wedding these days?"

O'Malley waved a dismissive hand, but Will placed several coins into it. "Thank you for doing it, even if it isn't legal by England's standards."

"Glad to help. Where are you off to next?"

"We're going to continue south. Mayhap as far as Aswan before we turn around."

"And after that?"

Will chuckled. "Rome. I've promised Barbara for years I would take her."

"She the one you left behind when you joined the navy?"

Nodding, Will said, "She is. Mother of both my boys. The oldest is married and lives in Catania and David is…" He glanced around. "Is no longer in here."

"Not yet married?" the reverend guessed.

"Too young," Will affirmed.

O'Malley sounded a snort. "He going with you to Rome?"

"Yes. We're on his Grand Tour," Will explained.

Chuckling softly, O'Malley slapped Will's knee. "Keep an eye on him."

The others had begun to file out of the house, and Will stood to go, "Thank you again for doing this."

"It was my pleasure." He walked with Will to the front door and waved as the first of the hantours jerked into motion.

"What's next for you?" Will asked.

"A nap," O'Malley replied, grinning as he shook Will's hand. "Safe travels."

Will nodded and hurried to join his wife in the last hantour.

CHAPTER 45
TWO LOVERS IN LUXOR

wo hours later

Tom closed the hotel room door behind him and let out a sigh of relief. "I thought I was never going to be rid of them," he whispered, driving home the bolt. He turned to face Helen, his eyes rounding at seeing her framed by the window. Dressed as she was with the afternoon light surrounding her, Helen appeared almost ethereal. "Hello, my beautiful bride."

Helen giggled. "Hello, husband." Standing at the window, she had been watching Diana and Randy as they headed back in the direction of the temple. She was dressed in the nightrail and blue silk wrapper she had been wearing the night before. "Rid of whom, darling?" she asked, stepping closer to face him. She began unbuttoning his top coat.

"Randy and David and my uncle and your father," he replied, his head dropping to watch what she was doing. "Everything is all set for the rest of the trip, but we have two more nights here at the hotel," he explained.

"Then I do hope we are going to enjoy traveling together," she teased. "We'll share a cabin, will we not?"

Tom swallowed, not having thought that far ahead. "Well,

I'd much prefer to spend my nights with you than with David," he replied. "He snores."

She giggled. "How will we travel?"

"On *The Dendera*. Mahmood has agreed to take us. He is provisioning the ship now, and his daughter will continue seeing to Bradley," he explained, noting how her fingers had moved to his waistcoat buttons.

"You mean your new little brother?" she teased.

Tom chuckled. "He is, isn't he?"

"Will we be interrupted?" she asked, grinning when he placed a kiss on her forehead.

"They don't know which room we're in," he said in a whisper.

"You've been drinking," she murmured, although there wasn't any censure in her voice.

"Your father insisted. A glass of brandy." He watched as she finished unbuttoning his waistcoat. "I... I could help."

She pushed the garments from his shoulders and pulled up on the sides of his shirt until the hem was free of his pantaloons. "You could," she said softly. She lifted her fingers to his cravat, deftly undoing the knot.

He removed his coats and helped with unwrapping the length of silk from around his neck. When her warm hands slid up the sides of his torso to lift his shirt, he inhaled sharply.

She paused. "What's wrong?"

His stunned look turned to one of amusement. "Uh, I guess I'm a bit ticklish," he murmured.

Grinning, she arched a brow and continued to help rid him of the shirt. "Good to know," she whispered.

"You're going to use that against me, aren't you?" he asked. He sat down on the edge of the bed and removed his Hobys and stockings.

"Maybe," she replied.

He reached out and pulled her so she was standing directly

in front of him, her knees between his. With his hands at her waist, he pressed his face into her belly.

Spearing his hair with her fingers, her nails scraping his scalp, she felt him shiver. When he inhaled deeply, Helen giggled. "That tickles," she said, squirming in his hold.

When he pulled away, he glanced up at her and grinned.

"You're going to use that against me, aren't you?" she asked.

"Maybe," he replied. He stared at her a moment before lifting his hands to push her wrapper from her shoulders. The garment fell to the floor, forming a puddle at her feet. "I adore your hair like that," he said. "I was going to tell you last night, but..."

"I slapped you before you could?" she guessed.

He nodded. "I didn't realize how golden it is," he whispered. "And curly," he added, twirling a finger through the wavy ends, his knuckles barely grazing the fabric covering her breast.

"Are you going to remove my nightrail? Or should I?" she whispered.

Tom audibly swallowed. "How about I take off my pantaloons at the same time as you remove your gown?" he suggested.

Helen gave it a moment of thought before she nodded. "All right." She stepped back, reached down to gather up the hem, and had it well past her knees before she stopped.

"What?" he asked, his heated gaze on her bare thighs. The bottom ruffle of her nightrail still hid the curls at the top of her thigh from view.

"Why aren't you taking off your pantaloons?"

He stood up, which had him once again so close to her they were nearly touching. "Apologies. I, um,.." He hooked his thumbs over the top edge of the garment and started to push it down as Helen resumed lifting the nightrail over her head.

His manhood, already engorged and standing straight out from his body, made it difficult to finish undressing. He returned to sitting on the edge of the bed, his legs nearly free of the knit fabric when he paused and stared at her.

Completely nude but for the golden waves of hair almost long enough to curl over and around her nipples, she looked glorious in the light from the room's only window.

She was doing the same with him, her gaze directed to where his manhood jutted out from above his thighs.

Neither seemed to breathe for a moment.

"Oh, my goddess," he murmured when he finally found his voice. He reached out to place a hand at the side of her waist, his palm warmer than her soft skin.

"Oh, my god," she countered, although her comment didn't sound as reverent.

He glanced down and cleared his throat. "I take it you've not seen one of these before."

Her eyes rounded. "I should hope not," she affirmed. "Not like that." Although she appeared slightly frightened, she reached out with a forefinger and touched the tip, where a bead of moisture had formed. When his member seemed to move of its own accord and he made an odd sound in his throat, she quickly pulled her finger away. He captured it and brought it to his lips.

"Well, if it's any consolation, I've never seen a naked lady before. I mean, a living, breathing woman," he stammered. "I've seen them in paintings, of course."

"And statuary?" she suggested.

"Mayhap," he murmured. He reached for her other hand and pulled her towards him as he stood. When he had his arms around her and she was fully pressed to the front of his body, his manhood nestled against her belly, he groaned. He kissed her lips followed by her eyelids and then her forehead. "Do you understand what it is we're about to do?"

She nodded, her hand sliding down the side of his body and then to his manhood. When her fingers touched it, he inhaled sharply, and she paused. "Do *you* know what we're about to do?" She slid her other hand down to his hip, smoothing it into the depression above his thigh before sliding it over a firm buttock.

He blinked and swallowed. "Will you sit on top of me? Straddle me?"

It was her turn to blink. "In the book, is that the one called 'riding St. George'?"

Swallowing, he seemed confused for a moment. "What book?"

"The book about sexual congress."

His eyes rounded. "You've read a book about sexual congress?" he asked in disbelief.

"Haven't you?" she countered. "My father has a rather extensive collection of books in his library."

"No doubt," he murmured.

"So, are you going to lie down so I can... so I can climb atop you?" she asked in a whisper

He seemed to have trouble breathing for a moment. "Not yet," he said. "I wish to kiss you all over."

For the first time since they had removed their clothes, she grinned. "Might *I* lie down for this part?"

He nodded. "Yes, by all means." When she pulled away, he startled her by lifting her into his arms. "Allow me," he said, grinning as he turned and lowered her to the bed.

Following her down, he covered her body with his as his lips took purchase on one of her nipples.

Helen let out a yelp of surprise and giggled as he noisily kissed the tops of her breasts and nipples and the tender skin beneath.

"Spread your legs, my sweet."

She did his bidding, her thighs cradling his torso.

Feeling far too exposed as he worked his way down her

body with a series of licks and nips and kisses, Helen inhaled softly several times.

"I'm going to taste all of you," he warned from somewhere below her navel.

"Are you going to be engaging in that... in that Roman art?" she whispered.

His movements suddenly stilled, and he glanced up to see her head was lifted from the pillow, her face displaying a look of wonder. "That's my intention," he said. The lower half of his body was nearly off the bed as he smoothed his warm hands beneath the globes of her bottom and lifted them until she was forced to bend her knees and open herself to him.

Her head settled back onto the pillow and she reached down to place a hand atop his head, her fingers clutching his hair as his tongue sought her most private place. Inhaling sharply when his tongue made contact somewhere beyond her curls, she jerked beneath his hold. All at once, his tongue dipped inside her, the rough texture setting off quivers of pleasure deep inside her. Arching her back to take him deeper, she moaned and struggled to breathe. "Yes, oh yes," she whispered, her fingers still entwined in his hair. "Oh, Thomas," she whispered.

He responded with a moan but pulled his tongue out of her to flick it across something that sent sharp darts of pleasure through her abdomen before he drove his tongue back into her channel.

"I cannot... I cannot take any more," she whispered, her head tossing back and forth in the pillow as she tried to push his head away from her.

"You cannot because... you don't like it? Or—?"

"Oh, I like it, I do," she replied. "But I feel as if I'm going to faint from too much pleasure," she murmured. "Is this what's it's like for you?"

He lifted his head from between her thighs and blinked. "We're about to find out."

"I don't know if I have the strength to climb atop you," she said before a giggle suddenly erupted.

He lifted his torso with his arms and crawled up her body until the tip of his manhood was at her entrance, glad when she pressed her thighs to his. "Then we shall do it this way. Will you help me in?"

She seemed uncertain at first, but reached down with a hand to grip and guide his member until he was half buried into her. "Push," she whispered.

He groaned, pushing into her before pulling out an inch or so. He tried again to bury his cock within her wet channel, finally sheathing himself completely on the third try. His eyes closed and his expression conveyed his bliss. "I hope to God this isn't hurting you," he murmured.

She shook her head. "It just feels very... full is all," she replied. "You're terribly large down there," she added.

"Not too large, though. Damn but you feel glorious, my sweet, sweet goddess," he whispered. "I have to move now, though."

Her eyes rounded when he pulled almost all the way out of her before he thrust into her. She inhaled sharply, instinctively clenching on him when she felt his next retreat.

He groaned. "I'm... I'm not going to be able to hold on much longer," he warned. "You're so tight, so wet, so..." With his next thrust, his body seized, the cords in his neck straining as his eyes squeezed shut, and a most unnatural groan sounded from his throat.

For a moment, Helen feared for his life, but when she felt a sudden warmth deep inside, she understood what had happened. "I do hope you're not in pain," she whispered.

His eyes opened and he displayed a grin. "The exact opposite, my sweet. I have never felt such pleasure." He lowered his chest to hers, his arms nearly giving out as his strength seemed to leave his body all at once. "Hang onto me," he said as he rolled until his back was on the mattress and she was on top of him, her eyes wide with surprise as she gripped his shoulders.

"Oh," she said on a breath.

"Are you all right?" he asked, his labored breaths slowly returning to normal as his arms seemed to relax atop her back.

"I think so," she murmured, wiggling her hips and tightening her knees' hold on his sides in an attempt to keep his manhood from escaping her body.

He chuckled. "I'm not ready for more yet," he whispered.

"You mean, we can do it again?"

Chuckling softly, he moaned. "If you're not too sore." He moved a hand to the side of her face and stroked her cheek. "Did it hurt? I'm told it won't after a time or two."

She sighed, the warm breath washing over his chest. "Truth be told, I'm not sure what I feel down there at the moment," she replied. "Other than.... alive."

He frowned. "In a good way, I hope," he whispered.

"In the very best way."

Seeing his eyes were closed, she settled the side of her face onto the top of his chest, gratified to feel his steady heartbeat beneath her ear. She grinned at remembering his enthusiasm —his determination—to see to it she was pleasured before he took his own. Surely they would be blessed with a baby within the year.

A few minutes later, she joined him in slumber, her dreams of their upcoming travels.

hree days later
By the time they settled in their cabin on *The Dendera* for the beginning of what would be their wedding trip, The Honorable Mr. and Mrs. Thomas Forster had toured all of

Luxor whilst riding in a hantour, spent time—and money—in several of the shops, and had returned to the site of their proposal to watch the sun set over the desert.

Meanwhile, David had become good friends with his new cousin's brother, Bradley. "Do you realize, young man, that we are the only two left on this boat who are not married?" he asked one afternoon when they were on the upper deck, engaged in a game of cards. Although the babe didn't yet understand how to hold the chipboard cards—several were backwards so David could actually see their fronts—he did seem to grasp the concept of putting coins into the kitty as well as pulling them out when he won a hand.

"Bach'lors," Bradley replied, his grin wide.

David gave a start. "Bachelors, indeed," he said proudly. "Let's discover how long we can avoid the parson's mousetrap, shall we?"

Bradley dropped his cards on the table, and David's mouth opened in shock. "You won *again*?" he asked in disbelief.

The boy nodded and happily scooped up all the coins onto his pile, unaware of how David's attention had been caught by Tom and Helen as they lounged together in a large chair, their hands clasped together, as they watched the passing shoreline. Every once in a while, Tom lifted her hand to his lips to kiss the back of it.

Making a dismissive sound in his throat, David turned his attention to the scattered cards and scooped them up to shuffle them. "Another hand?" he asked.

Bradley nodded. "Bach'lors."

"You needn't rub it in," David groused, trying but failing to ignore the young boy's delight. "Even if you do have a point."

CHAPTER 46
EPILOGUE

*S*eventeen months later, Gisborn Hall, Oxfordshire

The whirlwind of a late harvest having abated with the last of the wheat bundled and brought in from the fields, the Gisborn heir and spare, along with their wives, settled into the comfortable settees of the upstairs parlor with glasses of port and claret.

At their grandfather's request, Will and Barbara had elected to remain at Devonfield House, at least for a few weeks. Although William Slater, Marquess of Devonfield, was still hale and hearty at the age of eighty-one, he had insisted it was time his son take on more of his responsibilities. Will agreed, but was especially relieved when David reminded him he wanted to take on the role of 'man of business' for the marquessate.

The Bellinghams were joined by Randy and Tom's parents, Henry and Hannah, who were in London for Parliament and had taken Grace with them for the Little Season. They wouldn't be returning to Gisborn Hall until the following month. With George away at school, the bustling household had settled into a quieter routine.

Quieter but not silent, for the cries of a newborn could occasionally be heard from the mistress suite in the north wing.

"I'm not sure timing our arrival from Europe so we could be here to help with the harvest was the best decision," Randy commented, eliciting a murmur of agreement from his brother. "Min must have blessed us," he added, referring to the Egyptian god of fertility and harvest. One of the tenant farmers, Tom Cavanaugh, had claimed this harvest had set a record for wheat and beans.

"I'd forgotten what it was like to work in the fields," Tom said, experimentally lifting a sore arm to test his shoulder. "Happily."

Randy patted his middle. "After eating all that food in Rome, I am glad for the exercise. I feared having to make an appointment with a tailor to see to larger clothes," he commented. Despite his words, whatever he might have gained in girth whilst on their Grand Tour was soon lost after they returned to Oxfordshire.

The trip to Gisborn Hall had been put on hold after their arrival back on British shores, though. The matter of both boy's marriages in civil ceremonies outside of England required a stop at the archbishop's office in Doctors' Commons. Once marriage licenses were procured, both couples were formally married.

And not a moment too soon, for Helen was visibly with child and due to give birth within the month. Their grandmother, Cherise, Marchioness of Devonfield, was ecstatic to play hostess for a wedding breakfast of monumental proportions. Despite her age—and their grandfather's—attendance at the fête proved the two were still well regarded in aristocratic circles.

Apparently her cook was of a mind to show off, for the cake had been topped with sugar molded into columns and arranged in her version of a Greek temple. An ice sculpture in the shape of Aphrodite graced the center of the main table, and the bread rolls had been stacked to form pyramids.

After such a boisterous affair and arriving home to see to the harvest, the four were happy for the quiet. A week later, Henry Thomas Forster was born.

Once he was wrapped in a blanket and handed to Tom, he stayed in his father's arms until the babe and his mother insisted he be released to her care.

"Bradley is apparently quite happy to learn he is an uncle, even though he has no idea what it means," Helen remarked with a smirk. "Mother wrote that she and father will be paying a call as soon as they can. I expect their arrival within the week."

For the next few days, Tom only left Helen's bedchamber to help with the harvest, which had Randy and Diana realizing they had misjudged the young man.

"Back when we were in Egypt—after I had shared a *hantour* with you," Diana said, directing her comment to Helen. "I recall asking Randy if I should be worried for Tom, and he said he was more worried for you," she said.

Tom scoffed, but before he could put voice to a complaint and defend himself, Randy was quick to add, "Because I wasn't sure you should be stuck with my brother."

Helen's eyes widened with amusement. She leaned to her left until her shoulder rubbed against Tom's. "It sounds as if you don't have a very supportive brother."

Tom lifted a shoulder, his face displaying a grimace.

Diana was quick to provide assurances. "Actually, I remember him saying 'he deserves a good wife as much as anyone, but if he can't abide her attentions toward a babe, I'm not sure he deserves her'."

About to claim he never said such a thing, Randy realized no one would believe him. Diana remembered everything she read or saw or heard. "I did, indeed," he finally admitted sheepishly.

"Well, he certainly abides my attentions towards this one," Helen said, referring to the babe she held in her arms.

"Usually," Tom said, a grin replacing his look of discomfort at having learned he had been the topic of conversation when they were on the Nile. He reached over and took the boy into his hold, placing him up against his shoulder. "But only when it's her turn to hold him," he claimed. "Now it's mine." He beamed in delight when the babe opened his eyes to stare at him.

Diana glanced over at Randy, wondering why he didn't show any surprise at hearing his brother's claim. "I may not have my wife's perfect memory, but I do remember finding you in the nursery holding Grace and George when they were babes," he said, referring to their younger sister and brother.

"I did," Tom acknowledged. "I rather adored the scent of them. That is, if their nappy was dry," he added. He turned his face so his nose was nearly pressed to Henry's head and he inhaled deeply.

"There is something about the smell of a baby," Randy mused, before taking a sip of port. "I look forward to it."

"I'm rather glad to hear it," Diana said softly, a wan grin aimed in his direction. "Especially since it seems Min blessed me before he did the harvest," she added in a whisper.

Randy's eyes widened with understanding. "You're... you're going to have a baby?" he asked.

Diana nodded.

His head fell back into the cushions of the settee, and h⟨ exhaled dramatically.

"You don't seemed pleased," she said, her brows furrov⟨ Her gaze darted to his brother and Helen, whose atte⟨ were entirely on their baby.

"Oh, but I am," Randy claimed, his face break⟨

huge grin. He took one of her hands in his and gave it a reassuring squeeze. "Incandescently so," he added. "Relieved, as well, though."

"Relieved?" she repeated in confusion.

He nodded before chuckling softly. "I was beginning to think I might have been cursed by those mummies we saw," he said.

Diana arched a blonde brow. "Who says you weren't?"

She giggled at seeing his sudden look of alarm.

CHAPTER 47
AUTHOR NOTES

Where did these characters originate?

If you've been a regular reader of my historical romances, you probably recognized Henry and Hannah Forster, Earl and Countess of Gisborn, and William and Cherice Slater, Marquess and Marchioness of Devonfield, from THE SEDUCTION OF AN EARL, Will and Barbara Slater, Earl and Countess of Bellingham, from THE CARESS OF A COMMANDER, Stella and Harry Tennison, Earl and Countess of Everly from THE EPIPHANY OF AN EXPLORER and THE JEWEL OF AN EARL'S HEIR, and David and Adeline Carlington, Marquess and Marchioness of Morganfield, from THE KISS OF A VISCOUNT. If not, you can still discover how they met and married since those novels are available at all major book retailers in e-book, paperback and audio formats.

The First Egyptologist

Khaemwise (c.1285-c.1224 B.C.), a son of Ramesses II, pursued a career in the priesthood of Memphis and devoted himself to the study of hieroglyphs and antiquities. He also designed the Serapeum, the catacomb for the sacred Apis bulls in the desert at Saqqara. As a result of his interests and activities, Khaemwise has been described as the first Egyptologist in history.

*N*apoleon Bonaparte
When Napoleon invaded Egypt in 1798, he brought with him (and abandoned them to stage his coup) 150 scientists, artists, geographers, and linguists. They orchestrated the massive looting of Egypt, sending off the treasure to the Louvre.

This crew of savants (the word used for scientists back then) made careful drawings and measurements of a large number of ancient structures. Their depictions were so faithful that they preserved inscriptions that have since disappeared.

All these surveys were published in *La Description de l'Egypte*, a 24-volume tome published from 1809 to 1824. It included maps, hundreds of copper engravings, and essays describing what they'd learned about Egypt. It divided Egypt into ancient and modern times, and launched the modern vision of ancient Egypt as we know it today.

La Description de l'Egypte was extremely popular. The structures, symbols, and images of ancient Egypt became fashionable features of European art and architecture. Encouraged by Napoleon's savant expeditions, the European fascination with ancient Egypt gave rise to archaeological museums in Europe, beginning with the Louvre opening the first Egyptian museum in 1827.

*D*ominique-Vivant Denon
Credited with discovering the zodiac on the ceiling of the temple at Dendera, Denon was a diplomat and

artist who had moved up in Parisian society, befriended King Louis XV, survived the Revolution, and attracted the attention of Napoleon. Although he was not included in the Commission of Sciences and Arts, he was invited by Napoleon to join the expedition.

Denon was the first artist to discover and draw the temples and ruins at Thebes (Luxor), Esna, Edfu, and Philae. Before then, most of the known Egyptian antiquities were pyramids and pieces of sculpture and stelae. When he first saw Dendera, just across from Qena, he realized what might be in store. He passed through the gate and was enthralled by his first view of the portico of the Temple of Hathor, writing, "I felt that I was in the sanctuary of the arts and sciences...Never did the labour of man show me the human race in such a splendid point of view. In the ruins of Tentyra [the Roman word for Dendera] the Egyptians appeared to me giants."

*G**iovanni Battista Belzoni (died 1823, age 45)*

A circus performer and fountain maker, six-foot-six Belzoni was from Padua, Italy. After stints in Paris and Holland, he moved to England and married an Englishwoman. While performing with a traveling circus as the "Patagonian Sampson", he met the future leader of Egypt, Mohammed Ali.

Ali invited Belzoni to Egypt, where he was hired by British general counsel Henry Salt to collect antiquities "whatever the expense" for "an enlightened nation."

While in Luxor, Belzoni met Italian Bernardino Drovetti, who had been hired by the French to do the same (his finds make up the Louvre Egyptian collection). Belzoni did his excavations in the Valley of the Kings, where he discovered the tombs of Ramesses the Great (also known as Ramesses II), and the tomb of his father Seti I. He was also credited with discovering and arranging for the transportation of the nine-foot-high head of "Young Memnon" that can now be found in the British Museum. When the Rosetta stone was deciphered it was revealed that the head of "Young Memnon" actually belonged to Ramesses the Great.

He also discovered the means to enter the entrance to the burial chamber in the second great pyramid of Giza. The sarcophagus of the pharaoh was there, but the chamber had been looted centuries before.

Belzoni's other notable find was Abu Simbel. With the help of a tourist, he scooped out the sand that nearly filled the temple.

He wrote of his adventure in *Narrative of the Operations and Recent Discoveries within the Pyramids, Temples, Tombs and Excavations, in Egypt and Nubia; and of a Journey to the Coast of the Red Sea, in Search of the Ancient Berenice; and Another to the Oasis of Jupiter Ammon.*

*H*oward Richard Vyse

Ever since Napoleon's engineers had explored the Great Pyramid of Giza, the monument had become a particularly potent symbol. In 1837, British military officer Howard Richard Vyse investigated Khufu's pyramid with civil engineer John Shae Perring. Their infamous use of gunpowder to blast open the structure revealed four new chambers.

*T*raveling on the Nile

A trip up the Nile aboard a native *dhahabîyeh* was reserved for only the most adventurous traveler in the early nineteenth century. Not only would he be expected to pay for the round trip (a forty-day round trip from Cairo to Luxor cost about £110 in 1858) but he would also have to provision it, de-bug and de-rat it, oversee the boatmen, and even have it repainted.

The Turkish word *howadji*, meaning "merchant" or "shop-keeper", soon became a term used by Egyptians for all foreign travelers. In 1851, the word was used by George William Curtis in his travel account, *Nile Notes of a Howadji*, referring to it as "the universal name for traveler."

By the late 1860s, the London travel agency Thomas Cook & Son began offering Nile excursions on steamers and luxurious dhahabîyehs. With their organization know-how and provisioning, they turned a three-month voyage into a 28-day sight-seeing tour, bringing many more visitors to Egypt. Soon, the exotic locales of Nubia and the oases of the Western Sahara Desert were offered as stops on the Grand Tour.

Your Invitation!
Do you crave historical romance filled with passion and red hot chemistry?

Come join me and my author friends in the Facebook group, Historical Harlots, for exclusive giveaways, chats with amazing HistRom authors, raunchy shenanigans, and more! https://www.facebook.com/groups/210213859981360I

ABOUT THE AUTHOR

A self-described nerd and lover of science, Linda Rae spent many years as a published technical writer specializing in 3D graphics workstations, software and 3D animation (her movie credits include SHREK and SHREK 2). Mythology, immortality, and ancient Greece have been lifelong interests.

A fan of action-adventure movies, she can frequently be found at the local cinema. Although she no longer has any tropical fish, she does follow the San Jose Sharks. She makes her home in Cody, Wyoming.

For more information:
www.lindaraesande.com
Sign up for Linda Rae's newsletter:
Regency Romance with a Twist
For articles on research and travels, read Linda's Rae blog:
Regency Romance with a Twist